Dreams Happen

Amandah Berkowski

Bloomington, IN Milton Keynes, UK

AuthorHouse™
1663 Liberty Drive, Suite 200
Bloomington, IN 47403
www.authorhouse.com
Phone: 1-800-839-8640

AuthorHouse™ UK Ltd.
500 Avebury Boulevard
Central Milton Keynes, MK9 2BE
www.authorhouse.co.uk
Phone: 08001974150

This book is a work of fiction. People, places, events, and situations are the product of the author's imagination. Any resemblance to actual persons, living or dead, or historical events, is purely coincidental.

© 2006 Amandah Berkowski. All rights reserved.

No part of this book may be reproduced, stored in a retrieval system, or transmitted by any means without the written permission of the author.

First published by AuthorHouse 6/6/2006

ISBN: 1-4259-4210-5 (sc)

Library of Congress Control Number: 2006904872

Printed in the United States of America
Bloomington, Indiana

This book is printed on acid-free paper.

Contents

Chapter 1	Outspoken	*1*
Chapter 2	Heartbroken	*10*
Chapter 3	Grievance	*15*
Chapter 4	Finding Hope	*23*
Chapter 5	In the Spotlight	*34*
Chapter 6	Hide and Seek	*44*
Chapter 7	Breathtaking	*62*
Chapter 8	Closure	*82*
Chapter 9	Departure	*94*
Chapter 10	Betrayal	*103*
Chapter 11	On My Own	*116*
Chapter 12	Reuniting True Love	*128*
Chapter 13	Comfort	*140*
Chapter 14	Rebirth	*150*
Chapter 15	Recalcitrant	*161*
Chapter 16	Reality Check	*170*
Chapter 17	The Birth of Our Creation	*183*
Chapter 18	Remaking Our Love	*195*
Chapter 19	Dreams Happen	*204*

CHAPTER 1

Outspoken

Life for some is so irresistible, but for a girl in the twelfth grade, it can seem like forever just to have something great happen to you. What is it about us that makes us believe that we have to fall in love and get married to the man of our dreams instead of going to college or having a really great job when we get older? Who thinks like that anymore? I would never have believed that my life would go so wrong until I had everything I'd ever wanted standing right before me, but too bad he was already taken

His name was Steven, and until this moment, I never thought I would say that, especially out loud. Yes, that's right, I said it in front of a crowd of people, but who could blame me? Christie was making a move on him; I had to say something. By the way, Christie was his girlfriend, and I was the crazy girl who blurted out I liked him to everyone in the hallway including, by the way, Steven. He probably thought I was some kind of freak to say that out loud, but if I was lucky, maybe he'd think I was joking.

My best friend was Lindsey; she was tall with short brown hair to her shoulders and green eyes. She was very slim and wore such beautiful clothes, which was probably why we got along so well. My name is Tara. My mom must have been crazy to pick a name like that, or maybe she

Header

wasn't, and Dad picked it out. My parents, by the way, were split up, but I was the only one out of my siblings that seemed to even care. I had two sisters. My older one was Sarah, and the other was my twin sister, Terran. I know what you're going to ask, Why were our names so similar? Well, it was because my mother was crazy when she picked them out, or maybe it was my father.

Terran and I were practically best friends, but she was away right then in Mexico for a school project. We looked identical; we had light brown hair, blue eyes, and were very tall and thin.

Our dream was to marry Clay Edison, but I'd settle for Steven if I didn't get to meet him. I knew it was probably unlikely that I'd ever be with Clay, but you never know, right? One of these days, I planned to meet him and get married and live in a big house and have lots of children. My older sister thought I was crazy to want to be with him, but I could dream, couldn't I? But maybe I shouldn't.

The beginning of my adventure started here, and the end was only another beginning that I chose not to speak of. Before my life turned into a roller coaster, it had been a regular school day, and my mom had been trying to get me up as usual. "Tara, get up for school and come grab some breakfast before you leave." I got up grumpy not wanting to go to school, because if I did I would have to face Steven and all the people that had heard me say I liked him in the hallway yesterday. I slowly climbed out of bed and had a shower then got dressed in the outfit I had laid out the night before. After I had dressed, I ran downstairs and had breakfast which consisted of a celery stick, a slice of whole wheat bread, and a vitamin. "Tara, aren't you going to have some pancakes?" my mother questioned me, as if what I was eating wasn't good enough.

"Mom, do you know how much fat is in those? Think of the syrup. I can't believe you asked me that."

"Sorry I asked." My mom giggled thinking I was overreacting about eating the breakfast she went out of her way preparing for me.

After I had finished breakfast, I got my books together and put them into my school bag about to leave. I then sat down on the white bench beside the front door beginning to tie my shoes when I heard my mother call me. I finished tying my shoes and put on my jacket and placed my purse over my shoulders, holding my book bag in my other hand. My mom stood at the top of the stairs and stared down at me. "Tara, don't forget to call your father; he's coming to pick you up after school."

"Thanks, Mom. I'll see you on Monday." I left my house knowing I was one step closer to having to face Steven and all the people that heard me say I had liked him out loud. I walked towards the corner where Lindsey and I always met up before school since she lived up the street from us. When I saw Lindsey, she was with some girl, but as I got closer, I realized that she had been waiting with Jennifer. Jennifer was the one I used to be friends with, but she stole my song that my sister and I had written. I walked over to Lindsey and hugged her then moved her out of the way glaring at Jennifer.

"Where's your pack of know-it-alls, or did they leave you and find another cat to lead the pack?"

"They're waiting at the bus stop. So where's your other half?"

"That's none of your business, is it?"

Jennifer stood in front of me trying to act as if she was better than I was. I turned facing Lindsey and pulled her away from Jennifer and whispered quietly as Jennifer watched us. "Why are you hanging out with Jennifer? You know she's bad news. She stole my song, remember? Plus, she put a move on your boyfriend at the homecoming game. She can't even be trusted with a secret. Remember she blurted out to everyone that Stephanie had a pimple on her ass, and everyone teased her and told her to pop it."

"I know, but maybe she's changed. She told me David put the move on her. Plus, it's not like David and I are an item anymore."

"You actually believe her? She's lying; you know she's good at that."

"Please give her another chance, for me?"

"Alright, but if she lies about anything or steals one more thing, she's never talking to us ever again."

"Okay."

Lindsey and I then told Jennifer that we would forgive her, and she invited us to have lunch with her and the Pussy Kats. We accepted, of course, and hurried to the bus stop and got on the school bus before we missed it. I sat beside Jennifer and Lindsey and the Pussy Kat clan sat behind us.

Header

"I wish Steven caught the bus, and then I could stare at him every day instead of just in the hallway by the boys' bathroom where his group of friends all hang out."

"Oh, Tara, you're so in love with him, aren't you?" Lindsey added quietly.

"Yeah, I guess I am, but not as in love as I am with Clay Edison."

"Clay Edison, woo!" Lindsey and I screamed in excitement out loud so the whole bus could hear. I seem to say things out loud a lot that I sometimes shouldn't.

"So when does your other half come back from Mexico?" Jennifer questioned me.

"Would you please stop saying she's my other half. We're sisters. Yes, we're twins, but lay off would you?"

"Somebody must have their period."

Right then, I moved over, and Jennifer slid off the side of the seat onto the walkway of the bus. "Oops, sorry. I really need to be more careful." I giggled with Lindsey as the bus came to a stop as we arrived at the school.

Jennifer got up quickly glaring down at me angrily then added. "I know that was an accident, so I'll let it slide this time."

"Oh, okay, whatever you say, Kat."

Jennifer glared at me snarling, not knowing what to say. "So are we still up for lunch?" Jennifer asked holding back her anger for me.

"Of course, would I give up a chance to spend time with you?"

Jennifer waved her hand in the air, and her three friends followed her like a pack of cats behind her.

They all looked like plastic. They had rich fathers who bought them whatever they wanted. The short one with the red hair was Carrel. She was quiet and just acted as if she just wanted to belong somewhere. The tall blond one was Karin, and she was full of herself and was the girl who always did the dirty work for Jennifer. The last one was Cherry. She had black hair and brown eyes. She was the easy one out of them all. Last but not least was Jennifer. She was a tall blonde and was good-looking, but her attitude was what would always hold her back. She wanted what everyone else had, no matter what it took to make that happen.

Lindsey and I got off the bus watching as the girls went into the school. I walked to my locker inside with Lindsey not even realizing that Steven was walking not too far behind me. We reached our lockers, and Lindsey and I slowly opened them watching as Steven strolled by us with a group of guys. "Oh, I wish I could just reach out and touch him." And so I did. I grabbed his shirt, ripping it in the back. I couldn't believe what I had done. I tore Stevens's silk shirt. Steven and his friends stared at me in silence. We could have cut glass with the tension in the hallway.

"What was that for?" Steven questioned me upset by the fact that I tore his shirt.

"I'm sorry. I thought I saw a bug on you. I tried to get it off."

"This was my favorite shirt. Now what am I supposed to do?"

"Well, I can sew it for you if you want."

He stood in front of me holding the rip in his shirt staring at me. "Yeah, like I'm going to trust you after you ripped my favorite shirt." He was silent then finished, "I remember you; you're the one who yelled out that you liked me in front of everyone."

I stood quietly praying that he wouldn't make fun of me, but he did, and who could blame him? I did embarrass him in front of his friends.

Every time his friends or he would bump into me, they would try to trip me or push my books out of my hands. "What did I ever see in that guy? In fact, he's not even a guy; he's a boy, a little child that needs to grow up."

"Yeah, just forget about him, Tara; he's not worth it."

"Oh, but he's so cute." I leaned against the lockers dreaming. "And, well, that's about it. Yeah, maybe he's not worth it."

Lindsey looked at me waiting for me to snap out of it and wake up to reality. "Come on, Tara; let's get to class before we're late. Tomorrow is another day to rip somebody else's shirt." Lindsey giggled.

"Hey, that's not funny. Well, it kind of is, I guess."

At lunch break, Lindsey and I met up with the Pussy Kats sitting at the "It" table next to the soda machine. Everyone stared at us as we entered into the area where everyone was afraid to go that didn't belong. The whole lunchroom was marked off in territories. The Its, which were the people that were at the top, the Alternatives, who were in the middle that were just respected, and then there were the Drops, which were the people who didn't matter. After we sat down beside Jennifer and her friends in silence, we took out our lunches beginning to eat. While we ate, we started a conversation about guys, which, of course, was the number one topic besides fashion.

"So did you see that really cute guy that walked by? Maybe we should invite him over here to eat with us?" Cherry commented, as she watched him take his seat in the It section across the way.

"No way, no guys allowed. It's so not appropriate for a guy to see a lady eat," Jennifer answered.

"Why can't guys see us eat?" The group leaned back and took a deep breath knowing Jennifer would react to my question.

"Just think of the crumbs that might fall out of our mouths or fingers. I can't believe you would even ask that. It's terrifying to think about. I have to get the picture out of my head, oh God." Her friends put their arms around her shoulder, comforting her. "Think of shoes, purses; remember the red dress in the window."

"Thank you."

I shook my head watching them hug over imagining crumbs falling from their mouths. "Oh, my God. I'm getting out of here. You're all strange."

I stood up and left the table as they stared at me probably wondering what was the matter with me, as if I had the problem. Later in the day, I caught up to Lindsey, and she told me that lunch wasn't the same without me. I thought Lindsey would have left with me considering the dramatic breakdown that Jennifer was still recovering from.

"Why didn't you leave with me?" I questioned Lindsey standing in front of the lockers beside the gym.

"I didn't want to be rude."

I giggled thinking to myself, *How can she even think that? Jennifer doesn't have anything physically wrong with her to freak out about. A guy seeing crumbs fall from her mouth? I mean, they're only crumbs.*

"Look, I just didn't want to leave with you because lunch was almost over, and I kind of agree about the guys seeing girls eat."

"You're joking, right?"

"Well, what if the guys judge us? We have to consider the crumbs that fall. Oh my God, what if they land on our shoes?"

"Oh, God forbid that happens. However would we recover from that?"

"I know it's so terrifying to even imagine."

I leaned towards her and put my right hand on her forehead. "Are you feeling okay?"

"Oh, Tara." Lindsey giggled. "I'm just fooling you."

"Thank God, I almost thought I lost you there." I then nudged her in the arm and finished. "Don't ever scare me like that. I could have been seriously damaged. I could have had one of those nervous breakdowns."

"Oh, Tara, quit being silly."

After school, I waited by the entrance doors of the school for Lindsey where we always met. I must have only waited for a minute or two when I saw her coming from down the hallway. She stopped in front of me with a smile upon her face from ear to ear. "Oh crap, I forgot about my dad. I was supposed to call him." I opened my purse and pulled out my pink cell phone and dialed his number before I wasted any more time.

"Dad, it's me Tara. I'm sorry I never called sooner. I forgot all about you. I mean, well never mind what I mean."

"It's alright, sweetie. I took the liberty of just driving to your school. I'm parked outside."

"You are? Where?" I looked around for my dad's red truck, but I couldn't see it.

"Look beside the crowd of people."

"Oh, there you are." My dad was sitting in the driver's seat smiling and waving to me. I closed my cell phone then placed it in my purse where I had kept it. When I did, I looked up seeing Lindsey staring at me smiling as if she had great news. We stood in silence until I told her I had to go and I'd call her later some time when I arrived at my dad's house.

"Well?"

"Well what?"

"Aren't you going to ask me why I'm smiling?"

"Okay, why are you smiling?"

"Well, this incredible guy just walked up to me and asked me out. His name is Ted, and he's so cute. We're going to a movie Monday night."

"That's great, Lindsey."

"On Tuesday, I'll tell you how it went."

I started to walk away from Lindsey towards my dad's car. I turned back and shouted so she could hear me. "I want details." I walked over to my dad's red truck parked at the side of the street and opened the door. My dad sat there staring at me, as I climbed into the truck closing the door and placing my bag on the floor of the truck in front of me where my feet lay. My dad began to drive away from the school in silence until he made it to a street called Barry Lane.

"So how was school today?"

"It was high school."

"Should I be worried?"

"No, Daddy, I meant it was just an average day in high school for me."

"Oh."

It was silent for a few minutes as he continued driving towards the restaurant ahead of us called Evens. "Remember I told you about me having a girlfriend last weekend?"

"What about it, Dad?"

"Well, I was hoping that you could meet her."

"Why would I want to meet her?"

"Tara."

"No, Dad, I can't believe you're starting our weekend off with that horrible news. It's bad enough you and Mom broke up not even confronting me about it until I saw you leave with a suitcase in your hand. Don't you care that Mom misses you? Don't you even think about her anymore?"

"Tara, your mother and I decided to move on."

"God, just don't talk to me about that right now."

"Well, she's living with me, and she's going to be there when we show up."

I glanced over at my father with tears not knowing what to say while remembering my mother and father fighting before he had left us. All I could think about at that moment was how I wished that someone could rescue me right at that moment and take me away from all of this.

That way, I could forget about my parents dating other people. My worst thought was building up. What if Dad and that woman got married? What would I do if that happened? How would I cope with that?

"Tara, don't judge her until you meet her. She's really nice, and she's really looking forward to meeting you and Terran."

"Dad, I said I don't want to."

"But, Tara..."

"No, Dad."

"Tara, she's going to be my wife whether you like it or not. You just have to learn how to accept that."

My father came to a red light, and I sat in silence crying wondering what I should do. I opened the door, grabbed my bags, and quickly got out, leaving my father yelling at me. I ran to the sidewalk and caught a bus wanting to get away from my father before I had to meet his new girlfriend.

CHAPTER 2
Heartbroken

I arrived at home seeing my mother holding the receiver as I entered into my house. "Where have you've been? I've been worried sick. Your father said you got out of his truck in the middle of traffic and left him there."

"Mom, you don't understand. Dad told me…"

"Go to your room. I don't want to hear it right now." My mom cut me off pointing her finger towards the stairs angry with me. "What did I say, Tara? Now."

I walked up the stairs to my bedroom while lowering my head towards the floor.

When I reached my bedroom, I went inside closing the door behind me. While I waited, I started on my homework that I needed to finish for school before Monday. An hour must have passed by before my mom had finally entered. I had already finished my homework and placed it back into my bag as my mom sat on my bed beside me. "So what happened, Tara?"

"Well, as I tried to say before. Dad told me that him and his girlfriend had moved in together, and he wanted me to come and meet her. I was upset, and Dad said that I have to learn to accept it because no matter what, they're going to be together. So I got out of the car when we stopped at a red light and caught a bus across the street."

"So you don't want to ever meet her?"

"No, I want to stay with you. I know if I meet her, they'll probably end up wanting me to stay with them instead of you. I don't want to live with him. I hate Dad for leaving, and he should have stayed and worked things out."

My mother placed her arms around me, hugging me and kissing my forehead smiling. "You don't have to meet your father's girlfriend. No one is forcing you, and no one will ever make you live anywhere you don't want to. You're eighteen now; you're almost an adult. You're old enough to make your own decisions."

"Thank you, Mom."

The weekend was over, and it was Monday. I got to school in the same way as I always did, but something felt different. I felt as if something bad had happened, but I just didn't know what. I saw Lindsey from down the hall waving to me with a friendly smile. We walked towards our lockers seeing Jennifer and the Pussy Kats standing in front of them, looking as if they had something to say to us.

"Hi, Tara."

"Oh, that's so sweet, waiting for me as if you care. Now move."

She moved away from my locker as I slid by her and unlocked my locker. "Aren't you going to ask why I was waiting for you?"

I got the books I needed and placed them into my bag, hung my pink jacket on the hook, then closed my locker door. I turned around staring at Jennifer with a look of boredom then added, "No." I walked past her, and she grabbed my arm. I turned towards her while glaring at her as she held my arm gently.

"Get your hands off of me before I make you, Jennifer."

She let go of me then stepped back staring at me with a smirk across her face. "As I was trying to tell you before you ignored me, I was going to tell you that I told my dad that I really liked Clay Edison, and I wanted to meet him in person." I smiled believing that she was about to give me the opportunity to meet him as she continued. "My dad got me tickets to see his concert on Thursday. He's going to fly me to Atlantic City to see him perform live in the front row. Isn't that just fabulous?"

"That's great. So how many tickets do you have?"

Header

"Oh, only four, but as you know, my Pussy Kats and I have to go together; we can't squeeze you in. I just thought I might tell you that I was going to meet him and maybe, just maybe, he'll fall in love with me."

"You little brat, I can't believe you. You don't even like Clay."

"Yeah, but I'd rather see him with me than with you, and also, what better woman than a woman with connections?"

"He's not going to like a woman with her daddy's connections, if that's what you're thinking. He's not that kind of man."

"All men are like that; you don't know what you're talking about. You're just jealous that I get to meet him first."

I then began walking as fast as I could away from them and entered the ladies' room as Lindsey followed. "Don't even listen to her, Tara, you know as well as I do that Clay doesn't like plastic. He wants a real woman with lots of love in her heart, a woman exactly like you, Tara."

"Thank you, Lindsey, but I'm just not feeling real great about myself right now. I miss my sister and my dad's with another woman. Jennifer is going to meet Clay, and here I am sitting in the ladies' room on the cold floor crying over a man I'll never get to meet."

"Don't say that; you don't know whether or not you'll meet him."

"Nothing good ever happens to me."

It was silent for a while as I sat in front of Lindsey crying when we heard my name being called on the intercom for me to come to the office. I stood up wiping my eyes preparing for the next bad thing that I knew was coming. I just didn't know what it was. Lindsey walked with me down to the office placing her arm around me trying to make me feel better.

When we arrived at the office, I told the front desk that I was Tara Heart and wanted to know what they had wanted me to come to the office for. I then glanced to the side of me seeing two policemen standing beside me. I knew something was wrong the minute they said my name.

"Are you Tara Heart?"

"Yes." I hesitated as they continued.

"Would you like to sit down?"

"No, I'm fine standing."

"I'm afraid your mother and father were killed in a car accident early this morning."

"What? I think you have the wrong people. They're separated."

"I'm sorry, but there is no mistake."

"What?"

I was silent holding my hands over my mouth feeling as though I didn't know what to do with my body. My eyes filled with tears as the teachers and Lindsey held me as I went limp. I fell to the ground still holding my mouth rocking, not knowing what to do with the information I had been given. They carried me over to a chair near the office, and I sat down. I placed my head down in my hands then glanced up looking around at the students staring at me as if my life had been a movie. I stood up taking a couple of steps towards Lindsey. "I'm okay, I'll be alright now." I started to black out feeling myself fall to the floor below not knowing what happened next. All I remember is waking up in a hospital bed after and seeing my sister, Sarah, standing in front of me with tears in her eyes.

"What's wrong, Sarah?"

"I don't know how to tell you this."

"Tell me what?"

"I'm leaving. I can't take care of you. I have to start my own life, and I can't do that raising you like Mom probably would have wanted."

"I can't believe you're not even going to try and take care of us; we need you."

"No, don't say that. You'll be fine. Someone will be able to adopt you. I'm only twenty-five years old. I don't even have my own place yet. I'm nothing."

"Yes, you are; you're everything. Daddy would have wanted you to at least try."

"No, that's where you're wrong, Tara. He wouldn't have cared. He's not even my real dad; he's yours and your sister's."

"What? No, he's not. What are you talking about?"

"No, Tara, listen to me. He wasn't my father. I found out when I was eighteen. Mom was raped, and I'm the outcome. There, now you know the truth. I'm nothing but an outcast in the world."

Header

Sarah screamed then suddenly let out a breath of air and fell to the floor. I climbed out of the hospital bed knocking over anything in my way screaming for help. "Sarah!" I cried as she lay on the hospital floor unconscious. "Sarah!" I knelt down beside her as I screamed. "No!" I was holding my sister's head in my lap crying for help as three nurses and a doctor ran into the room pulling me away from her and towards the door as I reached towards Sarah screaming, "No!" The door closed as I sat in a hospital chair crying. I couldn't believe so much had happened in one day. It felt like I was dreaming, and I was about to wake up from this nightmare at any moment, but I didn't. It was all real, and it was the worst possible day I could ever imagine. I had lost my family all in one day, leaving behind me and my sister. There were no stars for me to see in the sky that night; there was nowhere I wanted to be but dead. How could I live when so many I loved had died not even a moment before I even understood who they really were?

CHAPTER 3

Grievance

Shortly after the death of my mother and father, I had lost my sister Sarah by a stroke that had been triggered by stress. I was later placed into a foster home after being reunited with my only family member left, my twin sister, Terran.

The day had finally come when we had to bury our loved ones and find the strength to move past what had happened to us. We were alone in the world, and all we had was each other. Nothing seemed possible at this moment. All that was left for me to do was get through this day of my family's funeral in the best way I knew how. "Here I go." I held onto my sister Terran's hand as we walked together beside our other relatives that were going to the funeral as well. All I saw in front of us was a funeral that felt like a bad dream that was still taking place in my head. It wasn't; it was all real and it had all been happening, and there wasn't anything that I or anyone else could do to stop what was happening to us. All I could do was hold on tight to my sister as she did to me.

We watched as our mother, father, and sister, Sarah, started being lowered into the ground slowly. With tears running down my face, I turned to Terran crying and hugging her as she did me. We couldn't watch; we didn't want to have to say goodbye yet. We wanted to have God somehow bring them back, even though we knew that life after death was impossible.

After the funeral was over, my aunt, Edina, from my dad's side was having a get-together at her house for everyone. While we walked towards the cars parked beside the curb of the graveyard, I looked back

Header

at the stones where my family lay, remembering their faces. I faced forward again watching as our relatives drove away from the graveyard slowly. I stood next to my sister, Terran, waiting for our cousins, Frank and Emma, to get into the backseat. I helped my sister climb into the car then closed the door not wanting a ride. My uncle, Herman, looked at me as if he wanted me to get in. He rolled down the window then called to me. "Tara, get in the car. Let's go to Edina's. You'll feel better when we leave."

I began crying as he stared at me wanting me to get in the car so we could leave. "I can't. I can't go to some get-together and eat good food and think of my family. I don't want to live anymore." I turned and ran towards the gravestones, being careful not to trip. When I reached the streets again on the other side, I hitched a ride home with a stranger. I told them to drop me off at my friend Lindsey's house, where I could at least have some kind of reality check, as if I needed one right now. After everything that had happened, I didn't feel like I needed anything, but to die. I knew it was my fault that they had died. I just knew it. I shouldn't have made such a fuss about meeting my dad's girlfriend. I was so damn selfish.

When I reached Lindsey's house safely, I ran up to the front door knocking as tears fell from my eyes. "Tara." Lindsey pulled me inside the house hugging me then closed the door behind us after we had entered. "Where have you've been? Everyone is looking for you. Your uncle called, and your sister called crying."

"I was running away. I don't know where to go. I don't know what to do. I'm so lost. I'm so confused right now about everything that has happened. I don't even know where I'm going to live now that my parents are dead."

"Calm down, Tara, it's going to be fine."

"Calm down? How do you suppose I do that? How do you suppose I live past this day?"

"Quit talking like that. Quit being that way. You're just upset. Your uncle already found out about where you'll be staying."

"Oh yeah, where? With him? I don't think so. I'm not living with Uncle Herman and Cousin Taylor."

"Tara, please have a seat. Your uncle's coming to pick you up and take you home."

"Lindsey, why are you on their side?"

"Whose side? I'm worried about you. I love you, and all this talk about you wanting to die is really scaring me."

"I thought you were my friend."

"I am, Tara, but you need some time alone for awhile to get yourself back together again so you can have the dream I know you still want so badly."

"What dream?"

"Clay, remember?"

"No, I don't remember."

Lindsey moved towards me trying to comfort me until my uncle arrived to get me. I pushed her away and stood staring at her glaring as tears fell from my eyes. "Don't touch me. I thought you were different."

"I am. I don't want anything to happen to you. I need you to be okay."

"Why?"

Lindsey stared at me beginning to cry then answered, "You help me live. You lift up my spirit whenever I'm sad. Don't you understand? You give me strength."

I stood in front of her feeling like an idiot knowing I had hurt the best friend I had ever had in my entire life. "You give me strength, too."

I walked over to her crying with my arms open towards her. She placed her arms around me holding onto me as I did her. As we hugged, I heard her whisper into my ear quietly, "I'll always believe in you, Tara."

My cry became louder as there was a knock at the door. Lindsey let go of me to answer the door, and standing outside was my uncle, Herman, all in black from the funeral earlier that day. "Tara, thank God."

I turned towards him. "I'm ready now."

"You'll be staying in a foster home. Are you ready, or do you need a few more minutes?"

I took a deep breath almost as if I had to prepare for somewhere that I wasn't able to ever leave. I looked back at Lindsey crying, seeing that she had been crying also. "I'm going to miss you."

"I'm going to miss you, too, Tara."

Header

After I had said goodbye to Lindsey, I went outside seeing a lady in a blue blazer standing beside a black car waiting to drive me to the foster home. I got in, and I looked out the window at everything going by, as I was being driven by the lady in the blue blazer whom I thought of as my messenger until I got to know her more. I wasn't sure if she was the mom of the foster home, or if she was just the lady whose job it was to bring me there safely.

When I had arrived at the foster home, I never had expected the house to be so large. It was five stories and was as wide as the school I had gone to. When the car came to a stop, the lady got out and walked around to my side and opened the car door for me. I got out slowly looking up at the house nervously. I arrived with no baggage in my hands. I thought I would have to pick it up when I got signed into the house. I entered into an office then walked up to the desk and told the lady sitting behind the desk my name. "My name's Tara Heart."

The lady looked through her book nearby then answered quietly, "Yes, Tara, we've been expecting you." The lady pressed a button on the phone, picking up the receiver as I watched her. I never heard what she said, but she talked on the phone for awhile looking at me. After she had finished talking on the phone, she turned and faced me. "I sent someone to get you and show you around and where you'll be staying. Have a seat over there while you wait. There are magazines on the table."

"Thank you."

I waited not even five minutes when I saw a woman in a red blouse and black dress pants walk over to me smiling as if she had already known me. She held out her hand towards me. "Hi, I'm Tracey, and I'm going to be your guidance counselor to help you. If you have any questions, feel free to come to my office and see me." She placed her hand back down after I didn't shake it and carried on with introducing herself and the house I would be staying in. "There are many teenagers that live here including yourself that you have to respect. We all do our part around here, looking out for one another like we are family. There are many rooms of activities where you can hang out. We make this house as comfortable as we possibly can in order to help the teenagers cope with the process of entering so suddenly. You'll be sharing rooms with someone. There is one bathroom per room and also other bathrooms near the dining area as you'll notice living here for awhile."

She then walked me to my room which was a room with a purple door. "You'll be sharing with Shelby, and she'll be your roommate for awhile until we switch at the end of the year."

"What? Wait, I have a twin sister. Why aren't we sharing a room together? I want to be with her, or I'm not going to be living here. I lost my mother, my father, and my sister, and I'm not about to lose my other sister. She's the only family I have left." "That's alright. Calm down. We'll put you two together. We are so sorry about the mix-up." We walked away from the room towards another room, which had a pink door. "This room is empty, so this will be your room with your sister once I get her moved in." She opened the door, and all that was in the room were two twin beds, two night tables, and two dressers, enough for two people. "Where are the blankets and pillows?"

"Oh, don't worry. I'll bring you all your things including what was at your house that your sister had packed."

"Where is my sister?"

"She's in her room crying, but we'll get her here with you as soon as I leave."

"Well, hurry, go get her; she's probably crying because you split us up."

I walked into the room and sat down on the bed with the door wide open as Tracey left to get my things. I waited on my bed for her to arrive. I was beginning to hear voices in the hallway. I wondered who they were, so I got up and walked over to the doorway peeking around the corner to see who was there. "Jennifer."

Jennifer turned, staring at me with a girl with short brown hair to her ears and brown eyes. "Hi, Tara."

"What are you doing here? You're not in a foster home, are you?"

"No, do I look like an orphan?"

"No one looks like an orphan."

"This is my friend, Shelby; she's Steven's cousin. You do remember Steven, don't you?"

"How can I forget?"

Header

Jennifer turned and faced Shelby smirking and pointing at me. "Yeah, this girl shouted out to everyone in the school that she liked Steven, and then she ripped his favorite shirt. It was so funny I almost wet my pants watching."

I watched as they stood in the hallway talking and laughing about me as if my life was a joke. I turned around and went back into my room not able to take anymore rude remarks after everything that had happened. I sat back down on my bed with my head faced down hearing them standing in the doorway giggling trying to act as if they weren't there when they were. I looked up at them smirking at me with their faces all dolled up as if they were dressed up for some kind of date.

"Are you still upset about Clay?"

"No."

"What's wrong then? Is it that you're still jealous of me, and you're just starting to realize it now?"

"No, actually my mother, father, and big sister just died, and now I have to live in a foster home, and worst of all, you happen to be here."

"Oh well, that's a little bit believable, except for the mother and father thing."

"What are you talking about, Jennifer? Didn't you even hear? I figured everyone would have spread it around the whole school by now that I lost almost everyone."

"No, I didn't hear anything about that, but that's horrible. Sorry about that. It must be so awful for you to even be sitting here still alive while your family's dead."

"Shut up, just shut your mouth. Don't you have any respect for anyone besides yourself?"

"Not for you. You don't expect me to feel sorry for you, do you? Oh, you did. Well, listen up, because I'm only going to say this once, you're no good. You probably caused your parents' death. They're probably so happy that they don't have to take care of you anymore. You're just loving the attention, aren't you?"

"Shut up, just shut up." I started to cry breaking down from Jennifer's severe putdown. I slid down onto the floor off the bed and started rocking my body.

"I think we should call for help; she's really freaking me out."

"Maybe you should just leave her alone; she's had enough," Shelby whispered to Jennifer trying to get her to stop her harassment.

"No, this is what she does. She's just acting like something is really wrong with her so we feel sorry for her and tell her it wasn't her fault, when it was."

"Leave me alone. Please just go away."

I lay on the floor in the fetal position not knowing what else to do with myself. I was so upset, and my heart was racing. It felt as if it was about to burst out of my chest. I was starting to sweat. I was so upset and just wanted them to leave me alone. "Quit being a baby, Tara."

Just then, Tracey entered the room moving the girls out of the way seeing me on the floor in the fetal possession. "What the hell is going on, girls?"

"We didn't do it."

"Stay right where you are, you two." Tracey placed the things on the floor that she had been carrying and lifted me up into her arms and carried me into the bathroom to wash my face. She placed me onto the bathroom floor and wiped my face with a towel telling me it was alright now. She left the bathroom closing the door behind her. Tracey walked over to Jennifer and Shelby angry about their behavior towards me. "What did you say to her? And don't say 'nothing' because nothing doesn't make a teenager form the fetal position."

"Jennifer was saying it was her fault that her parents died, that's all."

Jennifer glared at Shelby and snarled. "You're such a rat, you know that?"

"At least I'm not a tramp like you are, flaunting your body in every direction just to get what you want from a guy."

Jennifer pushed Shelby, and she fell onto the floor then got back up and raged at Jennifer, punching and kicking her as the people around that had helped Tracey bring my things helped break the fight up.

"What is the matter with you two? Don't you have any concern for the safety we try to keep in this household?" They looked at Tracey still worked up in anger. "Shelby go to Miss Laker's office and sign yourself up for five hours of counseling for what you've done. Oh and don't try

Header

and squeeze yourself out of this one, it won't work." Shelby walked away from them towards the office as Tracey still stared at Jennifer. "So who are you and where do you live?"

"Look, lady, I don't have to tell you nothing. My daddy is a lawyer, and he won't let you say anything to me or do anything, so screw off."

"You need to watch your tone, Miss Thing, or I'll give your daddy a little wake-up call about what his daughter was doing."

"You don't scare me, Tracey. You're just a person just like me, and you're all talk and no action. Tara deserved everything that happened to her; she doesn't deserve anything."

"Get out of this house before I call the police, and they come and get you out themselves after taking that incredibly large stick out of your ass."

Jennifer's jaw dropped shocked that Tracey had said that to her, then she stormed down the hallway leaving quickly.

CHAPTER 4
Finding Hope

*T*wo weeks later, after my sister and I had been settled into our new home and after the first day of my move into the foster home, we were finally ready to go back to school. It was getting closer to Christmas, and everyone was getting excited for the Christmas concert that the school was going to be having.

It was Monday morning, and I got ready for school and got a ride to school from one of the leaders that worked in the house. When I was let off at the school, I took a deep breath and prepared to enter the school. As soon as I had entered, I noticed right away the change in people towards me. As I walked down the hallway, everyone stared at me, and I knew by their stares that they felt sorry for me. I saw Lindsey by her locker and walked over to her happy to see her again. We hadn't seen each other since she had wanted to give me the time alone I needed to cope with what had happened to my family.

"Hi, Lindsey, how are you?"

"I'm good. I'm sorry about Jennifer. I heard she harassed you on your first night at the house."

"Yeah, tell me about it. Her and her friend, Shelby, who just happens to be Steven's cousin harassed me, telling me it was my fault that my family was dead."

"They're such jerks." Just as we were finishing greeting one another, Lindsey looked over my shoulder. "Speak of the devil."

"What?"

Header

I turned seeing Jennifer coming towards us with the three Pussy Kats following behind her with their tails between their legs, or so I had imagined. "Well, well, well, look who's back, crybaby from the foster home."

"Why don't you keep your lips sealed and your ass clean from all those sticks you keep finding to stick up there."

"Oh, I was going to mention to you, before you went all fetal on me that…"

"Like I even want to hear what you have to say, Jennifer."

"Oh, you want to hear this; it's about Clay Edison's concert."

"What about it?"

"I went to it on Thursday, and he was so nice to me. He even let me ride with him in his limo. We got along so well, and he couldn't stop talking about me. We have so much in common."

One of the Pussy Kats walked up to Jennifer and whispered to her quietly, "I thought you said you mentioned Tara and he kept asking about her."

"Shut up, Cherry."

"What was that, Jennifer? You actually talked about me?"

"No, I just mentioned you and what you looked like, and Cherry here talked about what kind of person you are, and he kept asking about you."

"Really?"

"Well, that's because Cherry said you were some kind of nice person which was a lie. Anyway, I told him that you were phony, and he deserves someone much better than trash, someone like me."

"Ha, like you, that's funny. You're nice? You have got to be kidding me."

"Don't laugh too hard because Clay's seeing me again on Friday at my house, and only the Pussy Kat clan, as you call them, can come. So eat dirt, Tara."

I watched as they flicked their hair towards me then walked away in the direction of the other Its standing down the hallway to the left of us. "Don't even listen to her; she's just trying to rub it in because you like Clay."

"But what am I supposed to do? I don't think I can take any more of this. I'm so tired of being hurt. I'm so tired of crying. I haven't even come to terms with losing my family. I can't seem to accept it. I keep thinking they're at home waiting for me to get home from school. What if it was my entire fault that they're gone? What if I would have accepted my dad's girlfriend? Then maybe they wouldn't have left that day, and they would still be here."

"You need to talk about this, Tara."

"I can't. I have to just move past this."

"You can't just forget about this; it isn't that easy."

"What else can I do?"

"Let's go shopping today, and we'll make it special and have a girls' day out, just the two of us."

"I don't know."

"Come on, let's go; school can wait for one day."

"Are you serious?"

"Yes, come on." Lindsey grabbed me by the arm, and we left the school and got on the nearest bus and went to the mall to shop our troubles away.

When we arrived at the mall, it was full of teenage girls surrounding the center of the mall where the fountains were. We thought nothing of it and carried on looking at clothes. I was too depressed to even think about clothes, but I did it anyway to please Lindsey. She had been trying so hard to make me feel better, and I didn't want to let her down, so I tried to smile, acting as if I had forgotten about what had been bothering me that day. As the time passed by, it seemed as though my tears were building up inside. The more I smiled, the harder it was to hold myself back from crying. The worst thing that could happen was to break down in front of a mall of screaming people, who, by the way, were kind of making the situation worse. I left Lindsey in one of the clothing stores after telling her I was going to see what the people were screaming about by the fountain. As I got closer to the crowd, I squeezed my way through the people and saw who I would never have believed I would ever see in my life. It had been none other then Clay Edison.

I had envisioned this day, but never did I picture it would be so blah. I suddenly didn't care. I picked up a piece of paper off a table nearby and got in line to get his autograph even though I was about to break down and cry. Maybe when I got closer, I'd be able to forget about my problems and move on. After Lindsey had caught up to me and saw that Clay was there, she went crazy screaming and ignoring that I was even there. Who could blame her? She had everything to be excited about. She had her family, whereas I didn't.

When my time came to meet Clay, I walked up to the table he had been sitting behind with two bodyguards, and I looked at him knowing that he could see that I was about to cry. Tears began to fall from my eyes uncontrollably as he watched me. He leaned towards me then whispered quietly so only I could hear him, "Are you alright?" "I'm so sorry." I was about to turn away from him when he grabbed my hand staring up at me. "No, wait. What's wrong? Maybe I can help."

"My family just died three weeks ago, and Jennifer is harassing me, and I don't know what to do anymore. Now look at me. I'm standing here telling my life story to Clay Edison. I must be crazy." I then let out a loud cry and fell to the ground. Clay saw me and got up then walked around the table and picked me up into his arms carrying me as his bodyguards surrounded us. Clay carried me towards the back entrance of the mall over to his limo as the limo driver held the car door open for him. He placed me inside onto the back seat then slid over on the seat toward me. The door closed, and the driver got in quickly and began to drive away from the mall. Clay turned towards me on the seat then wiped the tears away from my eyes gently as I stared at him.

"You must have wanted to meet me so much considering what happened to you recently."

"I don't know what to do anymore. I feel like I'll never be able to get past this. Have you ever felt like that?"

"I'm sure everyone has at least once in their lives."

"I wanted so much just to ignore it, but I couldn't. I saw you, and I lost it. It's so hard to believe I once believed in a dream, and you were part of it, but what good is a dream when you know they never come true?"

"What was your dream?"

"It's stupid. You out of all people wouldn't want to hear about it."

"That's not true. I'm the one who asked, didn't I?"

"I know you're just being nice because you think you have to, but it's really a stupid dream."

"Tell me."

"Are you sure?"

"Positive."

"My dream was to marry you." My face turned beet red as I placed my head on his shoulder so he couldn't see how embarrassed I was, even though he knew.

"That's not so stupid. It's kind of sweet."

"Really?"

"I think you're the most honest person I've ever met. You are also the only one who never tried to grab me and yell into my ear that you want to sex me up because I'm the measure of a real man."

"They say stuff like that to you?"

"Oh sure, they say more than that, but those are things that I don't even want to remember."

"Then let's talk about something else."

"Okay, what would make you happy right at this moment?"

"Anything?"

"Like what?"

"Well, I've always wanted to sing to you on a stage, but there's a spotlight just on you and me so you're the only one I can see that I'm singing to."

He stared at me smiling as I glanced down at my hands then back up at him. "You make a man feel so wanted when you say things like that. Where have you been all my life?"

"My name's Tara."

"Tara what?"

"Heart."

"That's pretty."

"So tell me, Clay. Do you have many girlfriends?"

"What woman am I going to find that will really listen to me?"

"Jennifer."

"Jennifer." Clay giggled then questioned me. "You know about Jennifer?"

"Of course, she rubs it in my face all the time that you and her are an item, and you're going to see one another again on Friday."

"Jennifer said that? Well, she's full of herself. I never even talked to her that much."

"Really?"

"She showed me a picture of a girl named Tara, and she said all this horrible stuff about her and for me to watch out. I couldn't stop asking about you."

"You saw me before today?"

Clay cleared his throat, knowing he now had to explain himself to me. "Yes, actually I saw you in person standing beside the school one day."

"You knew who I was before you even met me today?"

"Yes, I knew it was you when you stood in front of me, but I didn't want to ask you out when you were almost in tears."

"You were going to ask me out if I wasn't crying?"

"Well, I was actually going to ask you no matter what. I just saw that you were about to cry, and I wanted to be the one to take care of you."

"I'm flattered, but why didn't you ask me sooner when you saw me standing beside the school."

"I couldn't even find the words. When it comes to such a beautiful woman such as yourself, how could I ever find the words to even ask you?"

I glanced down at my hands then back up at him smiling. "You think I'm beautiful?"

"Yes."

"You're so sweet."

"And you're beautiful. You make me feel so comfortable. It's almost as if I'm back home."

"Really?"

"I know this probably isn't a great time to ask, but would you mind going out with me tomorrow?"

"I would love to, even if it was just to sit here and talk to you."

"Where should I pick you up?"

"Oh, maybe this was a bad idea."

"Why?"

"You might think different of me once you know where I live."

"I'm not so sure of that. I know you must be in a foster home considering you lost your family."

"You don't think that's a turnoff?"

"No."

"You're sweeter than I ever imagined you to be in person."

"And you're much more beautiful than I ever imagined you to be." I smiled looking at him with flirtatious eyes, fluttering to his every movement as if he was the only person I wanted to be with at this moment.

There was then silence in the limo as we stared into each other's eyes. I didn't know whether to lean forward and kiss him or wait for him, and then it happened. The limo stopped; we pulled up to the most incredible-looking hotel I have ever seen in my life.

The driver got out and walked around the limo over to Clay's door and opened it. He got out as I watched him. He then turned towards me and held out his hand for me and helped me out. "Where are we?"

"This is where I'm staying."

"Really? Wow. It's so tall. I mean…"

Clay smiled as he led me by the hand into the hotel. When we entered, people stared at us as we walked over to the elevator and walked inside with one another. I watched as Clay told the man inside the elevator his room number. "Up on fourteen, sir."

"That's high."

"It is?"

"I've only lived in a two-story house, never a fourteen."

"I can't wait to show you the view; you're going to love it when you see it."

"I hope I don't get scared in front of you."

"You don't have to worry about that, Tara."

"I know, but I just don't want to look like a fool in front of you."

"That's not possible."

I giggled turning my head away from him as I smiled feeling wonderful inside. When we arrived at his door to the hotel room, he pulled out the key from his jacket pocket while smiling at me. Clay turned and faced me, then the door, and I walked in. He closed the door, walked towards me, then placed his hand in mine and slowly walked me towards the window. "I want to show you something." I looked out the window with a smile across my face as he stared at me. I glanced over at him seeing him smirking at me.

"Thank you."

"For what?"

"For listening to me when I was at my lowest."

Clay turned towards me, looking into my eyes, then placed my hands in his as I stared at him in silence. "I'm so glad you decided to come to the mall today, Tara."

"Why is that, Clay?"

"Because I have this feeling that you're the one for me."

"If all this talk is just a game you play to get me into bed with you, then…"

"No, of course not, Tara. I'm not putting on a act to get you into bed with me. I'm still trying to comprehend that such a beautiful woman is in my room with me."

"Why wouldn't I be? You seem like a great guy."

"Because I have never met such an honest woman in my life. Every time you smile, I get chills. You're an angel."

I started to blush so I leaned forward and placed my head on his chest embarrassed. He knew exactly what to say at exactly the right moment. I wasn't sure if he was really into me yet, but all my thoughts pointed to yes. He put his hand on my chin lifting me up to look at him. "You don't have to hide from me, Tara. I'm not going to tease you because you're blushing."

"I'm not blushing."

He smirked, almost laughing, then he leaned forward kissing me. I felt the magic in our kiss. You know the spark that every woman looks for within a kiss. He had that feeling of everlasting eternal love, and I felt it in his kiss. "You're so beautiful." He walked with me towards the sofa that was nearby still not taking his eyes off of me.

"I think I should probably go now, Clay."

"Have dinner with me."

"I would love to, but I have to go."

"Well, at least let me take you home."

"But what if everyone sees me get out of a limo with you?"

"Let them."

"You don't mind?"

"Why should I? Hell, I would love for everyone to see me with you." I smiled then watched as Clay walked away from me and called his limo driver to meet him downstairs. When we finally left his room and entered the lobby, we went through the doors towards the limo. I linked Clay's arm leaning close to him as I looked around.

"It's so weird having everyone open doors for us."

Clay just smirked at me, as if what I had said was cute to him. When we were in the limo and I was being driven home, Clay held my hand smiling at me.

When we arrived at my foster home, the driver pulled over a block from the house. The driver stayed in the limo as Clay and I sat in back staring at one another in the same way we always had. "Isn't your driver going to come around and open the door?"

"No."

"I thought he always does that?"

"Oh, you're right, he does, but not this time. I'm going to let you out myself." He opened the door and got out then reached his hand in helping me out as I smiled at him. We stepped away from the door and began walking towards the house.

"How come we're so far away from the house?"

"Oh, that way it really feels as if I took you home." Clay smirked at me as if something was up.

"You planned this, didn't you? I don't know how you did it, but you planned it, right?"

"Maybe."

I stared at him wondering what was going on then questioned him. "When did you plan it?"

He stood silently as if he had to think about what to say. "While we were at my house. Remember I was on my cell phone in the other room?"

"No."

Clay looked down at the ground knowing he had been caught.

"What is going on? I don't understand how you planned all this. We were together the whole time, remember?" I was starting to get very confused. I didn't want to show him anger, but he wasn't telling me anything.

"It's nothing, Tara. Don't worry about it."

"I just need to know what you're hiding. Why won't you tell me what it is?"

"Come on." Clay pulled me gently towards his limo and opened the car door wanting me to get in again.

"Clay, please, I don't want to go anywhere with you unless you're honest with me."

"Okay, I planned it a week ago. Lindsey was supposed to bring you to the mall today, and we were supposed to meet, but it happened differently. You started crying and here we are."

"That's all you can say is, 'Here we are'?"

"Well, it's just that I've been so nervous to even meet you. I wanted it to be perfect when I met you, and it was."

"Oh."

"You're not mad at me about this, are you? I never meant it to upset you."

"I'm not upset, I was just confused."

"Thank God, you scared me there. I almost thought you were going to run for it and never want to see me again."

"I scared you. I was afraid you were hiding a big secret about how you knew me or something."

"No, I wouldn't keep anything that big from you. I really care about you. I've been planning to be with you for a while now."

"I thought you just knew about me from Jennifer."

"I did, but..."

"But?" I waved my hand as if to signal for him to carry on.

"Look, I have a confession to make to you."

"What is it?"

"Well, I knew you for a much longer time than what I told you."

"What?"

"I've known you for about two months now."

"How did you really find out about me?"

"Do you remember walking downtown where I live, and you saw a black limo parked outside on the street."

"Um-hmm."

"Anyway, you commented about how rich people always show off by parking their money so it's displayed on the street for the less fortunate to drool over. Then I remember the last thing you said, 'Except Clay Edison, he would never flaunt his possessions, he's such a man.'"

I began to laugh with him as he finished his story.

"You started spinning around in circles with your arms spread open like a bird, then bumped right into my friend leaving him drenched with his hot cup of coffee. You began giggling at him as he jumped up and down from the burning sensation."

"Right, the man that yelled at me and said I spilt his coffee all over his new suit. He even wanted me to replace it, so I reached my hand into my purse pulling out enough penny rolls for a coffee and placed it into his hand."

"Well, remember you thought you saw someone behind the other side of the limo?"

"Yeah."

"Well, that was me watching. I couldn't stop laughing at what you did, and I didn't want you to first meet me laughing my ass off."

"Oh, Clay."

"You made me laugh even harder when he told you that he had meant for you to replace his suit and not his coffee. So you started trying to take off his suit so you could replace it. He asked you what you were doing, and you told him you were going to bring it home with you and trade it with one of your daddy's. I couldn't believe how wonderful you were. You made me laugh so hard. After that day, I knew I needed to find a way to meet you." He then linked my arm in his and walked me towards the house again, as we laughed about the story he had just told me. When we reached the entrance, he leaned toward me and pressed his lips upon mine leaving me speechless. "Goodbye, Tara." "Goodbye, Clayton."

CHAPTER 5

In the Spotlight

The next day, I was feeling as though I was healed finally from everything that had happened. Then I heard the news that my sister had gone to live with her grandparents as if she was already giving up. The afternoon came, and I prepared myself for the date I would be going on with Clay later in the evening. Then as I was getting ready, I heard someone knock at my bedroom door, so I opened it not knowing who was there. "Jennifer."

Jennifer pushed me inside and closed the door after we entered my room together. "Where were you yesterday? People are saying that they saw you with Clay Edison."

"Yeah, so? What's it to you who I'm with?"

Jennifer grabbed me by the shoulders glaring at me. "I'm only going to tell you once, and if you don't listen, I'm going to make your life a living nightmare. You hear me? You stay away from Clay, he's mine, and we're an item."

"You're not with him. He said he never even talked to you that much. He was more into me."

"He said that? Well, we'll see about that one, now won't we?" Jennifer released her grip on my shoulders then stormed out of the room. I didn't know whether to be worried or not think anything of her behavior towards me about Clay.

Hours had gone by with me waiting downstairs by the curb for Clay to show up, but there was no sound to be heard and no limo in my sight. I was only going to wait twenty more minutes, and so I did, but still no Clay Edison. "He forgot about me. He just used me, I guess. I knew it was too good to be true." I got up off the ground from sitting on the curb and went back inside. When I entered my room, I tore off the red dress I had just bought and burst into tears. I didn't understand how a man could be so head over heels for me and then turn around and just give it up like it had meant nothing. My sadness returned, and I had nothing more to be grateful for. I climbed underneath my bed covers and turned off the light holding a picture of my parents in my hands crying.

"Oh, Mom, you always knew what to say when I was upset about something. I miss you all so much, and I wish I didn't have to go through all this on my own. I really like Clay. I don't understand how he can just walk away like this without even telling me the reason as to why he never showed up."

A week had gone by of my not even hearing from Clay. I was still very upset with him about what he had done. I grabbed my things for school and left the house quickly thinking about how Clay just stood me up. When I reached the street, I started walking towards the school noticing a black limo following beside me at the same pace that I had been walking. I stood where I was, looking into the window trying to see who was inside of the limo, but I couldn't. Suddenly, the limo came to a complete stop, and Clay Edison got out, stood in front of the door, and stared at me. I just stood in front him surprised that he was even here waiting for me outside my house as if he cared. Clay reached into his pocket pulling out a photograph then tossed it towards me onto the ground. I bent down and picked it up then stood back up looking at the picture closely. I saw that it was a picture of Brandon and me. I had dated Brandon about one year ago. I flipped it over onto the back and read. "Clay Edison is such a phony." It hadn't even been my writing, but I knew right then that he had believed that it was.

"Why did you stand me up? I got all dolled up for you for a date that I thought you were excited about."

Clay stepped towards me in anger. "Jennifer told me about that man in the picture."

"What? Brandon? What about him?"

"She told me that he's still your boyfriend and that is a recent picture to prove it."

"You have no idea what you're talking about. Brandon and I went out last year, and then he got killed in an airplane on his way to Minnesota at Christmastime. Also, the writing on the back isn't even mine. If anyone wrote that, it's Jennifer. So don't you dare stand there and make me feel stupid. As if I'm the one to blame for our confusion. If it's anyone's fault, it's yours for believing that I would lead you on like that."

Clay looked down at the ground then walked over to me placing his hands over mine looking at me in apology. "I'm so sorry, Tara. I didn't know."

"Yeah, that's right, you didn't, but for what it's worth, I'm not so sure I can be with you right now. I can't believe that you would even believe that I was with another man even though I let you kiss me."

"I'm sorry, just please don't leave angry with me. Come sit in my limo and talk about this."

I glanced down at our hands then heard a crowd of people coming from down the street screaming Clay's name. "We have to leave now before they catch up to us."

I pulled away from him as he stared at me. "I'm sorry. I can't." He then got back into his limo and was driven away quickly before the crowd caught up to him. I stood where I was wondering if I had really made the right choice in not going with him. I knew that if I had gotten in, he would think that it was alright for him to believe any kind of rumor and expect me to be there for him to blame me for something I never did. I had to take my stand now and be strong so he didn't start thinking I'd let him treat me in any way he chose to just because he was Clay Edison. If he was going to be with me, he was going to have to show me that he could earn my full respect back somehow. I just didn't know what he could do to earn it.

After school, I slowly walked towards my house with Lindsey thinking about Clay. I hadn't even told her about Clay and what had happened that day in the mall. "Lindsey?"

"Yeah."

"I have something to tell you."

"What is it?"

"Well, remember the day we went girl shopping and Clay had been signing autographs in the center of the mall by the fountains?"

"Yeah, why?"

"Well, I had gone up to get his autograph, but when I approached him at the table, I started crying and fell to the ground. He picked me up and carried me to his limo where he wiped the tears from my eyes. We ended up hitting it off, and he took me to his hotel room where we kissed. It was so incredible."

"I knew he liked you."

"Yeah, but we got into an argument about how he believed Jennifer that I had been with Brandon still, and I told him the truth. Then he wanted me to come sit with him in his limo and talk."

"Well, did you?"

"Well, no, how could I? He stood me up. He ditched me on our first date because of Jennifer."

"Oh, Tara, you should have got in his limo. He'll probably never come back."

"You think so?"

"Well, you did blow him off after he apologized."

"Oh my God, what have I done?"

"Well, I guess nothing because there he is."

"Where?"

I turned around then saw Clay pulling up beside me in his limo once more. The car door opened, and he got out as quickly as he could. "I'm so sorry, Tara. Let me make it up to you."

I looked into his eyes as he stared at me waiting for my answer. "Okay, but only for a minute." We then got into his limo and closed the door. I felt the limo drive away from Lindsey. I sat beside him not looking at him. My legs were turned towards the other door away from him. He moved closer and placed his hand on my chin gently turning me to face him. "Would you believe me if I said I was sorry?"

"No."

"Well, maybe after tonight, you will."

Shortly after the limo came to a stop, I watched as Clay bent over and pulled out a gift box from underneath the seat. He placed it onto my lap waiting for me to open it. I smiled then ripped open the gift and saw that it was a long pink gown with pink satin shoes to go with it.

"Put it on."

"Here? In front of you? Uh, I don't think so."

Header

"Come on, I won't look. I'll turn around to face the back, alright?"

"Fine, but no peeking."

I took off my clothes and pulled the gown over my head. All you could hear was the crinkling of the dress as I struggled to put it on. "Do you need any help?"

"Yeah, kind of." Clay turned around just as I had finally gotten the gown over my head and past my shoulders. "Clay, don't look."

"But you said…"

Clay turned back around as I finished getting dressed. I sat down putting on the pink shoes to match the beautiful gown he had given to me. "Okay, I'm ready."

Clay turned around and faced me smiling while he checked me out. "You look…beautiful, breathless." As he was staring at me, we then heard a knock at the window, and Clay opened the door. When he did, three hairdressers entered the limo with us picking at my hair as Clay closed the door. All I remember is them telling me to turn this way and move that way. After they had finished with my hair and makeup, they left the limo. Clay then got out and turned towards me holding out his hand waiting for me to grab it. I sat there scared of what I would be going outside to.

"Aren't you going to take my hand?"

"Are you kidding me? I don't know what's out there. For all I know, there could be people out there."

"Well, there are people; you're right about that one."

"Where?" I placed my hand over his, and he helped me out being careful that I didn't tear my gown. As soon as I got out, I looked around and saw I had been standing on the red carpet in front of many photographers taking our picture as I smiled in the best way I could, being surprised and all. "What are we doing here?"

Clay leaned towards me, and he whispered, "I'm apologizing."

"Oh, don't, you don't have to do that, not in front of so many people at least."

"Oh, Tara." He giggled as I linked his arm and he walked with me into the building with all the other people following behind us. When we entered, he took me into the back where he showed me to a group of strangers and left to go somewhere. The group of strangers handed me a song and told me to go practice with the band before the show started. I had no clue how they expected me to sing a song I had never seen before within an hour.

After the time had run out for me to practice the song, the band told me I would sing it great. I got on stage as the curtains opened to a dark stage. Suddenly, there was a spotlight that shined upon me. I was suddenly surprised, and I started to giggle. I then saw another spotlight shine upon Clay sitting directly in front of the stage in a seat below. I heard the music begin as I stepped forward beginning to sing the song I had memorized. The thing that was great was I had only been singing to Clay, so even if I messed up, I knew it was only Clay and I and also the band that would even know about it.

When I had finished the song, the whole room lit up, and I saw that it had really been millions of people that had heard me sing, also, and they all started applauding. They had really loved my performance. After I got off the stage, I jumped into Clay's arms as I laughed, telling him he was so crazy for getting me to do that.

"Let's go, shall we?"

"We shall, but no more surprises, okay?"

"Oh." Clay looked at me with puppy eyes as if he had another one up his sleeve.

"It doesn't involve people, does it?"

"No."

"Alright, one more."

"Oh."

"What? There's another one after that?"

"Just one last one."

"Okay, go on, show them to me."

He held onto my hand as we hurried to the limo and got inside, closed the door behind us, and felt the limo drive away. Clay looked at me and smiled. "Close your eyes, beautiful." I held them closed tightly as I felt him place something around my neck. "Okay, open." I looked in the mirror that was in front of us beside the bar, and there hung a diamond butterfly necklace around my neck.

"Do you like it?"

"I love it, but…"

"But what?"

Header

I turned and faced him. "You didn't have to do this."

"Do you not like it?"

"No, it's not that. It's just that you didn't have to; that's all."

"It looks beautiful on you."

I started to blush with embarrassment as he stared at me. "If this is the other gift, what's the last one?"

"This." Clay leaned forward, pressing his lips upon mine kissing me. He lay me down on my back on the seat as we began making out. I was sinking into his love and falling into his kisses that were so irresistible. All I could see as we kissed was our wedding day flashing before my eyes. I saw as I walked down the aisle to the man of my dreams, which was Clay. We then felt the limo come to a stop, and we stayed where we were kissing as he as he lowered the shoulder straps of my dress.

"Oh, Tara, you're so beautiful." He sat up above me then tore open his silk shirt he had been wearing that day. Suddenly, I realized what we were about to do. He kissed my lips, my neck, and my chest, dragging his hands all the way down to my ass.

"Stop, stop, I can't do this, I'm sorry." I sat up and quickly changed into the clothes I had been wearing before he had given me the dress as he watched me confused. I moved away from him, opened the door, and then I ran out.

"Tara, come back." I heard him calling my name as I started to run hurrying down the sidewalk looking back seeing him close the door and turn the limo around towards me. Suddenly, I felt like I was being chased. I ran into a clothing store nearby. I tried to find a back entrance before he found me feeling very embarrassed about what had happened. What was I to do? I had to leave him there even though he looked so good without his shirt on. I couldn't believe I had stopped Clay Edison from having sex with me. Any other girl would say I was crazy to do that. I was only eighteen. I wasn't sure if I was quite ready for a man in my life yet. As I stood at the back of the store looking at the doorknob of the back entrance, it finally came to me that I knew I had made a mistake by running away from him without talking it through like I probably should have done. I turned around and saw Clay standing in front of me with his silk shirt snapped up the wrong way. It looked as if he had buttoned it up in a hurry. He was breathing heavily as he stared at me trying to get his words out.

"I don't know what happened back there, but I'm sorry it happened."

I stood staring as he walked up to me and placed his hands upon either side of my arms staring at me. "Was it me?"

"No, it's not you, it's me."

"Do you want to go somewhere?"

"Why?"

"Well, for one, there are photographers staring at us taking pictures as if there was something to see."

"Fine."

He walked with me holding my hand as we walked outside past the crowd back into the limo to take us somewhere. We drove to his place and went upstairs to his room still recovering from what had happened. When we entered, I walked towards the sofa and sat down waiting for Clay to come sit beside me. He walked over to me then knelt down between my legs on his knees, staring at me. "Oh, Tara, what am I going to do with you?"

"What?"

"Well, you always push me away. I try to get closer to you, and you push me away."

"I only did it once, so what are you talking about?"

"Please just talk to me. Do you really want to be with me, Tara? If not, don't lead me on."

"Clay, don't make me sit here and feel as though you really can't see that I want you as badly as you want me."

"I'm just confused. I'm trying to contemplate this whole situation of ours."

"Clay."

Clay rose to his feet and walked away from me putting his hands through his hair as if he was upset. I stood up watching him stare out the window. "Are you mad at me, Clay?"

"No, just frustrated."

"About what?"

He turned around and faced me then lowered his hands. "About what? You turned me on so bad. I thought we were about to go further, but you stopped me. That wasn't as bad as you running out of the car as if I had forced myself on you."

"Clay, I didn't mean to. I wanted you to, but I…"

"You what?"

"I couldn't do it. I couldn't go through with it, and it was too soon."

Clay placed his hands at his sides walking toward me again slowly. "Well, you should have thought about that before you let me go so far."

"It all happened so fast. I didn't realize what was about to happen until you tore off your shirt staring down at me. What do you want me to say, besides I'm sorry?"

"All I want is to know whether you're attracted to me or not?"

I walked up to him and pressed my lips upon his, kissing him gently and showing that I was. I started taking off his shirt and running my hands through his hair. I saw his facial expression turn to excitement at my every touch. "I want you, Clay." I kissed his shoulders, apologizing as I looked up at him waiting for him to react to my actions.

Suddenly, he started kissing me back, whispering that he was so attracted to me. "Oh, Tara, I want you so bad." We started making out standing up, taking each other's clothes off staring at one another. "Wait, don't just go through with this because of me."

"I'm not."

"I think you are." He pulled away from me looking as if he had thought that I was just trying to please him so he wouldn't be upset with me anymore, which was probably true. "I'm not mad at you. We don't have to do anything."

"We don't?"

"No, all I want is to be able to spend time with you."

"I want that, too."

"Well, let's just forget about all that has happened and start over."

"Are you sure you can let go of this?"

Clay looked at me and lifted me up as I wrapped my legs around him. He carried me into his bedroom and stood by the bed smirking. "I don't know." He then dropped me onto the bed and jumped on the bed right after I had landed laughing. He started tickling me as he snarled and laughed making funny faces.

"You're so funny, Clay." He lay beside me on his back as I lay on mine.

"Tara, do think that everyone in this world has somebody out there for them?"

"I think that many people aren't given the opportunities to meet the man or woman they truly want."

"Why do you think that, Tara?"

"Well, just look at the world around us. I mean, there are categories of people. There's the stars and there's the people that are fortunate and the ones that are not which are forgotten."

"What are you saying exactly?"

"What I'm saying is that before I met you, I was just an ordinary girl praying for something out of my reach. I was dreaming of being able to share a life with you just like many other girls out there. There are so many girls out there that are praying for a man they will never get the chance to meet just because of the size of their wallets."

"Well, you and I met."

"Well, sometimes fate is stronger than money, and love was more powerful in our case; that's why we're together."

"You're such a wonderful person, Tara. We used to be these strangers that thought about one another but never thought we would ever be together. Now, we're like this couple that argues and talks about life, laughing our asses off at everything we do."

"That's because you're so damn funny."

Clay sat up, leaning over top of me and smiling down at me. "And you're so damn sexy. It's going to be really hard not to go further than kissing you."

"Well, maybe we should then."

"No, not until you're ready. Don't just do it for my sake; do it for yours, too, okay?"

"You're so considerate of my feelings."

"I would never want to make you feel as if you had to sleep with me."

"Oh, Clay."

CHAPTER 6
Hide and Seek

I awoke from my dreams feeling refreshed from my night with Clay after he had dropped me off late last night. We kissed and said goodbye until tomorrow, which was now today. I rose up from my warm covers and sat up seeing Lindsey in a chair looking at me with today's paper in her hand.

"What are you doing there just watching me sleep like that?"

"Oh, I came for this." Lindsey stood up placing the paper on my bed faced up so that I could see the front cover. She stood there crossing her arms towards me waiting for me to read what it said.

"What's this?"

On the cover there appeared a picture of Clay and me on the red carpet and also another one of us in a clothing store. The writing below the red carpet picture stated, "Clay Edison was seen with a new woman in a long pink gown. She sang for an opening act before the awards were announced. Stars said that she had a beautiful voice." Under the picture, there was one of us in the clothing store. I started to read. "Clay Edison seen with another woman later that evening as they then ran back into his limo together. Everyone said she was an ordinary girl that he had just offered to take into his car, without knowing her." I placed the paper down onto my bed and looked at Lindsey seeing her stare at me with open eyes.

"What is this all about, Tara? Who is this other woman?"

"That's me. I went to the awards ceremony with him."

"But it doesn't look like you."

"Yeah, that's because three professional hairdressers did my hair and makeup." "Oh, wait, let me see that again." She picked up the paper trying to see if she could determine that the other woman had been me. "Oh, it is you, sorry, I can't tell unless I really look at it closely." We sat and talked for awhile, as I told her all about the time I had with Clay and how much fun we had together. "You're so lucky to be able to sleep with Clay. He's so hot."

"Actually, we haven't even done anything yet. We're more into kissing and talking right now."

"Are you telling me that in the time you've spent with Clay, you two haven't done IT?"

"Well, we almost did when we were in his limo driving back from the awards ceremony."

"What made you stop? Was he bad?"

"No, nothing like that, it was me. I stopped him from going any further. I wasn't ready."

"Man, he must have been upset."

"Yeah, he was, thanks for reminding me."

"I didn't mean it like that. I meant that guys always get frustrated when girls lead them on as if they're about to, but then they don't. Guys are hound dogs; they constantly want sex."

"I don't think Clay is like that. He's more of a man that will wait for me." "Really?" Lindsey was silent for a couple minutes, thinking about something. She then leaned forward with a big smile upon her face. "So did you see his, uh, you know?" "Lindsey."

"What?"

She started giggling and asked again, "Well, did you?"

"No, I told you we didn't get that far."

"You should spend the night at his place and peek when he's sleeping."

"Lindsey."

"What?"

"I think he would probably find it pretty weird if I just spent the night without even doing anything. Also, imagine if he woke up seeing me pulling on his boxers taking a quick peek. That would be so embarrassing for me and for him, don't you think? Having him actually looking up at me wondering why I'm checking his package out as if I had permission."

"Well, you do. You're with him, so his package is yours."

"Since when is it mine? It's on his body."

"So? It doesn't matter where it is. All that matters is where your hand is when you're claiming your possession."

"Oh, Lindsey, I think you need better things to do in your day rather than thinking about how big my boyfriend's package is. Next, you'll be telling me to look at his hand just to find out."

"Hey, now, there's an idea."

"Lindsey, you're so wild, you know that?"

Just as we finished our conversation, we heard a knock at my door, so I got up from the bed and answered the door. I was wearing white socks and a Winnie the Pooh T-shirt with boxers and my hair tied back in a ponytail. I opened the door and saw Clay standing outside my door all wet from the rain. He stood there dripping with water from head to toe checking me out as he smiled.

"Hi, Clay."

"Hey, sweetie, can I come in?"

"Of course, would I say no to you?" I let him in looking down the hallway seeing girls peeking out their doors. I smirked, feeling special that Clay was with me. I closed the door and went into the bathroom with Clay to help him dry off, then I walked over to my dresser and took out some clothes of mine that would probably fit him until his clothes were dry. I handed them to Clay as he giggled, knowing I was insisting that he put them on. "Here, they're warm, they're dry, and they're just for you to wear until the ones that you have on are dry."

"Okay, but I better still feel like a man when I come out."

"You will."

Clay closed the bathroom door and changed his clothes, hanging his wet ones over the shower. I told Lindsey to leave before Clay came out of the bathroom wearing my clothes. After a couple of minutes of waiting, I called to him. "Aren't you finished yet?"

"Yeah."

"Well, come on, I want to see how you look."

"I don't want to. I look weird."

"Come on."

The bathroom door slowly began to open as Clay stepped out. I couldn't help but burst into laughter at how he looked. "What?"

"You look good." I let out a much harder laugh trying to hold it back, but how could I? He looked like he was busting out of my belly shirt and my boxers on him were so small I could almost peek without having to wait until he was sleeping. He took the shirt off, giggling and realizing he was silly to even try it on.

"I'm changing back into the wet ones."

"No."

"Well, then I'm walking around naked." I was silent as he stared at me waiting for me to reply with some kind of remark of some sort, but I didn't. I wasn't sure if I liked the idea or if I was just daydreaming about what it would be like if he did. "You don't mind if I'm naked?"

"Yes, I do."

"Well, then why didn't you answer?"

"Where are your boxers you wore here?"

"What makes you think I wore boxers here?"

"What did you wear then?"

He smirked not saying anything. I knew just by his silence what he meant. "Sorry I asked."

Clay went back into the bathroom, took off my boxers, then replaced them with a towel that he had wrapped around his waist, coming out right after.

"There you are, my pretty-in-pink man."

He sat on the end of my bed with a pink towel wrapped tightly around his waist. "Don't laugh; it's not funny. I feel like a woman in this towel."

"Don't be silly, you look fabulous, Mrs. Edison." I giggled as he got up, about to go back into the bathroom embarrassed. I grabbed him by the arm telling him not to. "I didn't mean it. I was just trying to be funny."

"I know you were."

"Come sit down on the bed with me."

Clay glanced at my messy bed that hadn't been made, smirking at me as he started making the covers perfect.

"Are you cleaning my room?"

"No, just making myself comfortable; that's all."

I then pulled him down onto the bed beside me and stared over at him.

"What are you doing, missy?"

I laughed as I watched him stare at me with one of his eyebrows raised. "So what do you want to do today?" I asked Clay as he noticed the paper on the floor that had fallen off the bed, most likely when he had been making the bed.

"What's that?" He picked it up reading it. "Did you see this, Tara?"

"Yeah, why?"

"Don't take these articles seriously; they're just there for entertainment."

"Some entertainment, using other peoples lives as news, making everyone seem as though they're worse off than what they really are."

"Please promise me you'll never let this stuff get to you."

"I promise."

I looked at Clay knowing that he had been worried that I would believe what the articles would eventually say. As the time went by and more people found out that we were together, they'd suddenly have more to say about us. They'd follow us around waiting for a time when they could try and build up a good story, snapping their cameras, making their films. Everyone needed space to breathe, but when you were a star like Clay Edison, it kind of went with the territory to be plastered everywhere in the world.

They made stardom so hard to reach, so the road there would prepare you for what you would eventually have to end up dealing with once you made it. Suddenly, everyone would want to know your deepest, darkest secrets and all the things that you enjoy doing. That way, they would know you enough to write about you in a way that they made you out to be the person you dreaded the most in life, your opposite. Like the saying always goes, "Keep your friends close and your enemies closer"; that way, when they wanted something, they'd know how to get it. After all, what are friends for, right?

After thinking for awhile, I watched as Clay placed the paper down onto the bed and turned towards me. "What were your parents like?"

"Clay." I moved away, crossing my arms, offended that he would even bring them up after I had finally moved past what had happened.

"I thought you said that I had helped you accept what happened to them."

"I have accepted their death."

"You haven't accepted it; you just tore them out of your life and replaced them with me as if they're replaceable."

"Let's just drop it, okay? If I don't want to talk about them, then let's just forget about them, alright?" I moved towards Clay kissing him on the lips trying to get him to forget about my parents. I would have rather had sex with him when I was not ready than have to talk about my parents. Clay placed his hand over my lips gently, preventing me from kissing him.

"What? You don't like my kisses anymore?"

"That's not it."

"What is it then?"

"I want to help you. I really want to know about your parents."

I cleared my throat, walking away from him towards the bathroom. "No, I can't do it, I told you."

Clay raised his voice as he said, "You put your foot down and that's it? You want me to be honest with you all the time, but you won't budge."

"Fine, you want to know, I'll tell you. They were the most wonderful parents in the world. Yeah, they were loud, yeah, they fought when they were together, but there was this feeling they gave me when they showed me love. I loved them." I was silent placing my hand to my mouth struggling to finish. "Oh, God, Clay, I miss them so much." I fell to my knees crying as he knelt down beside me wrapping his arms around me comforting me as I let my sadness out. "I need them. Why did they leave me? Why did they just give up on me?"

"They loved you; they couldn't help not leaving you. I'm sure they tried their best to stay with you, but it was too hard. Their bodies couldn't take it, so they let the angels deliver them to God."

I looked up at him in tears. "I didn't know you were spiritual."

He smiled letting me know he was, and I knew right at that moment that he was definitely the one that I was meant to be with. He was the only man that would ever understand me, I mean really understand me, as if he could see my soul.

"I feel so alone when you're not around. I feel as if when you're here, I can do almost anything."

Clay stared into my eyes then kissed my forehead. "Do you want to come with me?"

"Where?"

"Everywhere."

I thought about what he could have meant by "everywhere." I imagined that being anywhere with him was exciting and wondered what it would be like going everywhere with him. "Where exactly is everywhere, Clay?"

"I could get you out of this place. You could come live where I do."

"Where's that?"

"Well, it would mean you would have to go where I do since my career makes it hard to stay in one place all the time."

"Oh, I would have to think about that."

"Just think of all the fun we'll have together."

"That's asking a lot of me, Clay."

"All I'm asking is that you consider it. After all, what do you have to stay here for besides Lindsey?"

I looked away from him offended, then I faced Clay once more. "That's not fair, Clay."

"Well, I'm sorry, but I'm just upset that your heart can't decide a simple question of whether you are willing to be with me or not."

"Clay, listen to me. We just met a little while ago, and you're starting to act as if we're together. Are you that certain that I'm the only one for you?"

"I don't know what I'm feeling. All I know is that when I'm looking into those beautiful eyes of yours, there is no one else I would rather be with than you."

"I feel the same way, but I'm scared."

"What is there possibly to be afraid of, Tara?"

"I don't know. Just give me some time to think about things before I make the decision of going anywhere with you."

"What is there to think about, Tara?"

"I have to figure out if this is love I'm really feeling for you or not."

"Who said anything about love, Tara? All I asked is why your heart can't decide whether or not you want to be with me."

"You know what I meant, Clay."

"Obviously, I didn't."

"Why are you being like this?"

"How did you think I would react to you not answering my question as if you don't feel as I do?"

"You want to know the truth, Clay?"

"Yes, it would be helpful at this moment."

"I'm afraid of getting close to you. I'm afraid the closer I get, the more likely you'll probably be taken away from me as quickly as you came into my life."

"You don't have to worry about that, Tara. If we're together, it's forever. I'm not going anywhere."

"Not even you can say when God will take you. Look how my family ended up."

"Please, just don't compare our lives to how your family ended up; we're different people, facing different lives."

"I'm just scared, that's all."

Clay stood up, walking away from me in silence not knowing what to say. "Are you hiding something from me, Clay?"

Clay turned around to face me and raised his left eyebrow. "What would make you think it's me that's hiding something?"

"You never act like this, especially to me."

"If anyone's hiding something, it's you, Tara."

I looked down at my feet about to cry from feeling as if our relationship was about to end as quickly as it had begun. "Don't you dare direct your anger at me as if I'm nothing to you now."

"Well, maybe it's you that doesn't feel the same as I do."

"Well, that would probably be a good thing at this moment since you're acting as if I'm the problem."

"What?"

"You know what I said, Clay."

"Yeah, I do, you're implying that I'm the problem."

I paused wiping the tears from my eyes staring at Clay as if I didn't know who he was at the moment. Clay looked as if he was bothered by something, but I wasn't quite sure what it was. "Clay."

"No, don't bother explaining, I understand."

"No, you don't."

"Tara, I can't believe you gave me up, just like that."

I stared at him with a firm, steady look wondering what to do and then the words came to me. "Get out, just leave."

Clay looked surprised by what I had said. "What? You're ending it?"

"No, Clay, you must be confused, you're the one who chose this."

"You know what your problem is, Tara? You can't tell if something's real or not. I think you're just not grown up enough to make the decision of being with me."

"Get out, Clay."

"I'll leave, but don't come crying to me when you realize you were wrong."

"You found me; you gave me life again. You showed me love, and now you push me away without an explanation as to why."

"Tara."

"Leave, I said, I don't want to see you anymore."

Clay stood in front of me staring at me as if he already had regrets about what he had done. "Tara."

"Just leave, Clay."

Clay went into the bathroom and put on his wet clothes then came out placing the pink towel he had worn onto the bed beside me as if to say goodbye. He walked over to me about to kiss me, but I pulled away from him and he walked over to the door then left. I stood beside my bed in tears then walked towards the door and locked it. When I turned away from the door towards my bed, I heard a knock at the door.

"Tara, Tara, open the door; I'm sorry. I didn't mean it. I'm so sorry."

"Go away, Clay, just leave."

"No, I want to talk."

"You've done enough, now leave me alone." I ran to the door leaning my back up against it trying to hear every word.

"No, Tara, it's important; I need to tell you."

"No, go away. I don't want to be with you."

"I know you don't mean that, now open the door before it's too late."

"Too late for what?"

"Open the door, and I'll tell you."

"I don't trust you, now leave."

"I'm not leaving you, I love you."

"Why don't you just go away? It was a bad idea for us to be together. Why did you carry me to your limo? Why did you like me so much?"

"Because…"

"Because why?"

"Because you make life more interesting. My life was boring before you. You were a bright light that lit up my life with such beauty. It wasn't until you that I knew how to love. I fell in love with you, just as you fell in love with me."

I leaned against the door then rose up to my feet walking towards the bed picking up the pink towel and holding it to my nose. I smelt the fresh scent of Clay that had been left behind from his body as I started to cry more, missing his touch already. I listened to hear more of what Clay still had to say to me, but I heard silence. I walked over to the door and slowly unlocked it, trying to be as quiet as possible. I turned the doorknob and opened it slowly peeking outside my door for Clay. I saw a glimpse of him turning the corner down the hallway towards the office. I stood where I was thinking about why he would leave so soon. Where would he be going? He wouldn't just give up just like that. He was up to something. I had to get out of there.

I looked around at everyone staring out of their bedroom doors trying to figure out what was going on. I ran back into my room, threw on an outfit, and left locking the door behind me as quickly as I could before Clay came back. I didn't know where I was going to hide out. All I knew was that if I stayed, Clay would find some kind of way to get into my room and see me. I was frightened of what he was keeping secret from me. I didn't want to stick around and find out more bad news. I couldn't handle anymore right now. I had been falling in love with him. I had to fight with myself just to make the choice I did by leaving. I thought of his expression when he found out that I was not even in my bedroom anymore. I just prayed that he wouldn't hold that against me. I wanted so much to be able to work things out, but he was so rude to me that I wanted more just to run away from my problems as I always had. What could I have done differently, and if I had, would it have turned out better than it had? I was afraid to even think about what would have happened if I stayed and forgave him just because he asked politely. I knew in my heart that something would have been different. I knew that if I let him kiss me and love me just giving my full self to him, he would have thought he could always treat me like crap when something was bothering him.

I ran down the hallway in the opposite direction of the way he went, trying to find a back entrance and leave before he found me. I saw an exit sign in front of me and ran to the doors trying to push them open, but I couldn't. I tried even harder, struggling as my heart pounded feeling as if it was about to burst. I looked down seeing a bolt lock on the handle. I let out a silent cry of fright and ran in the direction Clay had gone. I had to hide behind the columns in the hallway in case Clay came back to my room while I was leaving. I ran but I had to slow down as I thought I saw someone coming towards me in my direction. I was stuck behind the column that was right beside my door. I planted my feet against one another and held my arms in, being sure no one would be able to see me if they were in front. I then heard someone standing in front of the column that I had been behind in front of my door. I held my breath trying not to make any noise to be caught. I then heard a door unlock as I slowly peeked around to see who it was. I saw Clay look behind him trying to make sure no one was watching him.

I watched as he entered my room slowly, as I stayed where I was not knowing what to do. I thought that if I walked past the room, he would most definitely see me. I didn't know where he was in my room. All I knew was that the door was wide open and Clay was inside about to find out I was not in there. I heard Clay's voice from inside my room, so I listened the best I could. I noticed he was on the phone. "Yeah, she's not. Look, I want you to find her. No, you do what you can. Her life may be in danger." I thought I heard him wrong, so I listened more closely trying to hear him correctly. "Yes, Jennifer Bunkston. I'm going to be heading over to Kevin's so you better have some kind of information about where Tara is before Jennifer finds her." I heard him hang up the phone with a loud noise. I didn't hear Clay come out, so I stayed as still as I could. I then heard him nearby. He must have been leaning against the column I had been hiding behind. "Where are you, Tara? Why didn't you let me in?"

I was about to walk around to him, but I held back, afraid of what he might say to me if I had. I had to wait until he was gone, but he stayed for so long leaning against the column as if he could sense me. "Where are you, Tara? It's like I can almost feel you. You're so close, but I can't see you. I can almost smell you, taste you, and feel your every touch."

"Do you always talk to yourself?" I then heard a woman's voice speak to Clay. I wanted to peek around the column to see who it was, but I couldn't. It was too risky to even try.

"I'm looking for Tara Heart; have you seen her?"

"Yeah, I saw her just a little while ago."

I suddenly couldn't move; it was like I was paralyzed by the sound of the answer "Yes."

"Where did you see her go?"

"Oh, I saw her peek out her door and look at you down the hall, and then she went back in her room."

"No, she's not there. I checked."

"Oh, wait a minute, I saw her again running down that hallway towards the back doors."

"What doors?"

"Down there. I'll show you."

I saw as Clay ran past the girl down the hallway towards the doors quickly. He passed right by me not even noticing me standing behind the column still as I have ever been in my life. I slowly walked around the column before they saw that the door had been locked and came back towards me again. I knew for sure they would find me if they returned to my room. I was walking around the column when I felt my foot get cut. I looked down and saw a nail sticking out from the bottom of the column and a part of my sock had come off. I quickly ran down the hallway not even thinking about anything but getting away as fast as

Header

I could. I reached the office and bumped into Tracey at the front doors. "Whoa, no running in the house, Tara. You have to be more careful when you're in a hurry somewhere."

"Sorry, excuse me."

I walked around her towards the doors to leave. "Oh, Tara, did you get to see the young man that I gave your key to? I think he said his name was Clay. He showed me a picture of you two together for proof so I let him have your key."

"Yeah, we talked, and now we're playing hide and seek, so I've got to go hide before he finds me."

"Oh, okay, I'll see you later, Tara. Have fun."

"I will."

I ran out the doors and left as fast as I could, going towards Lindsey's house. I knew she would know what to do next, because I didn't. Meanwhile, Clay arrived at the back doors finding out they were locked. He knew that I would have had to run back towards where he went so he ran back towards my room. When he came to the column beside my door, he noticed a piece of fabric with blood on it attached to a nail at the bottom of the column. He bent down, picking it up and looking at it. "It's Tara's. I remember this pink print on the bottom of her sock that she was wearing today."

"Are you sure?" the girl with him questioned him. She was not so sure you could tell from a sock.

"Yes, I'm sure." He was silently putting it to his nose, smelling the scent of me still left on it. "It even smells like her still. She must have been standing here when I was…She heard me. She knows, oh my God, she knows. I've got to get out of here."

"Wait, don't you want to know my name?"

"Why?"

"Because I'm one of your fans, and I want to remember you as a singer that asked me, a poor little foster girl, my name."

"Fine, what's your name?"

"My name's Susan; maybe I'll see you around sometime."

"I doubt it."

Clay hurried past her towards the office bumping into Tracy, as I had done not to long ago. "Whoa, watch where you're going, young man. Oh, hey, it's you, Clay, right?"

"Yeah, sorry, excuse me, I've got to go find someone."

"Oh yeah, you're playing hide and seek with Tara."

Clay stopped where he was and looked at Tracy once more. "What did you say?"

"Oh, I bumped into Tara just a little while ago. She said she was playing hide and seek and had to go before you found her."

"Which way did she go?"

"That way." Tracey pointed to the front doors as Clay yelled to her a thank you and hurried through the front doors to find me before Jennifer did. "Oh, Tara, why do you have to be so stubborn?" Clay asked himself as if I could hear him.

He ran to where his limo had been parked, but it was gone. He looked around trying to see where it could have gone. He reached into his jacket pulling out his blue cell phone and calling his limo driver, Steve. "Steve, where are you? I told you to wait outside for me."

"No, you didn't; you said to leave with Tara."

"Yeah, when I get in with Tara. Does it look like Tara's with you, because I don't see you."

"No, Tara's right here in the back of the limo. She said you gave her permission for me to take her somewhere."

"She's there with you right now?"

"Yeah, like I said, she's in the back."

"Well, put her on."

"Okay, hold on."

Clay waited standing in the middle of the empty street waiting to hear my voice. "Sorry, Mr. Edison, she told me to tell you, she's not in the mood to talk to you right at this moment."

"Well, you tell her, that I want to ask her about why she left and took my limo to add to what she has already done."

"Hold on." Clay waited for my answer pacing back and forth in the middle of the street frustrated. "Sorry, Mr. Edison, she said if you want to talk to her, you're going to have to outsmart her somehow."

"Oh, my God, Steve just turn the limo around and bring it back with her in it."

"I don't know; she's demanding that I drive her somewhere."

"Steve, whose limo is it?"

"Uh, yours, sir."

"Then do we have a problem?"

"Uh, now we do, Mr. Edison."

"Why?"

"Because she just got out of the limo and left."

"Well, catch up to her; you have the limo."

"Hold on, let me turn this baby around."

Clay waited patiently for Steve to find me as he walked over to the sidewalk towards the school that I had gone to. "Okay, Mr. Edison, she said she'll only get back in the limo if you promise not to make me drive her there."

Clay was silent for a minute as he thought of what to say next. "Fine, she can have you drive her anywhere she pleases as long as she talks to me for ten minutes on the phone right now."

"Okay, hold on, I'll ask."

Clay lowered himself down to sit on the curb of the street and wait for Steve's answer. "Clay." Clay stood up shocked to hear my voice. "You have five minutes."

"Oh, Tara, you don't know how good it feels to hear your voice right now."

"What do you want, Clay, besides to blame me for everything."

"I'm sorry about everything, Tara. Why don't you just let Steve drive you back to where I am?"

"Sorry, Clay, it's not that easy. I'm not so sure I could handle that."

"Listen to me, Tara. Jennifer talked to me and told me she was going to kill you. She's been sending me threats for a week now. You have to come get me, and I'll help you. I don't want anything to happen to you. I think I'm in love with you. Now, please just tell Steve to drive you here."

"Why would she want to hurt me?"

"You know that answer as well as I do. She's mad about us. She blames you for me not wanting to be with her."

"How do I know you're not just making all this up so I'll come back to you?"

Clay was silent taking a deep breath then blowing it out. "Because I know you heard me when I was in your room on the phone."

"How do you know about that?"

"Because I saw a piece of your sock attached to a nail at the bottom of the column beside your room."

"You know about that, huh?"

"Please, Tara, this isn't the time or place for you to get embarrassed. I need to see you to know you're alright. I said I was sorry. What else do you want me to say?"

"Oh, Clay."

"Yes, 'oh, Clay' is right. Now take a deep breath and get Steve to drive you to where I am, alright?"

"I don't know if I can do that. I think I need some more time to think."

"What would you possibly need to think about? Just let whatever you're confused about wait. I need to see you again. I miss you. I can't breathe without you. I need you here with me."

"If you can't breathe, how is it that you're breathing now?"

"It's an expression, Tara."

I giggled as I listened to Clay get frustrated about me not wanting to come to see him as if I needed him as much as he needed me. "This isn't the time or place in our lives to be making jokes, Tara. Now just come to me as soon as you can; that's the least you can do for me."

"I don't know if I can. I'm so embarrassed right now."

"Why?"

"Because I've messed up the greatest thing I've ever had in my life, and worst of all, it's with Clay Edison, people will think I'm crazy."

"Forget about them, they don't matter."

"How can you say that? They're your fans. Your fans make you Clay Edison."

"No, they may make me popular and earn money, but only you make me Clay Edison."

I was made speechless by what he said to me. I climbed inside the limo as Steve closed the door behind me. I quietly whispered to Steve to drive me to where Clay had been, but to park where he couldn't see the limo. The limo began to drive away as I continued my conversation with Clay on the phone.

"That's very sweet of you to say, but I'm not sure I can believe that you mean everything you're telling me."

"You have to, because I'm telling you the truth."

"Maybe you are, but there is still a possibility that there are more secrets that you could be hiding from me." I heard Clay take a deep breath as he began to sniffle as if he was beginning to cry. I had never heard him cry before. I didn't know what to say, so I said the first thing that had came to mind. "Are you crying, Clay?" It was silent except for the sounds of his sniffling on the other end of the phone.

"Yeah, what does it matter now? You'll probably never want me back. Oh poor Clay Edison, he already has everything, why would he need just one woman when he can have anyone he wants? But the thing is, I don't have everything because I don't have you."

"Oh, Clay, it's alright; you don't know what's going to happen in the future; maybe this is for the best."

"How could being apart be for the best? The reason I asked you to come with me everywhere before was because I'm going on tour again and didn't want to be separated from the one I love. I wanted to be with you and to come home to you no matter where we live, even if there are wheels underneath our house. It will still feel like home if you're there with me, sharing my life. I wanted you to meet my family, share with me a life that is memorable. You have my heart forever, Tara, I mean that."

"Oh, Clay, I don't know what to say."

"Well, 'I love you' would be a start."

I heard silence on the phone as Clay yelled, "Oh crap!"

I got scared that something was happening to him. My heart started to race as I yelled to him on the phone. "Clay, Clay, what happened? Are you okay? Oh God, don't leave me! I love you so much. I want to be with you forever."

"I'm fine; it just started to pour down rain. I'm soaked."

"Do you need to borrow my clothes again?"

"No, that's alright. I deserve this, for treating you the way I have."

"It's not all your fault, Clay. You just have to understand I'm still going through accepting my parents' death."

"I thought you said you had."

"Forget what I said. I love you, and I'm sorry, too."

"You really mean what you said a little while ago about wanting to be with me forever?"

"Yes."

"Then why aren't we together."

I got out of the limo and walked towards Clay who was standing on the sidewalk looking at his feet while on his cell phone. I stood there ten feet away from him as I began to speak in a low, quiet voice. "I think I should go now."

"Why?"

"Because I'm standing in front of you, baby." I saw as Clay lifted his head in the rain and dropped his cell phone as did I. We walked over to one another slowly and stared into each other's eyes as if we hadn't seen each other in years. When I reached him, he leaned toward me and pressed his lips upon mine as we kissed in the rain. "I always wanted to kiss in the rain."

Clay looked at me smiling with the biggest smile from ear to ear. He picked me up and turned me around with him as we danced in the rain like we were in heaven. "Oh, Tara, never leave me again."

"Only if you never push me away from you."

"Never."

"You look really sexy when you're all wet, you know that, Tara?"

I giggled as I finished. "Oh, Clay, I'm so achin' for your bacon, baby."

CHAPTER 7
Breathtaking

After the day Clay and I kissed in the rain, I finally told him that I was willing to leave everything and go on tour with him. I had packed my things and was on my way over to Lindsey's house to say goodbye. Clay waited at his house for me while the limo dropped me off in font of Lindsey's house. I got out of the limo and closed the door behind me with a couple of gift bags in my hands for Lindsey. I walked up to her front door and began to knock on her door, waiting for someone to answer.

As I waited, I began to hear the door unlock as I prepared myself for what to say to her. "Oh hi, Tara. Lindsey's upstairs in her room."

"Thank you, Mrs. Shook."

I made my way up the stairs towards Lindsey's room slowly. I peeked inside her room seeing her sitting on her twin bed listening to music on her Discman. I walked up to her taking the headphones off her ears. "Hey, girl, how are you?"

"I come bearing gifts."

Lindsey looked up at the gift bags in my hands.

"Here, they're for you."

"What for? It's not my birthday, you know."

"I know that, silly."

Lindsey opened the gift bags after I had placed them into her hands. "Wow, a beautiful red dress."

"Yeah, I knew you would like it."

Lindsey placed the red dress on the bed beside her and opened the other one. "Wow, red shoes and a purse to match. Thank you, Tara. I love them. They're beautiful." "You're welcome, Lindsey."

Lindsey placed the gifts down on the floor and reached for my hand pulling me down beside her. "So what's going on? Why did you really come bearing gifts for me, and I know it's not because you were just thinking of me."

"Okay, you know me too well. I have to tell you something, but I don't want you to freak out."

"Food fell from your mouth and landed on your shoes in front of Clay, right?"

"No."

"Really?"

"Lindsey, I need you to get serious for a minute."

"Sure, what is it?"

"I've decided to go on tour with Clay for six months. I really want this; please don't be mad at me."

"Let me get this straight. You're going on tour with Clay, a man that is fine and sexy and has money in his pocket, and you think I'd be mad at you."

"You're not?"

"Hell no, girl, I'm mad at him for not inviting me."

"Lindsey."

"I know, I know, I'm talking about your man."

It was silent for a moment while I thought about whether or not Lindsey was mad or excited about the decision I had made. "So you're not mad at me?"

"No, Tara." Lindsey was silent and then finished, "Have you two even done IT yet?"

"No."

"Oh God, girl, you're going on a six-month tour with this man alone, and you haven't even done IT?"

"No."

"Oh lord, girl, you're about to be laid."

"What makes you think that?"

"He's not just going to sit there and watch as you get undressed in front of his hungry eyes expecting nothing to happen. Girl, he wants your ass badly. Why don't you give it to him? After all, it's Clay Edison. I'm dying to know the measure of that man."

"Lindsey."

"I know, I know. I'm just teasing. It's just that he's so sexy. I'd like to take his hand and place it on my..."

"Lindsey, don't you dare finish that sentence."

"Sorry, I can't help it; he's just so yummy in my tummy."

"Quit playing, Lindsey. I'm sure Clay wouldn't like it."

"Well, when he's not here, us girls tell, and if we're being honest like I love to do, I still wonder how big his..."

I placed my hand over her mouth preventing her from finishing her sentence.

"Tara, you promised we would always share everything."

"Not boyfriends."

"Oh, but I really want him; he's so special to me. Please, I promise I'll let you go first."

"No way."

"I just want a measurement, that's all."

"No, Lindsey."

"Fine, I'll drop the subject but only if you get me one of his boxers before you leave."

I thought about it for a moment then answered knowing she might stop after I did what she said. "Fine, I will, but after I do, no more wanting to measure my man, alright?"

"It's a deal." We shook on it, making it final. I finished saying goodbye and called Clay on my cell phone as I sat in front of Lindsey who was watching me.

"Hi, baby." Lindsey giggled and started making sexual faces towards me.

"So when are you coming, Tara?"

"I'll be on my way in a few more minutes."

"Did she take it well?"

"Well, kind of, I guess."

"What does 'kind of' mean?"

"Oh, I'll tell you on the way to the airport, alright?"

"Okay."

"Oh, before I leave, can you leave one of your boxer shorts out?"

He was silent as I saw Lindsey giggling and whispering to me for me to tell him to sign it. "Oh, Clay, can you sign them as well?"

"Why on earth would you want my boxers and for me to sign them? You have the real thing, you know."

"It's not for me; it's for Lindsey."

"Tara, you're not supposed to tell him that." Lindsey nudged me trying to stop me from giving away anymore information.

"Who was that?" Clay questioned me.

"Oh, it's Lindsey, and she was telling me to be quiet about how it was her idea about the whole boxer shorts thing."

"Oh, I see, and why would she want my boxers?"

"She thinks you're sexy and wants to know the measure of a real man like you," I struggled to say as Lindsey tickled me and I laughed still trying to talk to Clay.

"Tara, you tell her I'll give her what she wants as long as she can guess the size of my..."

"Clay."

"I was only going to say foot."

"Yeah, sure you were. That's what they all say." I covered the phone telling Lindsey what he had said for me to ask her.

"Wait, let me think. It's a trick question, right?"

"I think it's just a question, Lindsey."

"I'm going to guess the size of his palm to his index finger."

"I don't think it's that small." I released my hand from the receiver and told Clay what Lindsey had said. "Lindsey said it's the length of your palm to your index finger."

I heard Clay giggling as he replied, "Okay, tell her she has her pair of autographed boxers."

"Really? It's that small?"

"Oh, I didn't know you would think so small of me, Tara. I do have long fingers, you know."

I was quiet for a moment looking at Lindsey laughing at what I had said as if I didn't understand what they were talking about for a minute. "Oh, you two were talking about your..."

"Well, what did you think, Tara?"

"Oh sorry, I don't think you have a small, well, you know. I didn't want to make you feel, uh, how do I say this?"

"It's alright, Tara, take a breath. You really aren't ready."

"Ready for what?"

It was silent, then he added to me, "Ready to go."

"Now I'm ready."

"You are?"

"Yeah, of course, I can't stop thinking about how much fun it will be to be with you all the time, day and night."

"Oh wow, I didn't expect that much, but okay, that's great, more is better."

"Hey, wait, what are you talking about. I'm confused."

"We're talking about you being ready."

"I know, ready for the tour with you, right?"

"Oh, now I'm confused."

"Clay."

Clay giggled in the background as we quickly finished our conversation. I told him I'd be at his house in about a half hour or so. "Bye, my love, I love you."

"I love you, too, Clay."

"Oh wow, that felt wonderful."

"Bye."

"I love you, Tara." I giggled blushing as he said my name aloud.

"Are you blushing?"

"No, I don't blush."

"Oh, you do so blush; you blush every time I say your name."

"That's not true. You can say my name four times, and I know I won't blush. I promise."

"Okay, let's just try it out then, for my sake. Tara, Tara."

"Okay, okay, you were right, I'm all red."

"Man, you're so in love with me. I didn't even have to finish saying your name, and you blushed."

"I know, I'm such a girl."

"No, it's cute. It makes you seem like more of a sweet girl than I already know you are."

"Oh, Clay."

We hung up the phone. I placed it back in my purse and looked at Lindsey knowing I wouldn't be able to see her after today. "What about the boxers? How will I get them? You're leaving."

"Don't worry about them. I'll have someone drop them off when we leave for the airport, I promise."

I rose up off the bed as did she. We walked over to one another. We stood staring at one another getting prepared to say our goodbyes. "So, you be good when I'm gone," I told Lindsey smiling and trying not to tear up.

"And you be bad while you're away." We giggled as we began to hug, squeezing one another with all our might, thinking if we held each other tightly enough, we would still be together. "I'm going to miss you so much, Tara."

"I'm going to miss you, too."

"Don't forget me, okay?"

"You don't have to worry about that, Lindsey. There isn't a girl in the world that could replace you."

"Really?"

"Yeah, really. After all, where am I going to find another girl who wants to measure my boyfriend's package all the time?"

"Well, that's true, only I would ask that, but I didn't say it to hurt you, you know."

"I know."

"You're my best friend forever."

"You're my best friend, too."

We burst into tears, holding one another for almost an hour or so it had seemed, but really it had only been five minutes. I left her house after saying goodbye and wiping my tears that fell from my eyes. I walked out of her bedroom and down the stairs of her house, reaching the entrance. I opened the front door and closed it behind me as I began to walk towards the limo which was still parked waiting for me outside Lindsey's house. I reached it and opened the door, climbing inside gracefully. As I closed the door, I was driven away. I was left just looking out the window at Lindsey from her window waving goodbye. She had the saddest expression upon her face. I wasn't sure if Lindsey would be able to make it without me. It might have been only six months, but to a best friend, even a day could seem too long. I never regretted leaving her behind, though. After all, I was where she even wanted to be. I was the luckiest girl in the world right at that moment in my life. I couldn't believe I had found love so young, and it being Clay Edison was a bonus. If I had known that I would be sharing my life with Clay Edison, I probably would have gotten some kind of boob job to impress him. Just joking, my body was just fine the way it was. After all, if Clay liked it, I was going to have to say I completely agreed with his opinion, wouldn't you?

I arrived and parked outside of Clay's hotel building, waiting for Steve, the limo driver, to come around and open the door for me. The door began to open, but instead of Steve, it was Clay opening the door and getting in beside me.

"Clay, I thought you were going to meet me upstairs?"

"You don't have to blush about it, Tara. You already have me."

I nudged Clay. "Hey, watch it, don't make me get you."

"Well, then I better tease you more, because I want to be got, especially by you, Tara." My face became redder as I thought about what he had meant by what he had said to me. "I'm gonna getcha. Na, na, na, na, boo, boo."

Clay pushed me down gently with my back towards the seat. He started tickling me everywhere. "Clay, stop, that tickles."

"Well, that's the idea." I couldn't stop laughing, considering he was still tickling me as I felt the limo start to drive away from the hotel. "Hey, stop, does Steve know we're moving?"

"No, I think we should tell him. The steering wheel might have him hostage, making him drive."

He giggled, laughing at his own sarcasm as I acted serious. "No, I'm serious."

"So serious, come on, you know I planned it. You know I like to spoil you." I looked at Clay trying not to smile. "It's alright, you can smile, and I won't laugh." I giggled. I could never be serious with Clay. I always ended up laughing at some point. How could I stay mad at him? It was a challenge to hold anything against him. He was too cute to be mad at. He had such a cute little manly face, with those tiny little beady eyes that would sparkle like diamonds, which were a girl's best friend. Also, that body he had was so good-looking. He was tall and had an incredible sense of style. He was sweet yet serious, at times, but no matter how much he sometimes bothered me, he was everything I'd ever wanted in a man.

I sat beside Clay in the limo, as we held one another's hands as we were driven wherever Clay had planned. "So where are you planning on taking me?"

Clay smiled and answered, "Somewhere really special."

"Like where?"

"Oh, I was thinking we would have dinner at a romantic restaurant, then we'll do a little dancing."

"Uh, I don't mean to be rude, but can you even dance?"

"Yeah, I can move a little, I guess."

"That's alright; we'll make it special, even if we have to dance swaying our hips from side to side."

It was silent for a few minutes as I looked down at myself disgusted. "Clay?"

"Yeah, Tara?"

"How are we going to go out for dinner with me looking like this?"

Clay looked down at the outfit I was wearing, which was a T-shirt and blue jeans. A smirk then appeared on his face. "You look beautiful just the way you are. It doesn't really matter what you're wearing, you always look beautiful."

"But, Clay, what about the dress codes? Won't they refuse to serve us?"

Clay was silent looking as if he had been thinking about what I said, "Well, I guess we should get you changed into some dancing shoes."

"Uh, it's not just my shoes that need changing. Just look at me, my hair, my clothes, my face. God, Clay, if I walk into a restaurant wearing this, they'll kick me out."

The limo came to a stop as I finished. Clay then opened the door and climbed out. Standing in front of the open door, he reached his hand out to me. "Come on, Princess, give me your hand."

I placed my hand in his as he helped me out. I looked around seeing a salon and a store that had the most beautiful gowns in the display windows.

Header

"Clay, did you plan all this?"

Clay smirked, letting me know he did. He always had some kind of surprise up his sleeve no matter what it was, and he always made it special for me. "Oh, Clay, this is so wonderful. You shouldn't have. I don't deserve all this."

Clay pressed himself up against me with his arms around my waist, looking into my eyes. "Are you kidding me? You are the kindest person I've ever met, and if anyone deserves this, it's you. It's the way you love me. Man, what more can a man ask for?"

"Really?"

"Of course. Now, let's go get you dressed up for dinner."

"Okay."

I held his hand as he walked with me into the hair salon. When we entered, Clay stood beside me with his arm around my waist as the professional hairdresser greeted us. He was saying a whole bunch of mumbo jumbo about what he was going to do for me. He had an accent, but I wasn't too sure what kind of one it was. He led me by the hand to the chair as Clay waited in the waiting area where the magazines were. He sat down as I sat in the chair waiting for the hairdresser to do whatever he planned to do with my hair. He walked up behind me and started running his fingers through my hair as he talked to me. "My name's Piercen, and I am you hairstylist for this evening. Now, here's what I'm going to do. I'm going to put some streaks into your hair to bring out your eyes and skin. Your hair will go up in a bun of curls with a beautiful rose that I will place into the clip that holds your hair up." I shook my head yes as he began styling my hair.

An hour passed by and he finished my hair and began on my makeup. When Piercen had finished with me, I looked in the mirror not even believing it was me. My hair and makeup looked phenomenal. I couldn't wait to show Clay what it looked like. Piercen then had one of his helpers bring out something that had been in the back for me. It was a long pink gown with spaghetti straps, with the shape of a heart at the back.

"I love it. It's beautiful."

"I'm glad, Mrs. Edison, because it's for you to wear with your husband, over there."

I leaned toward Piercen whispering, "You're mistaken. We're not married."

"Oh sorry, but you seem so in love. It seems like you are."

"Thank you."

"Oh, well, come, come in the back and put this beautiful gown on, and then you can show your guy friend, boyfriend, whichever he is. Okay, it will be great."

"Do you think he'll like it?"

"Don't worry about it. You look marvelous. You even smell good, you know."

"Okay, I'll go put it on."

I took the dress from the helper and went into the bathroom to change into the beautiful gown. I put on the dress and fluffed it in all the right places, so it was perfect. I stared in the mirror at myself, admiring how I looked. "Hi, Clay, how do I look? Oh no. Uh hi, Clay, do you like it."

I stopped preparing myself to show Clay and opened the bathroom door. I walked out passing all the hairdressers who were staring as I passed by. I was about to pass Piercen when he stopped me. "You look smashing, doll. Now, go get him, tiger. Err."

I giggled laughing at Piercen and walked over to Clay. I stood in front of him as he was reading one of the magazines. "Clay, how do I look?"

Clay glanced up to my voice, staring at me like he was in another world somewhere. He rose up to his feet, standing in front of me as he looked me up and down smiling in awe. "Oh, wow, you look so..." Clay stopped clearing his throat.

"That good, huh?"

"Are you kidding me?"

He walked over to me holding my hands and staring at me, not wanting to take his eyes off of me. "Man, wow, I've never seen anyone so beautiful in my life."

I watched as his face turned beet red, and I began to smile. "Now who's blushing?"

He giggled and stared at me, keeping in the moment. "Yeah, wow."

"Clay, are you alright?"

Clay stayed still. The only movement he made was when he looked me up and down as if he couldn't take his eyes off me, not even for a minute. "Wow."

"Clay, are you sure you're alright?"

Clay finally raised his head up towards me and looked at me. "Yeah, I'm okay. It's just…wow."

"Okay, okay, enough with the wows. Aren't we leaving?"

"Leaving? Oh yeah. Um, hmm." Clay raised his right hand running his fingers through his spiked hair. "Ah, where are we going again?"

"The restaurant, remember, your surprise?"

"Right." He linked my arm in his as he led me outside towards the limo. When he opened the limo door, we got in and he sat beside me not moving, not even saying anything. I must say, I was kind of getting freaked out by the way he was acting. I leaned towards him nudging him in the arm. "Clay, are you sure you're okay?"

He shook his head yes trying to bring himself back to reality. "Wow, I'm sorry, Tara, but I'm not sure I can do this."

"What? Go out for dinner?"

Clay was silent staring at me as my expression urged him to go on. "Yeah, for dinner. I'm not quite ready for it. Is it alright if we stay in tonight?"

I looked down at my beautiful dress, then back up at Clay. "Are you sure? I'm already dressed up, and I was kind of excited about dancing with you. Why would you ask me, if you were going to change your mind after you got me all excited about it?"

"I'm sorry I got you excited about it. I was really looking forward to doing it, also, but it's just that…" Clay stopped in the middle of his sentence, trying to get away without finishing.

"What is it, Clay? What stopped you?"

"I don't want to sound corny or anything, but you did. The way your hair is, that dress, your eyes, God, your whole body is, wow. Sometimes, I don't know what to say to you next. You're just so beautiful; you're so full of life."

"That's sweet and all, but I still don't see how my beauty could stop you from taking me out to dinner."

"You see, Tara, I don't know what to do when I'm with you. I wanted to make this night so special for us. I can't go through with what I was going to do. I don't know if I'm ready to say something to you."

"What are you hiding from me? What is it, before I get all worked up like last time and begin to freak out like before?"

"No, please, whatever you do, don't go all ballistic on me."

"Well then, tell me what's going on once and for all."

"Hold on, I'm thinking how I should tell you this."

I sat there in the limo not able to move or make any sound as he just sat there in front of me in his black suit in thought. I moved closer to Clay and placed my hand upon his as he looked up at me. "It's alright, Clay, if you don't want me to go on tour with you. I'd understand if something came up. Just please don't leave me up in the air wondering all the time what's going through that head of yours, alright?"

He smiled at me and placed his left hand on my right cheek as he began to speak in a soft, gentle voice. "You're so understanding, you know that?" I leaned towards him as I wrapped my arms around him hugging him, knowing I probably wasn't going to be going on tour with him. "I wanted to make this night so special for you so when I told you I couldn't take you, you would at least have one romantic night with me to remember."

I pulled back staring at him. "You're breaking up with me?"

"No, I'll be back in six months to see you. I'm just not allowed to take you with me."

"Oh, how come?"

"My agent said it might be too hard on my career dating someone so young and so on."

"Hmm, well."

I leaned back and began to take off my dress as Clay just stood there watching me, as if he had planned all of this. I sat in front of Clay in my underclothes upset with him. I then placed the dress on Clay's lap as I sat wearing only a bra and a thong. I opened the door to the limo still looking at Clay as I started to climb out. He gripped my arm as I turned and fell onto the floor of the limo by the seat staring up at Clay. Clay giggled wondering why I had taken off my dress and tried to leave.

"Where are you going, Tara?"

I cleared my throat. "Don't you remember? You were beginning to tell me that you broke up with me."

Clay started to laugh, closing the door and staring down at me.

"Oh, Tara, I wasn't braking up with you. I was trying to throw you off-guard, silly. Do you always have to be so dramatic about everything?"

"What? You weren't trying to blow me off?"

"No."

"Then what were you doing?"

Clay slid down off the seat beside me as he giggled, reaching into his inside pocket. "I was going to ask you…" Clay pulled out a ring box and opened it towards me as I sat at the bottom of the limo in my underwear. "Will you marry me, Tara?"

I let out a big laugh and smiled so big, shocked at the way he had asked me. "Yes, yes, of course I will, Clay. Are you kidding me?" He took the diamond ring out of the red velvet case placing it on my finger as we giggled at the way it had all happened.

"Oh, God, I thought you were really going to leave in your underwear. You scared me there."

"I scared you? I thought you were dumping me. Why did you have to scare me like that?"

"I was trying to throw you off-guard."

I giggled once more holding my hand where the ring lay as I looked at it sparkle. "You didn't have to do it that way."

"Well, it worked, didn't it?"

"Yeah, you're lucky. I could have run out in the dress and got away faster, then what would you have done?"

"Well, then I would have had to chase you."

"I don't know if you would have caught me. I'm pretty fast."

"No, you're sneaky, not fast. You wanted to leave a mark before you left."

I smirked at him as he leaned me back lying on top of me and staring at me as if he had won a grand prize. "You think you're so smart, don't you? Planning all this, you silly willy."

"What?" We rolled on the limo floor trying to tickle one another to see how loud we could get the other to laugh. Of course, he won. I had always been a sucker when it came to tickling. I lay beside Clay cuddling with him on the floor of the limo as I looked up at him with the cutest face I could come up with.

"Are we still going dancing?"

Clay looked at me starting to laugh. "Hey, don't give me that face. I said I was going to take you, and I meant it. I just wish you wouldn't have taken off your dress."

I smirked looking up at Clay making an open-mouthed expression almost like I was about to meow, but not. He laughed for a while telling me the cutest line I had ever heard.

"Pipe down, pip squeak."

"Hey, Me-Moo."

We giggled some more as I began to get up off the floor with Clay to put back on my dress.

When I had finally gotten my dress back on, I looked at Clay sitting on the seat beside me trying not to laugh for some reason. "What's so funny?"

"Your hair's just a little messed up."

"Oh my God, how bad is it?"

"This much." Clay showed me with his fingers the size of an inch.

"Oh my God, what am I going to do? Look at me." I looked at myself in the mirror in front of me so embarrassed. I had pieces of hair sticking straight up every which way, and the rose that was in my hair had its petals missing. All that was left of it was the stem. "Look, just look at me. I'm ruined. Now I know how it feels when those girls get crumbs on their shoes."

Clay reached out his hand placing it upon mine for comfort. "It's alright, Tara. Calm down, let's just go back into the salon. I'm sure they'll be more than happy to fix it."

He opened the limo door as we both got out and closed the door behind us as we walked towards the entrance doors of the salon. I glanced at Clay seeing him laughing. "Stop laughing. It's not funny."

"I'm sorry. It's just that I can see our reflection in the window in front of us. You look like me now, you know, with the spikes."

"Clay."

He burst out laughing as I stopped where I was staring at him. "Come on, sweetie, you look great."

He opened the door for me as I walked into the salon trying to figure out the words to describe my hair mess. Piercen saw me then walked over to me quickly placing his hands on either side of my shoulders. "Oh, no, this is bad, but don't worry, I will fix it." He looked at Clay with a funny expression on his face. "It's very bad idea to do hanky-panky when I finish hairstyle. No more, let it set, okay?" He walked over to Clay patting him on the back. "Don't look so sad. It's alright. You okay, no problem, I fix the spikes."

Clay looked at me as I did him. "I like him," I whispered to Clay as Piercen brought me over to the chair and began to fix my hair for the second time. As he styled my hair, I looked at the ring on my hand admiring it as it sparkled.

"Oh what's this? You married so fast; people grow up so fast. They walk out and come back married in minutes."

"No, we're engaged, that's all."

"Oh lucky man. He's Clay, you know, his hair like so. I think I seen him on a magazine once." Piercen looked at Clay waving then continued styling my hair in silence, as I waited for it to be over so I could leave this place and see Clay shake his booty on the dance floor the way he did on *Soul Seeker* to the song from *Slickers*.

After Piercen had finished my hair, he looked at me in the mirror in front of us. "There, now, tell that Clay that there well be no more hanky-panky before it sets."

I stared at Piercen in the mirror holding back from laughing at what he said. I got up off the chair and walked back towards Clay sitting in one of the waiting chairs reading another magazine. "Clay, I'm ready."

He then stood up seeing Piercen standing behind me watching. "Oh wow."

Piercen stepped around me in front of Clay shaking his right hand in the air. "No, touchy-touchy okay? You have to try and stay focused."

Clay cleared his throat with one of his eyebrows raised. "Look at her; it's kind of hard to stay focused when she looks so, wow."

"Uh, no." Piercen smacked Clay at the back of the head then finished. "No looky-looky."

Clay's face became red with anger. "See, that's better, good boy. Say you are Clay, let me show you." Piercen ran over to the table tray and dipped his fingers in gel then hurried back over to Clay and me. He ran his fingers through his hair styling it like Clay's then shouted. "See, now I Clay."

"I think we're going to leave now."

"Yeah, we're kind of in a hurry," I added to Piercen seeing him with his hands still open presenting his hair to us.

"No wait, I give you present. Stay here."

We waited by the door for Piercen to return from wherever he had gone to get something in the back. A couple of minutes later, Piercen came back over to us with a gift bag that he placed into Clay's hands. "I put gift in a hair bag, but that's alright, right?"

"Yes, that's fine, thanks." Clay opened the bag and pulled out a long length of connected condoms. We looked at Piercen curious as to why he would give us a gift of condoms. Hell, even hair would have been better. "Why did you give us condoms?" Clay questioned Piercen.

"Oh, they are good gift, no? You can use them for hanky-panky, but not now, okay? First, you go out and have a party, then you use present, okay?"

"Yeah, I don't know if I can accept this. It's really weird," Clay answered as I watched them talk to one another.

"No, it's a good gift for a good man. Did you know you were in a magazine? They said lots of things about you, good things, but lots. You go, come back when you all out or need hairdo, and I make you look like Clay."

"I am Clay."

"Oh, well, I make you spikes, okay? That's good, no?"

Clay placed the condoms back into the gift bag and opened the door for me, trying to get out of there as quickly as we could before Piercen said something else, and Clay lost it on him.

When we got back into the limo, we were then driven away to the romantic restaurant. When we arrived at the restaurant, we went inside, looking fabulous in our dancing clothes. The hostess guided us to our seats, and he pulled out our chairs seating us after greeting us.

He then placed napkins upon our laps leaving us as Clay and I began to start a conversation. The waiter who confirmed our planned dinner selection with Clay then interrupted us. When the waiter left, we were finally alone, but then Clay had to go to the bathroom, so I sat alone at the table waiting for him to return to me. I must have sat there for a good five minutes waiting for Clay. I just thought he had a stomachache or something, but I was wrong. I heard music begin to play from the other side of the restaurant. I listened in noticing the singer sounded like Clay. I thought nothing of it until I saw him walk around the corner towards me with a microphone in his hand singing. It was so beautiful. He came right up to me, as I placed my hand to my mouth blushing, of course. I couldn't believe he had done that. He sang to me as the couples around us watched from their tables smiling.

When Clay finished the song, he knelt down in front of me smiling at me. "Oh, Clay, you were wonderful. You did all this for me?"

He stood up and placed the microphone down as a slow song began to play. Clay faced towards me with his hand out for me to grab. "That's not all, Tara." I placed my hand upon his, and he helped me up, beginning to dance with me.

I whispered into his ear quietly as couples got up and danced beside us, "I didn't know you knew how to dance like this."

"I didn't, but I've been taking dance lessons for you so I can always dance away with you."

"Oh, Clay, you shouldn't have. Now I'm going to be blushing even more."

"That's the idea."

I giggled as we continued dancing with one another beside all the other couples who had begun dancing, seeing us. It was so incredible that I was with such a romantic man. There was no doubt in my mind that he was the one with whom I was meant to be. I didn't used to think too much of God until I saw Clay for the first time signing autographs in the mall. Even though I met him crying about my horrible life, I had no idea that he would mend my broken heart, and I would fall in love with him even though I didn't believe what was happening to me at that moment. All I had been thinking about was getting his autograph and seeing him. It wasn't until I spoke to him and heard him speak directly to me that I just knew. I was so surprised that he had even noticed me and had some kind of compassion for how I was feeling then. He knew exactly how to comfort me, at exactly the right moment. Then suddenly, I began to remember someone.

"Clay, what about Jennifer?"

"Oh, she was all talk, I guess, and no action."

"Well, that's nice to know."

The evening went on, and as the dinner and dancing came to an end, we headed home to get prepared to leave tomorrow for the beginning of Clay's tour and the start of something special. We got back into the limo. We were silent being tired from all the dancing that we had done. I snuggled up to Clay in the limo, feeling warm and fuzzy inside, just being the girl that was sitting next to him. Clay looked at me as we felt the limo start to drive away from the restaurant bringing us back to the hotel.

When we had finally arrived back at the hotel, I followed as Clay led me upstairs. The night had been perfect. There were so many emotions going through me at that moment. I didn't know whether to ignore them or commit to them like I should instead of always running away or ignoring them. We entered the room as Clay locked the door behind us, and we walked into the living room together.

"Do you mind if I get changed, Clay?"

"No, not at all, my bathroom's right over there beside the plant in the corner."

I went in the direction that he had pointed. I went inside and got undressed wondering what Clay was doing out there without me. I took my hair down and combed it straight then washed my makeup off. I stood in front of the mirror in my bra and underwear smiling that I was going to be sleeping in the same bed as Clay for the first time. I was so nervous to see him when I came out of the bathroom. He would probably be looking at me in excitement as he always had. I placed my hand on the bathroom doorknob and placed the other on the door preparing to come out. Clay knocking at the door startled me.

"Yes, what is it, Clay?"

"Are you okay in there? Do you need my help?"

I whispered softly to myself, "Oh, Clay, how do you make me feel so wonderful inside?"

"What?"

"Nothing, I'm coming out."

Header

I turned the doorknob, opened the door, and saw Clay standing in front of me looking at what I looked like in my underclothes. It was nothing new for him considering I had already given him a show of it in the limo earlier that evening. We began our night together watching a movie and eating popcorn while wrestling around on the floor laughing. We talked about so many things that night. We laughed, we smiled, and we gave kisses to one another. I was in heaven just sitting beside him. I couldn't believe how much fun we had been having. When the time came for us to fall asleep, Clay took off his clothes right in front of me. I watched as he took off his shirt placing it onto the sofa, then he pulled down his pants stepping out of them. He then stood in front of me in his basketball shorts. I looked at him feeling comfortable for some reason, even though we had been in our underwear in front of each other. Suddenly, I realized I hadn't even been blushing. I was feeling relaxed staring at Clay. I watched as he lowered himself down to me on the floor staring at me as if to say good night.

"What?" Clay asked me seeing the calm look upon my face. I leaned forward starting to kiss him, placing my hands on either sides of his face, feeling his heart tremble inside. I pulled away gently moving my eyes following his back and forth. "Oh, I see." He leaned towards me kissing me as he glided his hands along my skin, over my bra. He stopped for a second staring at me. "You're not blushing."

"That's because I'm ready."

He leaned towards me again kissing me as I kissed him passionately. He lifted my shirt over my head and tossed it to the floor. He laid me down as we kissed one another, feeling each other's every touch, finding every inch of one another's body, connecting in the most amazing way, throughout the heart and soul. I wasn't nervous. I was finally ready for the moment of love, which we would soon forever share, tattooing an emotional bond between us, holding one another together with the seal of God that would forever be strong whenever we were together, loving every moment that we shared with one another, never regretting our time and never separating our lives, but growing with each other and finding the most sacred thing in life, our souls.

We made love that night. We finally did it, yes IT, the commitment I was most afraid of in my life. I was so happy. I felt so loved, and I know he felt the same, also. We woke up next to one another under his satin sheets, still pressed up against one another. Considering we did it almost the whole night, we woke up so tired and could barely get out of bed. I guess those condoms Piercen gave us went to good use. I never told Clay this, but I took the first condom wrapper from the first condom we ever used, and I'm going to save it forever. I never wanted to forget this moment no matter what happened in our future. Yeah, I know what you're thinking, what a weird screwball to keep a condom wrapper. But just look on the bright side, I could have kept the condom. Oh God, I don't even want to think about that.

We lay in bed a little bit longer, just snuggling up to one another envisioning the way it all had happened last night. God, he was good. He was the real measure of my kind of man, wow.

CHAPTER 8
Closure

The next day, we were driven to the airport where we were going to catch our flight to Vancouver to start Clay's tour that was beginning there. Everything had been hectic there. People were trying to take pictures of us, and they were asking for the signature of not only Clay, but me also for some reason. We got caught in a crowd of reporters beginning to question Clay, as I stood beside him with my hand in his.

"Who's the girl with you? Is she related, or what can you tell us, Clay?"

"I'm sorry, no questions today."

We finally got past them, and when we did, Clay kept looking at me making sure I wasn't scared. He held onto me tightly making certain I didn't get separated from him considering I had never been on an airplane and also there were reporters everywhere waiting for any chance they could to get one of us alone. If I were to get separated from Clay at a time like this, it wouldn't have been pretty, if you can imagine me getting surrounded by cameras and people asking me millions of questions. I stayed with Clay as his bodyguards led us through the crowds of people and reporters leading us to our private plane.

When we had finally made it on the airplane, we took our seats and fastened our seatbelts preparing for takeoff as his bodyguards took their seats as well. Clay stared at me smirking.

"What are you looking at?"

"You." I was silent as my face started to turn red. "Why is it that you blush when I speak to you and look at you, but when we're about to have sex, you're as relaxed as a turtle in its shell, peeking out every time it's kafuffled."

"Kafuffled?"

"Yeah, meaning you only blush when your attention is directed to something you really enjoy."

"Okay, I think it's more facial expressions. When you tell me I'm beautiful, I blush. When you are about to have sex with me, I'm comfortable and relaxed. I think that's all it is."

"Yeah, sure, sure, you so want me. You are so kafuffled."

"I am not. I am as relaxed as a turtle like you said."

"So you admit your kafuffled?"

"What? No."

He just giggled at me succeeding in confusing me with his words so I agreed with him about something. When the plane began to take off, I started to get nervous. Clay held my hand so I could stay calm and relaxed. I must say, it did work. When we had finally made it in the air and my ears had popped a few times, we were allowed to take off our seatbelts. Clay took off mine then his own then began to whisper into my ear softly. "We're in the air, and the flight's going to be very long, and there's an empty bathroom all for us in the back. Do you want to try it out?"

"Clay, are you asking me to have sex with you in the bathroom?"

"Shh."

I looked around seeing that Clay's three bodyguards, Larry, Kevin, and Bruce, were staring at us, most likely because they heard what I had said.

"Well?" Clay waited for my answer wanting to sleep with me again.

"What the hell, why not?"

I got up and walked into the bathroom in the back of the plane waiting for Clay. Clay followed not too long after and met me in the bathroom. I let him in, closing the door and locking it behind us. We started making out, taking one another's clothes off in the tiny bathroom beginning to have sex. When we had finished, we rested for a couple minutes and put our clothes back on to go back out and sit down, but when I looked down I saw… "Oh my God, my shirt's in the blue toilet water," I said so loud that everyone in the airplane most likely heard me.

"It's alright; you can wear my shirt." Clay placed his shirt in my hands, and I put it on. "There now, you're wearing my colors."

I smiled as Clay walked out with me with no shirt on, and we walked past everyone staring at us as we took our seats. Clay put on his jacket so he didn't make anyone in the plane feel uncomfortable including himself.

We sat in our seats beginning a conversation when a lady stood in front of us holding out a tray of my blue dyed shirt that had fallen into the toilet water. "Is this yours?"

"No, I've never seen that in my life."

"Oh, really? Well, thanks anyway." The lady walked away as we laughed about it and continued our conversation.

"Clay?"

"Yes, Tara?"

"Do you think the flight attendant lady knew the shirt was mine?"

"I think she knows, but she's not going to try and prove it."

"So what's it like flying everywhere, going to see new places?"

"You like to jump from subject to subject, don't you, Tara?"

"Not intentionally, of course."

"No, of course not."

Clay giggled staring at me. "Clay, can you pass me those peanuts over there?"

Clay looked down, saw a bag of peanuts on his table in front of him, and picked them up. He held them out to me smirking, as I stared at him. "You want my peanuts, do you?"

"Yes." I took them from him, opened the bag, and began to eat them. I turned to face him seeing that he had been smirking at me.

"Are my peanuts good?"

"Yes."

"Are they just the way you like them?"

I giggled nudging Clay. "Clay, stop. I know where your mind is."

"Do you?"

"You're so dirty, you know that, Clay?"

"You know, if we were all alone on this plane, I'd…"

"Clay."

"Right here on this seat." I giggled as Clay leaned towards me, and I leaned my back up against the window. We began kissing one another passing the time by, enjoying every minute with each other. After all, who could blame us?

After we finally arrived in Vancouver after so many long hours, we were so tired from not having gotten that much sleep last night or on the plane. We headed out of the plane going outside where millions of fans had been waiting for Clay. Some reporters caught up to us asking Clay who I was. "Sorry, no questions today," Clay's bodyguards told the reporters who were holding cameras in our faces.

"That's alright," Clay added giving permission for the reporters to ask questions about us.

"Clay, are you dating this girl?"

"No."

"Who are you and what is your name, miss?"

I stepped forward answering one of the questions. "My name is Tara Heart."

"Where did you two meet?"

"At the mall."

"Are you planning on being together?"

"Yes."

"Clay is Tara going to be joining you on stage at your concert?"

"No."

"Can you sing, Tara?"

"Yes."

Clay looked at me smiling then back at the reporters while placing his arm around my waist. "That's wonderful. So will you be singing with Clay?"

"No, this is his concert. I wouldn't want to take the attention off of him."

"Tara! Tara!"

"Sorry that's enough for today."

Header

We walked through the crowds of reporters going through the gates to our limo which was waiting for us. Fans were grabbing at us while we walked by them. One even managed to rip a part of my pants at the side. "I got a piece of Tara's clothing," I heard someone in the crowd yell as I glanced down at my pants seeing a rip on the side.

"Clay, some girl just tore a piece of my pants off."

Clay giggled. "Yeah, sorry about that, the fans kind of get really wild at this time."

"It's okay; it's just now I have a big slash in my pants."

"Don't worry about it. I'll buy you another pair."

"Cool, shopping."

"Oh, Tara."

We reached the limo as the crowds of people watched us get in and drive away as they screamed for Clay. The limo drove us to our hotel where we went upstairs after checking ourselves in. We made ourselves comfortable, taking our clothes out of our suitcases and placing them into our dresser drawers. We got prepared to leave after putting our things away that were in the suitcases. We headed downstairs to be driven to his concert, so Clay could prepare for his songs with the band before the concert began. He opened the limo door for me, and I climbed in as he followed snuggling up beside me. The limo began to drive to the destination as we began a conversation. "I wonder what your concert's going to be like."

"What? Haven't you ever been to one of my concerts before?"

"No, sorry, I haven't, but if it makes you feel better, I haven't even been to anyone's concert before. This is all new for me."

"Oh really, then I should make this special for you then."

"How are you going to do that?"

Clay leaned back in the seat of the limo stroking his chin with his hand while smirking at me. "Hmm, I don't know, I was kind of thinking, call you up on stage and sing a duet with you."

"What? Did you already have it planned for that to happen?" Clay began to smile. "You did. You're so sneaky, you know that, Clay?"

"Of course I do."

"I don't know, Clay, I don't know if I'll be good enough to sing beside you. They might laugh or get mad at me for singing with you."

"No they won't; they're kind of expecting you to sing one song with me."

"What are you talking about?"

"That's why the reporters asked you that question when we got off the plane remember?"

"You told everyone already? I don't even know the song, and the concert's tonight."

Clay then reached into his pocket pulling out a piece of paper. It was the words to a song.

"Wow, you really did have all this planned, didn't you?"

"Come on, I'll sing it over with you."

"What's the song called?"

"'The Sway.'"

"Oh, that's a pretty song."

"You've heard it?"

"Well, yeah, I am a fan."

"Well, that's great then, now you have an idea before we practice."

"Well, okay, what part do I sing?"

Clay smiled then answered, "All of it except the beginning part. We'll be singing at the same time through most of it, except when it comes near the end where you'll be on your own, to do whatever flows at the end of the song, okay?"

"Okay, that sounds good." We began to sing it over together practicing for his concert.

"That was great, Tara, you sound as if you've been singing for years, you know that?"

"Really, I only sing in my room on a karaoke machine and in the shower sometimes."

Clay smiled at me with love built up within his eyes. "You sound like an angel, Tara."

"Thank you, Clay, but do you think your fans will like me?"

"I think they'll be your fans, too, after tonight."

"That's so sweet, Clay, but do you really want that?"

"Of course, they made me who I am today, and sharing something this special with you is a gift that had to have come from God."

"Alright, as long as you're okay with it, I'm okay with it, too."

We arrived at the place where Clay's concert was being held, as Clay turned to me smiling and placing his hand over mine. "Don't worry, Tara, you'll be fine." We then got out of the limo and went inside through the back entrance. I followed Clay down the hallway. We reached the directors who then showed us to our separate dressing rooms where our hair and makeup would be done and whatever else we needed to put on before the concert. I had no experience about anything that was going to happen, but I wasn't nervous for some reason. I felt comfortable that Clay was going to be singing beside me, so it was not like I was alone. I loved singing, and with Clay, it was a bonus. We had sounded so good together in the limo, and I just hoped that when I was on stage, I wouldn't mess anything up. I sat in the chair in my dressing room as three ladies came in and began to work on my look. One did my nails, one did my makeup, and the other worked on my hair. I must say I had never been pampered in my life until now. It felt really nice to be treated like a princess by other people.

I wished my parents could have been there with me, but in a way, I didn't regret anything; otherwise, my life might have turned out differently than it already had. I loved exactly how it was now. I couldn't have planned it better even if I had done it myself.

The girls finished my look as I rose up to my feet wondering what I was supposed to wear on stage. One of the girls left the room and came back with a beautiful outfit for me. It was a pink skirt with diamond butterflies all over it and a butterfly-shaped diamond top. It even came with pink high heels that also had diamonds. I had never had so many diamonds on my body in my life. The ladies helped me get my outfit on and placed a big butterfly clip in my hair. I felt so sexy in the outfit I was now wearing. I worried about Clay being able to concentrate when I walked up on stage looking so wow. Hopefully, he didn't sing his songs, only saying one word, "Wow."

As I stood in front of the mirror admiring myself, a director came in placing a microphone into my hands, telling me to come with him so he could get me set up. He led me down a long hallway towards the back of the stage where I had heard Clay singing a song called "Measure of Mine" to the audience. As he sang, I could hear the crowds of people screaming his name. The director led me to a door and opened it, walking me into the audience showing me where to stand in the front row. It was then that I began to feel butterflies in my tummy. I was so nervous, so I began taking deep breaths to calm myself down before I had to go up on stage with Clay.

I stood in the front row beside all his fans in the audience as I waited for my time to start singing and walk on stage. It was then that I thought about the song and how Clay was supposed to begin the song alone. It gave me a great idea for something. After he had ended the song, "Measure of Mine," he began talking to the audience saying the next song was going to be "The Sway." Clay winked his eye at me as I held the microphone in my hand smiling. He began the song as I added what I had planned to add while he was singing. While I did what I had planned, Clay smirked at me while singing, then he began the chorus with me. Everyone in the audience turned their heads staring at me as I walked up onto the stage slowly as the crowd screamed louder.

When I had made it onto the stage, we slowly walked up to each other standing in front of one another. He placed his hand on my side as I did the same as the audience screamed as we sang. We stared into one another's eyes singing as we began swaying our hips slowly from side to side. We let go of each other walking towards the front of the stage as we began the high part where we each had to do our own thing. I gave it my all, and when I sang a high key I didn't even know I had, the crowd jumped up out of their seats screaming and coming right up to the stage as I knelt down touching their hands. We finished the song standing in front of one another staring into each other's eyes as the crowd cheered louder.

After the song was over, we stood there beside one another thanking the fans for listening. I started to walk off stage waving, so Clay could finish his concert, but the crowd screamed my name for more. I felt bad because it had been Clay's concert, not mine, but what could I have done? Clay wanted me to sing with him. I just hoped he wouldn't get upset with me about it. Clay ran up to me turning me towards him preventing me from walking off stage.

"Do you know any more of my songs?" Clay stood there worried that I didn't. I stood in front of him in thought trying to remember any of them.

"Oh, wait, I remember a couple more. After all, I do have your CD."

"Great, which ones?"

"'When You Say You Want Me,' 'Magical Day,' 'Shimmer,' and…'"

"That's good. That's really good, Tara. Now do you know all the words?"

"Yes, of course."

"Great, come on, we'll have to finish this together, alright? And if there is a song you don't know, just do your own thing, okay?"

"Are you kidding me?"

"Does it look like I'm kidding?"

"No."

"Well, come on, I need you, Tara."

I stood in front of him staring at all the people screaming for us.

"Tara, please. You have to do this for me."

"But it's your concert, not mine."

"Look, Tara. I don't care whose name is displayed outside. All I know is if you don't do this, all these people will be let down."

I took a deep breath blowing it out slowly as I stared at Clay. "Alright. I'll do it."

We walked to the front of the stage together as the audience calmed down slowly. We began another song together as I danced around Clay giving the people something to scream about as Clay watched me trying not to laugh. The crowd loved hearing us singing with one another. I just hoped it was just because the crowd had got excited to hear a new voice with Clay because he had always sung alone before he met me. After all, I had no intention of wanting to steal Clay's thunder. I loved him, and all I wanted was for him to be happy, and if singing with him tonight made him happy, that's all I wanted.

When the concert ended, we walked off stage together where a group of security guards led us towards the back entrance where the limo waited for us to come out to be driven away quickly.

When we had gotten outside of the building, we got back into the limo to be driven back to the hotel. I didn't know if when Clay got me alone he was going to be mad or okay about what had happened on stage. Clay sat in silence not even looking at me. Then finally I broke the ice wanting to know what he was feeling about everything now.

"Clay, are you alright? You're not mad that they wanted me to sing with you, are you?"

Clay looked at me in silence with a straight face. I didn't know whether he was mad or just okay about it. "Uh, well, that was unexpected."

"Are you upset, though?"

"I'm just confused, everything went so fast. All I could think about was letting you end the concert with me. I'm just worried. What if they forget all about me, and they begin only looking at and listening to you?"

"Clay, listen to me, I never wanted to steal your fans. I never even wanted to sing, for that matter. This is just something that happened unexpectedly that we'll get through. I can tell you right now that I will never sing with you ever again. I didn't like taking away your thunder. I never wanted to make you feel less than you are. You are the real singer not me. You went through *Soul Seeker* and made it to the end. You're a winner."

"No, actually, I came in second."

"I don't care if you were second, Clay. You were the winner in my eyes, and that's all that should matter."

Clay looked at me about to cry and wrapped his arms around me. "You're so great, you know that?" I was silent not saying a word to him. We were almost to our hotel, and we were so tired and needed to get some sleep. Clay had to go sign some autographs the next day, so as soon as we got to the hotel, our plan was to go to bed. I was going to stay at the hotel while Clay signed autographs, because I didn't want anyone to direct any attention towards me. After all, this was just for him. He deserved every good thing that happened to him; that was how special he was.

Every day I woke up, I thanked God that he lined the stars up perfectly bringing us together, as if he had our best interests at heart. I wondered sometimes if God listened to every prayer made by every one of us in this world, taking a little piece of everyone and connecting it in some way to every other person in this world that had also made a prayer, bringing them together, forming a new bond between us. How else would you explain it when a person from a faraway place or a successful person met a person that was at the bottom and never stood

Header

out in a crowd? Life was so wonderful. It was wonderful how God made all the wonderful prayers come true, that were truly made from the heart. He always looked at the prayer, checking it out, only giving it to us if it wouldn't bring bad to our lives. For example, God listened to Clay's prayer and made it happen for him because it was going to bring him love. God needed for him to stand out in a crowd so I could find him and he could find me. Now, if that wasn't enough hope to have faith, I didn't know what was.

I stopped thinking about life as we pulled away from one another feeling the limo come to a stop. Steve came around, opening the door for us, and Clay got out. Clay reached his hand in helping me out carefully. We then walked inside the hotel holding each other's hands, so in love and swept up in the moment of the wonderful success of the concert. I could still hear the sound of the music in my ears, since I had heard it so close up, being on stage and all. When we arrived at our room, he unlocked the door and went inside, closing the door after me.

We entered and began to take off our outfits and hang them up in the closet, to be taken to the dry cleaners in the morning. We brushed our teeth and climbed into bed next to one another falling asleep right away. I wasn't used to all this. I'd never even been out of New York in my whole life, and even though I was only eighteen, it did not mean I couldn't use that expression. I was going to be turning nineteen in another month, and I never even told Clay about my birthday. I, of course, knew his, being a fan and all. It was November 30th. I could never forget that.

That night, I dreamt of marrying Clay. My father was walking me down the aisle, and my mother stood at the front by the altar crying because she was so happy I had found love. I looked the same as I did now. I must have been young, but that was okay; you couldn't always go through your life by the books making everyone else happy, but yourself. I knew that one thing that I would be missing when I did eventually get married was my parents and my big sister being there, standing beside me. I was still upset about their deaths, and it would forever haunt me in my life, but as time went by, I knew I'd be able to accept it. I was just having a hard time seeing it in the way God was trying to help me see it.

Header

Death comes to all living things, and sadly, it happens to the ones we most love and care for. All we're left with is their memories, trying to hold onto them as if they're still here as long as we remember them as they were and not how they died. I was beginning to understand myself as I spent more time with Clay. He gave me another chance at life, to change my ways and become an even better person than I had already been. I just didn't see why my twin didn't seem to show any kind of affection towards me after we both lost our family. You would think that she would have become closer to me, being my twin and all. I sometimes wondered how she was doing, but not so much anymore. I just couldn't figure out why. Maybe it was because if we saw one another, we were afraid when we would look into each other's eyes we would see our family that died within one another. That reason was a strong enough one to keep us separated no matter how long we were apart.

CHAPTER 9
Departure

Morning came so fast. The sun was shining in my eyes, and I glanced over beside me where Clay was supposed to be. He wasn't there. I wondered if he had already left to sign autographs in the big mall downtown. I pushed the bed covers off of me and got out of bed and went into the bathroom to take a shower.

I looked around the hotel room when I came out after starting the shower to see if Clay was gone. He was, so I got undressed and went into the bathroom again to get into the shower. I knew Clay would be gone for a couple of hours signing all his fans' autographs that looked up to him as I had.

I washed my hair and body standing under the water. I faced it letting the water gently drizzle down every inch of my body. I relaxed as the water cleansed my body while I thought about Clay. I couldn't get him off my mind; he was always there, living inside me. I believed he was my strength, and I couldn't think of any words to describe how he had made me feel inside.

I turned the water off and got out reaching for a towel that I had laid out on the counter beside the shower. I dried off and got dressed brushing my hair gently. It was kind of lonely in the hotel room without Clay with me to keep me company. I came out of the bathroom, walked into the kitchen, and made myself something to eat and sat at the table to eat what I had made. After I had eaten, I was feeling bored, so I walked over to the sofa in the living area and sat down turning on the TV. I flicked through the channels. I was turning the channels when I caught a glimpse of Clay on TV signing autographs. I turned it back to the channel and watched as the reporters were asking him more questions about me and who I was.

He didn't seem to mind answering them, though. He just told them what they asked and no more. You see, when it comes to fame, you have to be extremely careful what you say to the fans and the reporters. If you're not, they try and squeeze the juice out of you, making up a new story.

I sat there just watching him as I began talking to the TV as if Clay could hear me. "Oh, Clay, you look so cute on TV. Look at your sweet little eyes sparkling. I just want to reach out and touch you." So I did, finding myself on the floor in front of the TV touching the screen every time they showed Clay's face.

When the reporter had moved on to something else, I turned off the TV. I rose up off the floor and went back over to the sofa and sat down waiting for him to return, so I didn't have to be bored anymore.

An hour had passed by when I heard the door open, and I got up off the sofa and walked towards the door to see if Clay was home yet. "Clay, you're back! I saw you on TV. You looked so good, you were wonderful."

Clay walked up to me, lifting me up in the air and greeting me then setting me back down as he began to kiss me. I loved when he kissed me. It felt so soothing, and I'd never been kissed by anyone the way Clay kissed me. I'd also never felt the feeling that I did when Clay kissed me. He pulled away looking at me, beginning to check me out. "Did you miss me?"

"Of course, I did. I even watched you on TV. You looked so yummy on the TV screen."

"You saw me on TV? Wow. Let me guess, you were touching the screen when you saw me."

"How did you know?"

"I know what you're like. You're so in love with me and my body."

I grabbed the front of his shirt pulling him towards me. "Mmm, you smell really good."

"So do you."

"Thank you."

"Your hair smells really nice."

We walked into the living room where Clay took off his jacket getting settled on the sofa resting from all the signing. I walked over to Clay, climbed on top of him, straddling him as he looked at me as if wondering what I was going to do. "Are you tired?"

"No, but my hands are."

I lifted one of his hands up to my cheek holding it with both my hands beginning to kiss his hand gently. "Oh you poor thing. All that writing must be so exhausting for these fragile hands," I whispered in a sexy voice trying to excite him as he just stared at me smiling.

"You little tease. You know you're going to have to finish what you started."

"That's the idea."

I leaned towards him more beginning to kiss his neck as I ran my fingers through his spiked hair. I felt his hands upon my ass as I kissed him still running my fingers through his hair breathing on his neck. The sound of a woman's breathing to a man is so exciting to them. He lifted my chin with his hand as we began kissing on the lips. He was so sexy, and I always wanted him every time I saw him. I just couldn't get enough of his touch.

He then lifted me off of him lying me down on my back on the sofa as he ran his hands up and down my body. We started taking off each other's clothing as we kissed one another.

After we had sex, we lay beside one another on the sofa being careful not to fall off. "Oh, wow. You sure know how to please a man, don't you?" I giggled as I stared up at him staring down at me.

"I love you, Clay."

"I love you, too, Tara."

We lay there just talking for about an hour, just telling each other about our childhoods and about things that we liked. I mentioned to him when my birthday was, and he was really excited about it coming up in two months, on July 24th.

The week went by quickly filled with Clay having to meet fans and talk to reporters and be interviewed in front of so many viewers. It was finally the day when we had to leave Vancouver and go to the next destination where another concert was to be held. I was anxious to see him perform and also excited feeling that we'd most likely join the mile-high club on our way there as we had experienced before.

Clay and I packed our suitcases in the morning, making sure we didn't forget anything before we left to catch our plane. "Come on, Tara, we have to go; the plane leaves in an hour."

"Okay, I'm coming. I'm just trying to lift this stupid heavy suitcase of yours."

I struggled to pull the heavy suitcase as Clay saw me trying to pick it up. "Hey, hey. Don't lift that. Be careful. I'll get somebody else to move it. You're not supposed to take them downstairs anyway. I pay people to do that."

"Man, what did you pack in there, Clay? Bowling balls?"

"No, just things I'll need."

"Your suitcase is heavier than mine."

"That's because you pack light. Whereas I, on the other hand, happen to bring everything I think I'll need."

I giggled laughing at Clay trying to explain why his bags were heavier than mine. We left the room after the bellboys came and got our suitcases bringing them downstairs to place them into the limo. We got downstairs and went outside standing in front of the limo door. Steve opened the door for us, and we climbed in beside one another snuggling up as we always did. We watched out the limo window as we were driven away slowly leaving Vancouver behind and moving on to Seattle.

"Oh, Clay, this is so exciting to be going with you to see what you go through with the kind of lifestyle you set for yourself. I must say, you are the most intellectual man I've ever met in my life, and I can't believe I'm going to be marrying you. When the day finally comes, you are going to make me the happiest woman in the world just by saying 'I do.'"

"You're so cute, Tara. You are the cutest, kindest, most creative, sexiest, most beautiful girl I've ever known, and I'm so proud to be the one marrying you."

Clay and I leaned towards each other smooching as we snuggled with my legs crossed over top of Clay's knees. When we had arrived at the airport, we took a deep breath before we got out of the limo. We prepared ourselves for all the crowds that would be hounding us when we got out. The limo came to a stop as Steve opened the door for us,

Header

and Clay got out. He reached his hand in helping me out like the true gentlemen that he was. I held onto Clay's arm staying close to him trying to stay with him, as we were about to enter the airport where all the people were waiting. We entered surrounded by Clay's bodyguards keeping everyone at a certain distance. As we walked through the crowd of fans and reporters, there were millions of cameras flashing in our faces as we passed through.

When we had finally entered into the area closed off especially for Clay, I kept hearing someone calling my name from behind me. I knew it was a voice I recognized clearly. I turned, letting go of Clay's arm as he turned soon after I had, seeing why I had left his side. "Oh my God." Clay walked up beside me seeing me staring at Steven from school, who had been standing in front of me not too far away. I walked up to Steven as Clay wondered who the guy was and why I was going up to him.

"Tara, there you are. Lindsey told me you were here. I missed you." Steven walked up to me planting a long hard kiss on my lips right in front of Clay. I pushed Steven away from me staring back at Clay disgusted. "Ew, what the hell was that for?" Clay moved me out of the way with his arm shielding me as he stood in front of me, glaring at Steven angrily. Clay held his fist out towards Steven questioning him. "What in the hell do you think your doing kissing my fiancée?"

"Fiancée? She's my girlfriend. Lindsey told me she went on an airplane trip with a friend, so I thought I'd meet my girlfriend here."

I stepped up beside Clay as he stared at me confused. "He's lying. He's lying, Clay. I've never went out with him in my life."

Clay stared at me in disbelief. "Is this true, Tara? Are you dating him while you're engaged to me?"

"No, he's lying, I said. I would never do that. You know that. I love you."

Steven walked up to me again kissing me again without my permission. I pushed him away from me slapping him across the face, as Clay stood there just watching. "Don't ever kiss me, you jerk. What the hell are you doing trying to pull this crap on me in front of my fiancé?"

"What do you mean, Tara? You told me you loved me. You said I was the only one." Steven began to tear up wiping his eyes, as Clay turned to me again after seeing Steven start to cry.

"What the hell is going on, Tara? I thought you loved me. I thought I was the only one for you. We were going to get married, and now I find out this. Why, Tara?"

"Clay, no." I started to cry, pulling Clay close to me by his shirt staring at him in the face, with tears falling from my eyes. "He's lying; you've got to believe me. He's just acting like we're together."

I turned my head towards Steven glaring. "Tell him you're not serious. Tell him you lied, please."

"Why would I want to do that? I love you."

I cried even more noticing that Clay had believed every word from Steven's mouth. Clay placed his hands on either side of my arms lightly, looking at me as if he was about to cry. "Why, Tara? God. Why did you lie to me? What was I thinking trusting you? How come I never saw this coming? I'm so stupid. My friends warned me about dating a girl that wasn't in my line of work."

"But, Clay, it's not true." Clay pulled away walking away from me in silence. I watched as he paced back in forth in front of me holding his hands on his head. He lowered his hands walking back up to me standing in front of me staring. I could see tears building up in his eyes. He was holding back the tears as best as he could.

"Tara, I'm going to have to leave you from here. I'll get one of my bodyguards to fly you back home, to make sure you're safe," Clay whispered in a very upset voice trembling as he spoke to me.

"Clay, no. Don't do this. I love you." I pulled him towards me again wrapping my arms around him. I placed my hands on the sides of his face staring at him as tears fell from my eyes. I pressed my lips upon his gently. "I didn't do it, Clay. Believe me. I wouldn't lie to you. I love you. You know that."

He pulled me off of him not wanting to listen to me. "I'm sorry, Tara. I have obligations. I have a contract I can't break. I'll be back in four months. We'll deal with all this then."

"No, please, Clay. Let's settle this now."

"I'm sorry, Tara, I can't."

"Why not?"

Clay stared at me with an upset but straight facial expression. "I can't even look at you right now, Tara. How can I talk about this with you when I don't even believe you? Damn it, Tara. Why did you mess this up?"

"I swear, Clay. I never did anything with that guy. I swear it," I cried lowering myself down to the ground crying as Clay looked down at me and told one of his men to carry me on a plane to New York and take me back home. The man whose name was Kevin picked me up into his arms as I cried looking at Clay walk away from me about to enter the plane. "No, wait. Put me down. I've got to stop him. Wait. Clay no!" I got loose, and I ran up to Clay pushing him up against the wall kissing him and holding onto him as he tried not to look at me. "Please, don't do this to me, Clay. Please. I love you."

"I've got to go, Tara. Now go with Kevin."

"No."

"I said leave. I can't do this right now."

"But I love you."

"Leave me alone, Tara."

I backed away from him slowly with tears falling from my eyes as he stared at me with tears in his eyes. "Fine. Believe him, Clay. If you can't tell what's real from what's not, maybe we shouldn't be together."

"I'll be back in four months. I'll talk to you then."

He walked on the plane past me never looking back at me. I was so upset. I couldn't believe Steven had done what he had. I knew as soon as I arrived back home, I was going to find out what the hell had been going on. At this moment, I just wanted to crawl into a hole and die. I loved Clay so much. I was finally happy and now this. I got close to somebody and look what happened. They got taken from me, just like I was afraid of. I had no clue at this moment if Clay was actually going to come back for me, or not. He seemed pretty damn mad at me to even consider taking me back, but I had to have faith. We were engaged. He couldn't just leave me without trying to work this out. He was in love with me. He just needed time to sort through his thoughts, and I hoped that was all he needed.

I saw Steven and ran up to him hitting him as I yelled and screamed crying, "What were you thinking? I hate you. I hate you, you jerk." Kevin ran up to me pulling me off of him, picked me up over his shoulders, and carried me past Steven onto a plane back home.

As I sat in my seat on the plane, I thought about Clay and how he had believed Steven over me. I knew the only way he would take me back was if I found out some kind of proof that I hadn't ever dated Steven. I just didn't see how I was going to get that kind of proof. Who would know something about it and be willing to tell me? Then I thought to myself as I sat on the plane which was about to land looking at the empty seat beside me, *Lindsey must have seen or heard something.* She would know what to do, because I didn't. She had to know or my life with Clay was all over. If I didn't get to have Clay over some kind of stupid game of Steven's, I was going to die. I would seriously find a hole and lay down in it, as if I had already been dead.

When the plane landed, Kevin helped me up, grabbed my bags, and told me to follow him to the car. When we reached the outside of the airport parking lot, I followed him as he lead the way carrying my things to the car which was waiting for us. We reached the car, and Kevin opened the back door for me, and he closed it behind me. He picked up my bags, placing them into the trunk of the vehicle. When Kevin got in the car, he drove me to my foster home, to which I was really not looking forward to going. I was so upset and confused as to why all this had happened. I felt like someone was blowing air into me like a balloon and then sticking a needle in me until I popped. All I wanted was to reverse time to when I heard my name being called. I should have kept walking with Clay. It was my entire fault. I should have known better than to see why he had been at the airport. I was so stupid to even believe that Clay and I could ever be together. He had his dreams, and I had one but now it was ruined.

We finally arrived at my foster home as Kevin let me out and got my bags from the trunk and walked with me carrying them to my room. As we walked down the hallway, everyone that was in the hall stared at me. They were probably wondering why I was crying and also why I was with a strange man. We got to my room where I unlocked my bedroom door, letting Kevin come in to put my bags down on my bedroom floor. I stood in front of Kevin as he just stared at me. "It's alright, Tara. Clay will be fine. He just needs time to think."

"Do you think I did it, too?"

"No, I know you wouldn't do anything to hurt him. Clay just needs time to realize that. He's just stressed out about the tour, and now this, you see. It will be fine; you'll see. You take care of yourself. Clay told me to tell you if you need a ride anywhere I would be honored to drive you anywhere."

"Thank you, Kevin, but I know Clay didn't really tell you that, now did he?"

"No." Kevin then said goodbye, as did I. He left and closed the door to my bedroom behind him. I stood there in tears about what to do next with my life. What was there possibly left for me to do? I had nothing if I didn't have Clay. My dreams were shattered, and to think, one person caused this. How could Clay have believed him? I loved him so much.

CHAPTER 10
Betrayal

I spent a week in my bedroom just coming out to eat, being depressed about what had gone wrong at the airport. I couldn't get Clay off my mind. How could God possibly let this kind of tragedy happen to me? I didn't do anything wrong in my eyes, or did I? I was beginning to think that maybe we weren't meant to be together as I had thought. All I wanted was to lie in bed holding onto Clay as I had done just a week ago, which had felt like years ago. I knew I had to get out of my bed eventually, so I could find out who planned the airport scene and why someone would be so cruel as to do this to me. What did I possibly do to deserve such a painful, depressing tragedy that would haunt me as my parents' death had? My birthday was coming up soon, and Clay and I were supposed to go somewhere special, but now look. Now, all I could expect was a kind "happy birthday" from Lindsey, who probably still believed that I was having the time of my life with Clay Edison.

I lay in bed crying underneath my pink bed covers as I began to hear a knock at my door. I pulled the covers off of me and got up, slowly walked to the door, and opened it, seeing Lindsey standing in front of me. "I'm so sorry about what happened." Lindsey wrapped her arms around me, then pulled away as I let her enter, closing the door behind us. I walked over to my bed and sat down with my knees up to my chest watching as Lindsey did the same.

"Why didn't you tell me when it happened? I would have come sooner."

"How do you expect me to tell anyone when I don't even like telling myself what happened?"

"I didn't find out until today at school. I overheard Steven laughing about what he had done to you and how he actually got Clay to believe him."

"I hate Steven so much at this moment. At least I got some anger out when I hit him after Clay left me."

"You hit him? Damn, girl, he said he got those bruises from camping."

"Yeah, right. Like Steven ever goes camping."

"I know, but don't worry about him, Tara. He won't be bothering you anymore."

"Why is that?"

"Because I attacked him and started smacking him."

"Didn't you get in trouble for that?"

"Yeah, of course. Mrs. Jacob saw me, and now I have detention for a month, even though he deserved what he got for doing that to you."

"Oh, Lindsey, why did you do that? Now he's going to bother me even more. You probably aggravated him."

"No, I don't think so."

"How do you know?"

"Because a boy that gets beat up by a girl and cries telling me that he'll never do it again in front of his friends would be too afraid to try anything else."

I sat quietly as I looked at Lindsey trying to be happy that she was there, but all I could think about was how much I missed Clay. "Tara, you look so unhappy. What can I do to cheer you up?"

"Nothing, there's nothing anyone can do. I need Clay. I want things back to the way they were before all this. I deserve to have the truth about what happened at the airport."

"Oh, you don't know who planned it?"

"No, why do you?"

"Well, actually, I overheard Steven telling his friends about who set it up."

"What did you hear? I want to know everything Lindsey. Who did this to me?"

I leaned closer to Lindsey so I could find out what had really been going on that I wasn't aware of. "First of all, it wasn't entirely Steven's fault; it was actually Jennifer who had planned everything. She had paid

Steven off to go to the airport pretending he was your boyfriend while you were with Clay. She's such a little brat. She wanted Clay to leave you so she could try and arrange with her rich daddy to have Clay see her so he would lean on her for comfort."

"What? So you're saying the reason I'm not with Clay right now is because of Jennifer?"

"Yes, I'm sorry to say this, Tara, but I'm afraid that's the truth."

"How could she do this to me? Damn her."

I placed my feet down on the floor, got up off the bed, and walked over to the coatrack grabbing my jacket and putting it on as I found my shoes. I got ready to leave.

"Where are you going in your pajamas?"

I looked down noticing that I was still wearing my pajamas. I pulled on my shoes and tied the laces standing back up. "I'm going to kick that Pussy Kat's ass. She's not going to get away with doing this to Clay and I."

Lindsey got up off the bed and hurried over to where I was, grabbing me by the arm before I left to find Jennifer. "Tara, look at me. This is not like you. Don't just do this because you're angry. She doesn't deserve to know that she has won. If you go, she'll think that she got what she wanted."

I turned looking Lindsey in the face angry with Jennifer. "What do you expect me to do? Lay down in her crap and keep letting her pile it on top of me, poking me with sticks like I was some kind of experiment of hers?"

"No, all I'm saying is if you go do something to her, you will eventually regret it. Clay wouldn't like it if you beat her up. You're better than that. Don't do this because she did something to you; that would be going down to her level. Be strong like you are and prove her wrong. You have the proof now to get your man back, now call him."

I looked at Lindsey then at the phone wondering if she was right that I should call Clay and give him the proof he needed. "Well, pick up the phone and tell him the truth, then this mess can all be over, and you two can be back together like you were meant to be."

"I don't know; he might not want to talk to me. He really believed Steven, especially once he cried."

"Tara, who cares? Don't just let this time go by. Tell him now and get him back, before it's too late."

"But he doesn't want to talk about this with me until he comes back. What if he gets mad at me?"

"Come on, Tara. Don't be afraid. He loves you."

I walked towards the phone on my nightstand still wearing my jacket and shoes. I sat down on the edge of my bed and picked up the receiver, holding it to my ear as I dialed Clay's number. "Hello?"

"Hey, you're not Clay. Who is this?"

"It's his limo driver speaking, how may I help you?"

"Steve, it's me, Tara, remember?"

"How can I forget? You always look flawless."

"Well, thank you."

"So what can I do for you, Tara?"

"Is Clay there?"

"Yes, but he's not accepting any phone calls for awhile."

"Can you just tell him I'm on the phone, and I need to talk with him about something?"

"Okay, I'll try, hold on."

I waited for Steve to ask as I crossed my fingers hoping that Clay would be as anxious to talk to me as I was to talk with him. "Tara?"

"Yeah?"

"Mr. Edison told me to tell you that he'll deal with everything that happened when he returns."

"No, but God, Steve, just put the phone in his hand."

"I'm sorry I can't do that," Steve whispered into the phone.

"Please, Steve, I'll never ask another favor from you again if you just do this for me." I listened for his answer, hearing him take a deep breath. "Okay, hold on, I'll try, but if he hangs up on you, I think it would be best for you to just play hard to get." "Thank you, Steve."

I waited as Steve placed the phone into Clay's hands, praying that he would say something to me. I then heard noises from the background as I listened closely. "What do you want, Tara?"

"Oh, Clay, you don't know how good it feels to hear you say my name. I've got some news, Clay."

"Tara, not now. I'm not in the mood to talk about this kind of stuff while I'm on my way to another concert. Please, I'm upset as it is and need a break from you so I can figure out my true feelings for you."

"But, Clay, my news..."

"Tara, if this is about your birthday, I don't want to hear it. In fact, I'm hanging up."

"Clay, please, I thought you loved me."

"Oh, Tara, don't even use that on me. I don't want to speak to you right now, and if you can't accept that, I won't bother coming to see you. Now, don't call me back anymore."

"Clay, wait, just tell me one thing."

"What, Tara? Make it quick."

"Do you still love me?"

I heard a sudden silence, and then I heard, "I love you, Tara." I heard a click as he hung up after saying he did love me. I placed the receiver down and looked at Lindsey with an upset expression upon my face.

"So what did he say to you?"

I broke down into tears crying as Lindsey came up to me sitting down beside me on the bed wrapping her arms around me. "What did he say to you?"

I wiped the tears from my eyes trying to find the words to tell her what he had said to me. "He told me not to call him anymore, or else he wouldn't come around. He wouldn't even hear me out. He said he loved me, but I'm not so sure anymore if he really does in a way that he wants me to share a life with him."

"Oh, Tara, you know he loves you. If he told you he loved you still, then he does."

"I don't know; he might just be saying he does."

"You know just as well as I do that he's not like that."

"I shouldn't even bother. I should just go on with my life and accept that I wasn't meant to have anyone I really love."

"No, Tara, don't give up on the greatest thing you have ever had in your life. Great love only happens once in a lifetime; after that, it's just second best."

"I don't want to hurt anymore. I don't want him anymore. He can have Jennifer. I don't care."

"Tara, you don't mean that."

"I do; we'll be better off friends."

"Quit lying to yourself. Clay wouldn't like it."

"Lindsey, would you just stop taking his side and just accept my decision. It's not like he's even going to come back for me anyway. Look at him; he's gorgeous and sweet and the most kind, intelligent, wonderful man, and I'm just…" I took a deep breath then finished, "I'm just a poor little orphan who has no life and no reason for him to even want me as a wife. What on earth do I have to offer him?"

Lindsey took a deep breath then blew it out frustrated with me. "Love."

"Love? He doesn't love me. He just thought he did. If he loved me, he would have heard me out. He would have believed me when I said Steven was lying to him."

"You don't know how he was feeling; he thought he had lost you. He thought you didn't love him anymore, or you were just playing with his mind. Celebrities are sometimes like that because they're mostly afraid of when they meet someone and fall deeply in love with them that they'll end up turning around and hurting them in some way, leaving with not only their heart, but their belongings, too."

"I don't care about his money; that's not why I love him. I fell in love with his soul, and I thought he fell in love with mine."

"Tara, stop talking about him like that. Stop making him out to be the bad one. It's no one's fault but Jennifer's."

"Yeah, and now I'm going to kick her ass."

I got up off the bed as Lindsey grabbed my arm stopping me as she rose up and stood in front of me. "No, Tara, stop it. Snap out of it."

"Let go of me. Let me go, Lindsey, I mean it."

Lindsey held on to me with both her hands on the sides of my arms looking at me. "Tara." Lindsey slapped me across the face as I started to break down into tears. I fell to the ground crying as Lindsey knelt down beside me placing her hand on my shoulder.

"I'm sorry, Tara, but someone had to do it. You're acting like a child."

I wiped my tears, holding my cheek where Lindsey had slapped me. "It's alright, I deserved it. I shouldn't have acted like I did, I'm sorry. I won't do anything to Jennifer, but I'm still going to try and move on without him."

Lindsey brushed my hair away from my eyes staring at me as I cried sitting on the floor holding my face. Lindsey got up off the ground about to leave. "I'm going to go get you some ice. I'll be right back."

"Okay."

Lindsey left the room as I got up off the floor and ran out of my room and down the hallway leaving the foster home to find Jennifer. I didn't want to listen to Lindsey anymore. After all, what did she know? I couldn't even believe she had slapped me like she had the right to. If the tables had been turned, I would have never slapped her. She was my friend, but not anymore, not after that. I ran down the street towards the school in a hurry. I knew Jennifer and the Pussy Kats always stayed late after school dancing on the field outside. When I made it there, I walked around the school to the field. I saw Jennifer and her three friends dancing with a stereo playing. I walked right up to their stereo and pressed power, turning it off. I looked at them as they all turned towards me, walking up to me angry at the sight of me.

"Jennifer, right here, right now. I want to know why the hell you paid Steven off to pretend he was dating me while I was engaged to Clay. What the hell were you thinking, doing that to me? You had no right. I know you wanted Clay and all, but to stoop that low, that's just wrong."

Jennifer walked up to me until she was a foot away from my face. "I don't have any idea what you're talking about, Tara. I didn't pay anybody to break you two up."

"Well, Lindsey told me different. She overheard Steven say you paid him off to act as if he was going out with me at the airport."

"What the hell are you talking about? I didn't set any deal up. I got over Clay. I was just bugging you about him; that's the most I did. You need to lay off. You're really starting to aggravate me, you know that?"

I pushed Jennifer, then she pushed me back and I fell to the ground. She began kicking me as her friends surrounded me punching my face a couple times. I then heard Jennifer tell them, "That's enough. She's had enough." Jennifer knelt down beside me staring me in the face as I lay on the grass bleeding from their beating. "You had to start

Header

something, didn't you? I never made a bet. You should have believed me. From what Steven tells me, even though I shouldn't tell you this, Lindsey made the deal with him, not me."

I watched as Jennifer got up picking up her stereo and leaving with her three friends. I lay on the ground bleeding and trying to find the strength to get up off the ground, but I couldn't. I couldn't even hear anyone in the area. All I saw was grass. I prayed to God that someone would find me before dark. I must have lain on the cold grass bleeding for about two whole hours before I saw a man pick me up into his arms and carry me to his car placing me inside. I didn't know who he was, but he drove me to the hospital and brought me inside safely. I couldn't remember anything after that point; my mind was blank. I must have passed out or something from the pain. All I could think about was what Jennifer had told me about my best friend. I couldn't believe it had been the other way around. How could Lindsey be the one that did it? She was my best friend; we were so close. Why would she want to destroy what I had?

I remember having my eyes closed for awhile just lying in a warm bed covered in thermal blankets. I lay there as I remembered the incident at the airport when I had asked Steven why he was there. I then remembered him saying that Lindsey had sent him. I knew right at that moment that Jennifer had been telling the truth and not Lindsey. I had never expected that Lindsey would stoop that low, but that would explain her slapping me. All her jokes about Clay hadn't even been jokes; they were real feelings Lindsey had felt. Lindsey was using me to try and get closer to Clay, so she could steal him away somehow, and what better way than this?

I slowly opened my eyes and saw a nurse standing beside me refilling my IV hanging it above me. "Where am I?"

The nurse turned to me and looked at me staring. "Oh, darling, you're awake now. How are you feeling? Do you have any pain?"

"Where's Clay? Did he call?"

"Clay who?"

"Clay Edison, my fiancé."

"You're engaged to Clay Edison?"

"Yeah, why?"

"Can I have your autograph?" The nurse pulled out a piece of paper from her pocket and gave it to me with a pen.

"Are you serious? You want my autograph?"

"Of course I'm serious."

I picked up the pen and paper and wrote my signature on the paper giving it back to her. She was smiling at me.

The nurse left my side. She left the room as I closed my eyes for a minute, then I opened them as I saw Kevin walk into my room towards me. He placed his hand over mine with a worried expression on his face. "Kevin, what are you doing here?"

"Clay wanted me to check up on you, to see if you're alright."

"Oh, I see, that makes sense. Why would he want to see me looking like this?"

I turned over facing away from Kevin tearing up. "Tara, he couldn't come; he was busy. He had another concert."

"Just tell him to screw off. Tell him not to bother coming to see me when he comes back. I don't want to see him anymore."

"Tara, he does love you. He was so upset when he heard about you in the hospital. He almost cancelled his concert."

"Yeah, I bet. It really shows."

"Tara, he wouldn't have sent me to see you if he didn't love you."

I turned towards him sitting up. "If he loved me, don't you think he would have believed me when I said Steven was lying? He would have come to see me in the hospital. Hell, does he even know why I'm in the hospital?"

"Yes, the hospital told him you were beat up and found on the school grounds."

"Does he know why I was beat up?"

"No, but if you told me, I'd make sure he found out."

"I don't want him to know. He's got to figure this one out on his own. For once, I'd like to see someone prove to me that they had been wrong."

"I wish you could understand that Clay was going to come until Lindsey called him and told him that you were fine and didn't want to ever see him and that you had been dating Steven after all."

"Yeah, I bet she did."

"She did."

Header

"I know. I could believe that. She's messed up enough already, so why not more?"

Kevin walked up towards me placing his hand on my shoulder. "What did she mess up?"

"I don't want to talk about it. I know you'd probably tell Clay everything if I told you."

"Well, if it's going to bring you two back together, of course."

"You don't understand, Kevin. Clay doesn't need me. I don't deserve him. I have nothing to offer him that is worth loving me for. I'm just going to go on with my life and try and start over. I might move. I might stay. I'm not sure at this moment as to what I should exactly do."

"But Clay, he would be so upset if you moved. I just know it. Please don't move, Miss Heart. It would be wrong."

"I probably won't move. I'll probably just move on carrying on with my day without anyone getting in my way."

"Just wait for him to return. Don't just walk away from him. Let him return to you and then decide."

"Do you even realize that I have lost everything in my life? I've lost my friend, my family, and now Clay. What the hell do I have to give me strength to even try to wait? I can't wait. I have to forget about everything. I can't believe how much has happened to me this year."

"Tara, Clay will come back for you. Don't worry. He loves you. He's fine on stage, but when he enters his limo or is away from the public eye, he looks so upset."

"Really?"

"Yeah, really. Please just leave your heart open for him. Don't try and forget him. Just keep him a part of you until he returns back home."

"I guess, but please tell him I'm okay and I'll be fine."

Kevin said goodbye then turned away and walked out the door. I lay there just staring at the ceiling above me relaxing. I looked beside me on a table tray where there was a mirror, and I picked it up holding it in front of me. I saw that I had bruises on the right side of my face. I looked horrible, and I regretted trying to fight Jennifer. I should have figured it out sooner by what Steven had said at the airport, but all I heard that day was Steven telling Clay he was my boyfriend. I placed the mirror down holding it against my body as I lay staring at the ceiling again.

A couple of days had passed by when an unexpected visitor came to visit me one day. I was sitting up in the hospital bed eating my lunch as Lindsey entered my room. "I heard about Jennifer. I told you not to go down there." I placed my lunch down and moved the table away from the bed as I glared at her in anger.

"Don't give me that crap, Lindsey. What the hell is the matter with you? Are you insane? I know it was really you that set the whole deal up with Steven, so don't put on a big show for me as if you don't know what I'm talking about."

"How do you know?"

"Because Steven told Jennifer, and Jennifer told me. What did you think? I wouldn't find out somehow?" I took a deep breath then continued, "Why did you do it?"

"Why do you think I did it, Tara? You always get the guys you really want. You stole Clay. If I can't have him, you can't either. You don't deserve him. I thought Clay would only stay with you for a couple weeks, but as you two got closer, it made me sick to my stomach to hear that you were with the person I wanted. How could you stay with him? Why did you have to bring this on yourself? Everything was all fine until you got Clay."

"Are you kidding me, Lindsey? You did this because you were jealous of what I had? So all our friendship was to you was a person for you to use for whatever you wanted?"

"You're not much of a friend either, Tara. I have no idea what Clay saw in you. You're so selfish, you know that, Tara? You're always thinking about yourself, never giving people anything."

"Excuse me?"

"You heard me."

"God, all this time, I thought that Jennifer was the one that did everything disrespectful to everyone, when really it was you all along."

"You deserve everything you got, Tara."

"Get out. I don't ever want to see your face again, you hear me?"

"Yeah, I hear you loud and clear. Oh, by the way, Tara, have a nice life without Clay."

Lindsey left the room as I sat in my bed watching her leave my life, feeling happy that she was gone. I knew from that day on that I had to be strong and move on, going through each day one at a time until I

Header

eventually ended up in my future, wherever that might be. I had to be able to look at my life and find a way to see the good things out of all the bad that had happened to me. Although I couldn't see any good in my life right at that moment, maybe I'd find out what good would eventually come out of the bad. Some things are better left unsaid, just as some things are better left untouched. I didn't know how I was going to carry on considering everything that had happened so far.

I lay down in the hospital bed waiting to be released to go back home and start over again. When the time came for me to leave, I changed into my clothes and walked downstairs leaving the hospital. When I walked outside, I saw a limo parked in front of the hospital. I thought nothing of it until a man rushed over to me.

"Are you Miss Heart?"

"Yes, why?"

"Clay sent me to come take you home. He wanted to make sure you got home safely."

"Really?"

"Yes, Miss Heart."

"Well, tell him I said thank you for sending me a ride."

The man walked me over to the limo and opened the back door as I got inside looking at the empty seat beside me that Clay had always sat in. The man closed the door and got back in, driving me back to my foster home. I couldn't wait to get back home. I sat in the back of the limo looking in the mirror at the bruises on my face. They were almost faded, and I couldn't wait until they were gone. I couldn't wait until I could at least look beautiful again.

When I arrived at the foster home the man let me out and made sure I got inside safely then drove away. I walked down the hallway to my room seeing the teenagers saying hi to me as I walked by them. Everyone must have known about my whole life, but it didn't seem to bother me anymore. I reached my room and unlocked it going inside and closing the door behind me. The first thing I did was climb into bed and go to sleep. I wanted to get as much sleep as I could for school tomorrow.

I lay in bed looking at a calendar hung beside me across the room. I saw that there were only three more months left until Clay would be returning home. I smiled then closed my eyes falling asleep, feeling better about being home. I knew in my heart that everything would turn out

Header

well in the end as long as I was willing to wait for my broken heart to mend. I was ready, and I was not going to give up on my life so easily. Would you?

CHAPTER 11
On My Own

A month had gone by of me moving on, and I was beginning to feel a little bit better except for not being able to see Clay. I knew I would see him in two more months, so I felt good every time I thought about that. My birthday was today, so I was on my way to the hair salon to get Piercen to do my hair. I was going out to a dance club so I could have some kind of celebration to remember.

I got ready and opened my bedroom door, locking it behind me as I left to go to see Piercen. When I got outside, I saw a limo parked out front and started to walk past it until the same man that drove me home from the hospital ran up to me. "Miss Heart! Miss Heart!"

I turned towards him and stopped. "What is it?"

He caught his breath staring at me. "Clay sent me to drive you wherever you want to go for your birthday."

"What? Does he have some kind of signal when I'm leaving the house or something?"

"No, actually, whenever you call a taxi, Clay gets a phone call that you need a ride somewhere and that's where I come in."

I giggled then followed the man whose name was Brian to the limo. He let me in and drove me to the salon. I found it very amusing that Clay had connections with a taxi service. I sat in the limo as it drove away feeling warm and fuzzy inside as I glanced to the side of me on the floor of the limo. I got up off my seat and walked over to the other side of the limo pulling out some kind of gift bag that had been under some

116

kind of soft white blanket. I picked it up and carried it back to my seat sitting down and staring at it. I searched for the tag on it at the top, and it read, "To the woman I love. Happy Birthday."

I began to open the bag. Peeking inside, I saw a box. I pulled it out and opened it, seeing it was a charm bracelet. As I looked more closely, I noticed the charms on the bracelet represented our love for one another. There was a teardrop for when I cried the first time we met and a limo and also a microphone. The charm that made me laugh the most, though, was the one that said stubborn, for all the times we fought with one another. Brian parked at the side of the street, got out, and opened the door for me. I placed the gift bag down and got out of the limo, standing beside Brain. Brian glanced down at me seeing me struggling to put on the bracelet I had received.

"Miss Heart, would you like me to help you with that?"

"Yeah, could you?"

Brian placed the bracelet on my wrist then looked back up at me smiling. "I take it you found your gift in the limo then?"

"Yeah, did you know about it?"

"Of course, Miss Heart. Clay sent it to me for you."

"Hmm, that man sure gives me a lot for being mad at me."

I walked past Brian towards the salon. I entered and saw Piercen doing someone's hair. I stood by the door waiting for someone to notice I had been standing there. Piercen turned and seeing me standing by the door, he walked up to me kissing both my cheeks like a Frenchman. "Oh, Tara, you come for hairdo? I make it look perfect like before."

"Thank you, Piercen."

"I'll be a little while longer. Come, come, take a seat. Sit, make yourself comfortable." I sat down in the waiting area on a chair looking up at Piercen beginning to walk away. He quickly turned toward me again. "Oh, how is Clay? Is his hair still spiky?"

"Oh yeah, it's fine, but I can't say how he is, because I haven't seen him in three months."

"Oh no, why not? That's terrible! You come. I make your hair special."

I got to my feet following Piercen as he led me to the salon chair beside a lady whose hair he hadn't finished. Piercen called to one of the assistants. "Psst, come finish Mrs. Hurdle's hair, Megan. I've got a

Header

very special customer." Piercen walked up to me placing his hands on my shoulders and looking at me in the mirror in front of us. "Tell me everything. I want to know about this separation. Did he hurt you? I'd kick his arse. You are a special girl, and no one treats you like that."

"No, it's nothing like that."

I began telling him the story as he worked on my hair making it perfect as he always had. When I finished telling him the story, he was almost finished with my hair. "Oh, that's a terrible story; that Lindsey has some nerve, huh. Does she have a brain, no?"

"She took the most wonderful man away from me, just like that."

"Oh, that's okay. He'll come back, and one look at you, he'll be all over you like last time. Look, I'm Clay, wow, wow, wow. He so cute. You know his arse is so tight. I've seen a lot of great bottoms in my life, but his is…"

"Piercen."

"What? I just playing. I make jokes, no? I won't tell no more. He your manly man, I know, I understand; he good man. That Lindsey was a, well, you know. I surprised that the Pussy Kats never scratched you. They have claws, no?"

"Oh, Piercen, it's just a name I gave them."

"Oh, I get it, err…"

Piercen finished my hair and spun me around as I got down off of the chair. I walked up to the register with Piercen about to pay for my hairstyle as Piercen took a look on his computer, ready to tell me the amount for it. "So what is the total, Piercen?"

"Oh, you don't have to pay; you're already covered under Clay's account."

"What? I'm not under his account, and if I am, I didn't know anything about this."

"Well, that's what it shows, so you can go out with your bad self and get down and boogie."

I giggled at what Piercen said and walked out of the salon back towards the limo and got inside. I told Brian on the intercom in the limo where to drop me off next. "Brian?"

"Yes, Miss Heart, what can I do for you?"

"Can you take me to a dance club called Smashing."

"Sure thing, Miss Heart."

I pulled my outfit out of my bag I had brought with me and got undressed, changing into it in the back of the limo.

After almost ten minutes, the limo came to a stop, and Brian got out and made his way around to open the door for me. I climbed out standing in front of him as he closed the door and stood looking at me. "So should I wait outside for you?"

"No, you just go home, and I'll call a cab when I want to leave, alright?"

"I highly doubt that a cab will show up, but as you wish, Miss Heart."

Brian walked back to the driver's side as I went inside the club showing them my identification. When I entered, I saw so many people inside dancing, having the time of their lives. I, on the other hand, was just having an okay time, being by myself and all. I walked up to the bar and sat down on a stool ordering a drink. The bartender poured me a drink and placed it in front of me on the counter. I sat there on the stool taking sips of my drink as I saw a man sit down on the stool beside me. I could see from the corner of my eye that he was staring at me. Then he spoke to me. "So, pretty lady, what's your name?"

"That's none of your business, now is it?"

"I saw you from across the way and wanted to know if I could buy you a drink?"

I lifted my glass up swirling the liquid around. "It's already paid for, sorry."

"Well, how about your number?"

I turned towards him staring, as he looked me up and down checking me out. "I'm engaged, sorry."

"Oh, that sucks, who's the lucky guy?"

"His name is none of your business either, now is it?"

He got up and walked away being rejected by me. I stayed seated until I had finished my drink and then stood up and walked onto the dance floor beginning to dance. As I danced, girls nearby surrounded me starting to dance along beside me picking up my moves. We laughed together. I was finally having fun until the man at the bar came up to me drunk, pointing at me. "I know who you are. You're Clay Edison's girl, aren't you?" I stood in silence surprised that he knew who I was.

Header

"You were on stage with him at his concert." I still stood silently looking at everyone around me staring. "You said you were engaged." The man paused then finished, "Oh, I see, you're engaged to Clay."

I ran through the crowd hearing everyone beginning to take in the information from what the man had said to me while on the dance floor. I hid inside a closet that was beside the bathrooms. I looked down, reaching into my purse and pulling out my pink cell phone as I dialed the number for a cab. "Hi, I'd like a taxi to be sent to Smashing, the dance club."

"And who is the taxi for?"

I stopped while thinking of a name. "It's for Jane Lee."

"Well, thank you, it will be there in five minutes."

I hung up the phone placing it back into my purse hearing people running around the club looking for me. They were calling my name. I knew that some of the people had remembered me from when Clay and I got off the plane on our way to Vancouver a while back. I thought for a couple of seconds wondering how I was going to get out of there with all the people looking for me. I slowly opened the closet door sneaking past everyone, ducking so no one would see me.

When I had finally made it outside, I looked around for my taxi. I saw a limo that had been parked outside at the side of the street. I knew it couldn't have been Brian because I had used another name, so I stood outside waiting for my ride. As I waited, I saw the limo door open as Brian got out walking up to me smirking and shaking his head at me. "How on earth did you find out I needed a ride? I called a cab and used a different name."

"Oh, Miss Heart," Brain laughed. "You should have known better than that. It's voice-activated. He'll be able to know it's you no matter what."

"Damn it, well, just leave, I'll find my own way back. There must be a bus coming sometime soon."

I looked around as Brian stared at me confused. "Miss Heart, why is it you don't want a ride? Most people are happy to ride in a limo."

"Yeah, it's great and all, but he's supposed to be mad at me for something I didn't do, so he can stop all this crap because it's just making it harder for me to go through my day without thinking about him."

"Would you like me to tell him that?"

"What? You've talked to him?"

"Of course, every time you're in the limo, I'm in the front talking to Clay on my cell phone."

"Really? What does he say?"

"Oh, he asks what you're wearing and where you're going and stuff like that."

"Oh, I see." I was silent then looked up at the limo, then back at Brian smirking. "Is he in that limo?"

"No, but he's on the cell phone."

"Oh, really? He is?" I looked at the limo smirking then back at Brian. "Why don't you go tell Mr. Edison that I ran away and caught a bus, bye."

I took off running, taking off my high heels as I ran. I ran as fast as I could to a bus that I could see coming from up the street. I reached the bus stop as I got on quickly, waving goodbye to Brian as I passed him seeing him talking on his cell phone. I giggled sitting down on the bus amused by what I had done. I had never ridden a bus before so I sat up front and told the bus driver where I was going and he said he would tell me where to get off. I relaxed on the bus wondering what Clay was saying to Brian when he found out I refused the ride and took off. I knew he would be worried, but he made a big deal about me calling him, and then he turned around and did these little things for me as though he only had the right to stay in touch with me.

When the bus reached my stop, the bus driver told me to get off and walk a block, and I would see my foster home. I got off the bus watching as it drove away. I started walking down the street, beginning to see my foster home not too far from where I had been. As I had got closer, I heard a car coming from behind me speeding up and driving along beside me. I looked over at it seeing it was the limo. Brian was peeking his head out of the window telling me to stop. I stopped, as did he. He got out of the limo, placing his cell phone into my hands.

"What's this?"

"It's for you; pick up the phone." I stood there with the phone in my hands wondering if I should talk to him. Brian moved closer to me. "Please talk to him. I got in trouble because of the stunt you just pulled. Now fix it."

Header

I took a deep breath and placed the phone to my ear scared as to what Clay might say to me after what I had done. "Hello."

"Tara."

"Yeah."

"Is what Brian said true? Did you run away from the limo?" I paused, shaking.

"Yeah, why?"

"Why would you do that? You know how dangerous the bus is out there for a girl like you?"

"Are you lecturing me, Clay?"

"No, I'm just telling you I was worried. Was it so hard for you to get a ride in a warm limo rather than on a bus full of strangers that might find out who you are?"

"Oh, I already had that problem at the club."

"Why don't you just accept the rides I send you? I do it so you're protected until I return."

"Clayton, you are so, err, my God. First, you leave me at the airport. Then you tell me not to call you. Then you send me rides and pay for my expenses at the salon. Do you want to be with me? Do you believe me or what?"

"Tara, calm down. I told you we would talk about that when I return. I just did those other things because I was worried. I'm not there, and I'm worried about you." "Clayton, oh God, I'm hanging up because I can't take this. I have to move on. How can I be with you if you don't believe me? Stop sending me things, okay? I'm fine. I'll do everything on my own, and if something happens, something happens, alright? Don't even bother coming to see me when you return. I'm not going to wait around for you to talk about something that I didn't even do. Goodbye."

I placed the phone back into Brain's hands and walked towards the foster home. Brian picked up the phone placing it to his ear, "Mr. Edison?"

"Well, that didn't go too well, now did it?"

"No, Mr. Edison, it didn't."

"Put her back on for a second."

"Right away."

I turned feeling Brian place his hand upon my shoulder. I stared at Brian holding the cell phone out to me. "What now?"

"Please, Miss Heart."

I rolled my eyes taking the cell phone from Brian and placing it against my ear gently. "Hello."

"Tara, please. I know I said I wanted you to wait until I got back to talk about this, but let's just do it now."

"Wait a minute. You make me so mad, Clay. You don't believe me, and you make me leave without you at the airport. Then you blow me off on the phone. Screw you, Clayton. You should have told me before."

"I just noticed that you call me Clayton when you're mad."

"Clay, are you even listening to me at all?"

"Yes, and I don't think you should be getting so mad about this. How did you think I felt when I found out about Steven?"

"God, Clay. There was no Steven."

"Tara, please."

"No. Now screw off." I placed the phone back into Brian's hand as I stormed off towards my house. Brian picked up the phone placing it to his ear once more.

"Do you want me to go after her, Mr. Edison?"

Clay took a deep breath blowing it out upset. "No, don't bother. If she doesn't want a ride, that's fine. Cancel all connections with the cab services, alright? I'll talk to you soon, take care."

"Goodbye, Mr. Edison." Brian placed the cell phone into the limo and got in and drove away, as I carried on walking to my house. When I entered the hallway and turned towards my room, I noticed a girl standing beside the column beside my bedroom door. She was tall with dirty blond hair and blue eyes. When I reached her, she stared at me waiting for me to say something. I unlocked my door seeing her smiling at me. "Hi, I'm Carrie. I saw you at Clay's concert. I thought you were so great up there."

"That's nice, but I'm really not in the mood to hear about how great I was."

I opened my bedroom door about to enter as Carrie placed her hand upon my shoulder. I turned my head staring at her. "Please, can I come in and hang out with you? I'm new here, and I'd really like to have someone to talk to, especially someone that got to sing alongside of Clay Edison."

Header

"Sorry, but the last friend I had went behind my back and destroyed my relationship with Clay because she was jealous."

"Really, oh my God, that's such a horrible thing to do, especially to a friend." "Thank you, finally someone who agrees with me on this."

"So can I come in?"

"Sure, why not make yourself comfortable."

I let Carrie in, and I closed the door behind us, walked towards the bed, and sat down beside her. "So why are you here?"

"Oh, my mother died about a year ago, and my dad couldn't afford to take care of me anymore. He thought I would be better off in a foster home."

"I'm sorry about your mother."

"That's alright, I know she's still with me, as long as I feel her here and remember her. I know I'll be able to go through my days easily knowing she's out there watching over me from somewhere." I looked at Carrie as she told her story, without even crying like I probably would have. Carrie was silent and then began to question me. "So why are you here?"

"Oh, no big reason. I'd kind of like to forget about why and just move on so I don't have to remember it again."

"Oh, it must be sad; you shouldn't hide your feelings, and you can trust me."

"I don't even know you, Carrie, so how on earth do you expect for me to trust you?"

"Because I've never really had anyone to talk to in my life but my mother, and she's gone now. I'd really like a chance at being able to talk to someone who is not so into herself, like some girls I know."

"Well, that's really nice, but I don't want you to pity me if I told you my story."

"Oh, girl, you don't even have to worry about that. When I want to say something, I speak my mind."

"Well, okay, I'll tell you…"

I took a deep breath then began to speak, telling her everything that had happened to me as she listened. "Well, first my mother and father died, then my sister right after. My twin moved away to my grandma's. I was feeling so upset and down about myself just trying to cope with everything that had happened to me. After that, my best friend,

Lindsey, took me to the mall to try and cheer me up. At the mall, I saw Clay Edison signing autographs, so I went to get one even though I was almost in tears. When it was my turn to get an autograph, I fell to the ground upset. He picked me up and carried me to his limo and cheered me up. It felt so good to be in his presence even though I had been crying. We started dating, then we had arguments. Then we got engaged."

I stopped taking a breath wondering if she wanted to hear more of what I had to say.

"So what happened next?"

"Well, I went with him on tour having the time of my life, and I even sang on stage with him. Then on the way to Seattle from Vancouver, Steven, from my school, came up to me acting as if we were dating. Clay believed him because he cried and sent me home and left to finish his tour without me. I found out from Lindsey that Jennifer had paid Steven off to pull the stunt he had. But when I got beat up by Jennifer, she told me it had been Lindsey all along, who actually admitted it to me just a little while ago."

"Is that all?"

"What? You want more?"

"Well, only if there is more."

"No, that's about it for now."

"So you're not with Clay anymore?"

"I'm not sure."

"He didn't even talk it through with you?"

"No, he said at the airport that he would deal with everything when he comes back, but then he keeps sending me limos every time I call a cab to go somewhere." "Man, girl, you've got serious problems. You need to get some kind of activity to keep your mind occupied."

"Yeah, tell me about it."

"Have you ever thought of playing hard to get, so he'll decide faster what he wants?"

"I thought about it, but I'm not so sure how to do it."

"Well, that's where I come in. I know the perfect thing."

"What?"

"Well, first, when does he come back?"

"In two months."

"Hmm, yeah, that would work out great."

"What is it?"

"Do you know the day he comes back?"

"No, not really."

"Well, it doesn't matter; just don't give him any reason or chance to see or talk to you."

"Why?"

"Because I've got the best idea. You can sing, right?"

"Yeah, why?"

"Well, you could audition for *Soul Seeker*, and I know you'll get in. The reason being is because if you win, he will have to see you all the time which will make him want you so badly, he'll forget about everything that happened and move on. You'll end up with him again, and Lindsey will have to live with hearing about you two on the radio and television every day."

"Uh, I don't know; he might not like it if I don't stay here waiting for him."

"Tara, you have to make some kind of stand. He's your man. You have to fight for him before any other girl sweet talks him away considering that he's upset about you right now."

"Yeah, maybe you're right, maybe I should. I know I would be able to win. I'm a great singer, and the audience loved me at Clay's concert."

I stood up looking down at Carrie then finished, "I'll do it. So when does it start?"

"You go, girl."

"I want to be close to the man I love, so when is the audition?"

"Oh, it's in two months, so September 15th I think; yeah, that's right."

"That day sounds familiar for some reason. I wonder why."

"Oh, it's probably nothing."

"Yeah, you're probably right. Oh man, I'm so excited. I'm going to win Clay over with my voice and captivate his heart like he did mine."

Carrie smiled at me with a sweet look of innocence. She reminded me of someone I had met before. I just couldn't figure out who it was. "So what's your daddy like, Carrie?"

"Oh, well, he's a great man and loves helping people in the best way he knows how."

"What's his name? Maybe I've met him?"

"Oh, Kevin."

"Hmm, oh, I know a Kevin."

"Oh, but I don't think it's my father; he lives in Washington, D.C. now."

"Yeah, it couldn't be him then, sorry about that."

"It's alright; everyone makes mistakes."

"Yeah, I wish everyone else thought that way, too."

"Well, you can't change everyone."

"That's for sure."

We talked for hours in my bedroom telling each other different stories about our childhood and how our families were. I told her all about the Pussy Kats and to watch out for Lindsey and Jennifer. I finally felt like I was able to tell anyone my past since Carrie made it seem like it wasn't my fault, and she didn't once pity me for anything I had told her. She was the only friend I had now, and she was a friend worth keeping, considering the sweet nature she had towards everyone. I was moving on and feeling so great about myself again. I was ready to fight for Clay, and I was willing to do whatever it would take to have my man back that I deserved. This was the beginning of my new life, this was the most wonderful, memorable time I was going to remember forever. This was the beginning of where my dreams would take place. With a little faith and a good friend by my side, my future looked brighter than ever. I just prayed that Clay was still in love with me as I was with him, and wondered if so, how would I know for sure?

CHAPTER 12
Reuniting True Love

The time had finally come for me to audition for *Soul Seeker*; I was in Carrie's room getting ready to leave. Carrie did my hair really nice; it was up in a bun with diamond clips. I looked very beautiful in a red short dress that came to above my knees that had sparkles all over it.

Carrie looked at me while smiling. "Wow, man, Clay's missing out on something special. When he sees you on TV, he's going to flip. He won't know what to think about it."

"Yeah, I really miss him, but I have to think positive. The closer I get to stardom, the closer I am to Clay. If I can't be with him, I at least want him to know I can take care of myself."

"Okay, Tara, we should leave soon; it's almost time."

I glanced in the mirror in front of me then turned towards the nightstand, picking up my purse. I got ready to call a cab. "Oh crap, I can't call a cab; Clay will send a limo."

"So? What's wrong with that? We deserve a limo ride. Look at you, you're radiant."

"Yeah, we do deserve a limo ride; you're right." I pulled my cell phone out of my purse and dialed the number for a cab. "Hello. Yeah, I need a taxi at Seekers' Dale foster home."

"Okay, one will be sent to you in a few minutes."

"Aren't you going to ask my name?"

"No."

"Okay, bye."

I closed my cell phone, placed it back into my purse, and stared at Carrie seeing her looking at me. "They didn't ask for your name?"

"No, Clay must have cancelled it. I really messed things up with him, didn't I?"

I walked over to the bed, sat at the edge with my head down, and started to cry. "I miss him so much, Carrie; my heart hurts so bad. I don't know what to do. I'm trying to move on, I am, but it's hard when I love him so much."

"I know. It's alright. You'll be fine, and I'll be there when you audition. I'll be cheering you on so they give you one of those yellow slips."

"I don't even know if I'm doing the right thing auditioning for *Soul Seeker*. What if my life turns out worse than it already has?"

"I don't think it will. I believe good is going to come out of this. I feel it in my heart, Tara."

I took a deep breath and stood up, wiping the tears from my eyes. "Okay, how do I look?"

"Beautiful, now let's go break some hearts."

"Okay."

We left the room after putting on our jackets and shoes and locked the door behind us. We walked down the hallway as everyone that saw me in the foster home cheered me on including Tracy who had been beside the front entrance.

Meanwhile, Clay was back from his tour and was getting his hair done at the salon where Piercen worked. Clay sat in the chair as Piercen got ready to spike his hair like he had always worn it, while they began a conversation. "So, you're back from your tour now?"

"Yeah, I just finished with it, and now, I'm on my way home, but I wanted to stop by and get my hair done first."

"That's good. You came to the right place for that. I will give you the best spikes you've ever had, no?"

Clay sat quietly for a minute watching Piercen in the mirror styling his hair. "Oh, are you and Tara back together yet? She's such a doll?"

"How do you know about Tara and me not speaking?"

"Oh, she came in awhile back; she told me everything."

"She did. Oh, I see. She probably blamed me for everything, didn't she?"

"Oh no, not once. She had no reason to blame you. You did nothing wrong; you're a good man."

"Well, thanks, Piercen, but I don't feel like such a great man right now. I messed up everything. I really miss her, but if she was with Steven, what am I supposed to do? Share her with him?" Clay took a deep breath, blowing it out upset. "I won't. I won't share someone I'm in love with. It can't happen. I need her. I want to be with her. I don't want to have to see her with any other man but me, and she's my beautiful."

"What? Oh no, you don't know about Lindsey? You're going to be surprised. But just don't jump out of my chair and hit the ceiling. I get that a lot."

"What are you talking about, Piercen? What about Lindsey? What does she have to do with anything?"

Clay turned and looked up at Piercen who was still styling his hair. "Tara found out Lindsey had paid some Steven boy off to make it look like she had been cheating on you. Lindsey is a bad…Well, you know, she has no brain, and I want to kick her arse. Poor Tara got beat up trying to find out the truth so she could have you back. She took on three Pussy Kats for you. She told me that she tried to tell you on the phone once about it, but you blew her off like a cold breeze. It sounded so awful especially coming from such a sweet girl like Tara." Piercen looked down wiping his tears with his shirt as Clay watched him. "Oh, it makes me so sad, poor Tara dear."

"How does Tara know Jennifer didn't lie about it?"

Piercen sniffled. "Oh Lindsey admitted it, and also, hmm, oh yeah, she mentioned at the airport Steven had said Lindsey sent him."

"Yeah, I remember that, too."

Clay jumped out of his seat. "Hey, I told you not to jump; you could have hit your noggin on my ceiling. That would not be too good, your body feel pain and your head have bump, no?"

Clay stood up in front of Piercen thinking for a minute. "I've got to find her. I'm such a jerk for not seeing it before."

"Yeah, that's a good boy. You go get her, tiger, err."

Clay rushed passed Piercen out of the salon as Piercen yelled to him. "Wait! Your spikes are not perfect! Come back." Clay was gone, and Piercen stood with one hand near his face stroking his chin. "Oh no."

Meanwhile, back at the foster home, Carrie and I were outside waiting for our taxi on the side of the street out front. A couple of minutes later, the taxi showed up as we got inside, closing the door after us. We were driven away to the auditions for *Soul Seeker* that were taking place that day. "Man, I hope I remember my words when I sing. I don't want to look like a total idiot in front of the judges, especially Rage. Oh my God, what if I fall on my face?"

"Calm down, Tara; you're going to be great. They'll love you. You have enough personality to make five people."

We giggled as we watched out the window as everything passed by. I had seen a black limo drive past our taxi as I stared out the window at it and remembered all the fun Clay and I had in his limo. While we were being driven to the auditions, Clay had been on his way to find me. He ran out of the salon getting into his limo, telling Steve to hurry to my house. Clay sat and waited in the limo to reach my house so he could win me back for the misunderstanding that had been going on for months now. "God, I hope I'm not too late. If she's with someone else, I don't know what I'll do."

Steve reached the foster home and pulled up in front of the entrance where Clay opened the door and got out in a hurry to mend my broken heart. He walked quickly towards the doors, entered the house, and walked down the hallway towards my bedroom. He knocked on the door, and as the door started to open, he stood looking at a girl staring at him.

"Oh my God, Clay Edison's at my door. Can I have your autograph?"

"Not now. Where is Tara? Have you seen her?"

"Yeah, she's in Carrie's room; they share a bedroom now."

"Where's her room?"

"Down the hall." The girl pointed towards where he had come from.

"Oh my God, it's Clay."

"Hey, show me where her room is and I'll give you my autograph."

"Sure."

The girl opened the door more and walked with Clay, staring at him and fluttering her eyes at him while smiling. She came to a blue door and pointed. "In here. Now may I have an autograph?"

"Of course."

The young girl pulled on her shirt as Clay reached into his pocket pulling out a pen. He signed her shirt. Clay put his pen away then began to knock on the door. "Tara, Tara, it's me. Open up, I need to talk to you."

"She's not here; she just left."

Clay turned to see who had spoken to him, and when he turned, he saw it was Tracy staring at him. "Oh hi, Clay, what brings you here. Long time no see. Oh, by the way, nice hair."

Clay felt his hair with his hands then placed them back down at his sides still staring at Tracy. "Where's Tara? I need to find her; it's important."

"Oh she's playing hide and seek with you."

"What?"

"I'm just fooling; she left to go audition for *Soul Seeker* not too long ago with Carrie."

"Oh no, I've got to stop her."

"Hey, just wait here one minute, young man. Why on earth would you want to stop her from fulfilling her dream?"

"Because she's just doing it for me. If she gets in, we'll have too busy of schedules to even have a relationship."

"Oh, well, in that case, you go find her. Hurry!"

Clay hurried passed Tracy towards the doors as girls surrounded him asking him for his autograph. As Clay was stuck in the foster home being surrounded by hundreds of young girls, I had just arrived at the studio for my audition. I had to wait fifteen minutes until I could audition. I sat in the waiting area beside Carrie practicing my song quietly so people couldn't hear me. Timmy Thermal saw us and came up to us asking questions. "So what brings you to New York?"

"Well, Clay does actually."

"You're a fan of Clay Edison?"

"No, I'm..."

Carrie cut in, "She's his fiancée."

"Your Clay Edison's fiancée?"

I didn't say anything. I sat there thinking he would just leave not believing Carrie, but he didn't, he called people over to us. "Did you know Clay Edison is engaged to this girl?"

The boy he asked looked directly at me then answered, "Yeah, she performed on stage with him at his concert. I saw them. It was awesome. Tara, right? Tara Heart?"

I smirked at the boy agreeing with him.

"Really?" Timmy Thermal then brought more people over to us asking the same question until he finally believed that it was true about my being Clay Edison's fiancée. It was almost my turn to audition, so I waited beside the doors for the person auditioning to come out of the room.

After five minutes, a girl opened the door crying from not getting accepted as I pulled open the doors and went inside. I walked towards the judges and stood in front of them, as Rage looked down at his piece of paper then began to question me. "So I see here that you've performed at one of Clay Edison's concerts. Is that true?"

"Yes, it is, actually, Clay and I are engaged, and well, you don't need to hear the rest."

Eddy spoke out, interested, "No, please, we would love to hear about this."

I began telling them the story as I watched their expressions go from happy to sad. Pamela was tearing up when I had finished telling them what had happened.

"Oh my God, you poor thing," Pamela answered with a sigh.

"How do we even know you are who you say you are?" Rage questioned.

"Well, you don't; you either believe me or you don't. It's all up to you."

"Fair enough, so what song well you be singing for us?"

"'A Moment In Love,' by Kelly Taken." I was just about to open my mouth and start singing when I heard Timmy from outside the room yelling at someone.

"You can't go in there."

"Tara, don't do it; don't sing."

Clay came running in through the doors yelling for me not to sing. He then stood ten feet away from me facing me.

"Oh, hey, it's Clay Edison. Yo dawg, what's up?"

"Clay, would you like to join us?"

"Yeah, come on, Clay," the judges said, greeting him as we stood facing each other.

"Oh my God, Tara, I've been looking everywhere for you."

I stood in front of him silently still shocked to see him standing in front of me. "What are you doing here?"

"What does it look like I'm doing? I'm auditioning to be the next *Soul Seeker*

"Oh, come off it, Tara, you don't want this. You never wanted this sort of thing. Who are you trying to fool coming here?" Clay said as he walked up closer towards me.

"I do want this. I need to become *Soul Seeker*. There's nothing else left for me here." I held back tears so no one would see me cry, especially him.

"Oh come on, Tara, you're doing it to be closer to me. You don't have to hide your feelings from me. I love you."

"Wow, it's like we're in a soap opera."

I turned my head glaring at Rage. "Shut up." I then faced Clay again. "I am not just doing this for you. I want this. I can win. I'll prove it to you. I will make it to the top. You'll see, it's all for me, not for you."

"Tara, I don't want you to prove to me anything. I already know you can sing. I don't want you to do this. You're not being very fair to yourself." Clay walked up closer to me until he was five feet away from me.

"Clay, you make me so, God, just..."

"Tara, I know you never lied about Steven. Piercen told me everything. Why didn't you tell me?"

"Excuse me, I tried to; remember the time on the phone? But then you blew me off. You never even came to see me in the hospital, and now you're trying to say you're sorry?"

"How did you expect me to see you in the hospital? I was on my way to a concert. I can't just not show up."

"Why didn't you just believe me, Clayton? Why didn't you just let me explain myself? You never even gave me the benefit of the doubt."

"The girl's got a point, Clay," Rage said, interrupting our argument.

Clay and I turned, staring at Rage, then shouted, "Shut up Rage!" We faced one another once more as I took a step backwards away from Clay as he stared at me.

"What do you want me to say, Tara?"

"I don't know. Why didn't you believe me? Why didn't you just talk about it with me at the airport?"

"I couldn't talk about that with you at a damn airport, Tara. I thought you cheated on me."

"You should have figured it out that he was lying. In what period of time when I was with you, did I have time to be with Steven?"

"I'm sorry, Tara. I didn't mean to hurt you."

I then burst into tears crying breaking down in front of the judges. I looked at the judges for a second, seeing them starting to cry also. Even Rage was wiping tears from his eyes unless he had an eyelash in his eye.

"Oh, Tara, I love you, and I'm so sorry for all this mess. I want to be with you. I need you. You're my life. I never should have thought you would actually cheat on me. I'm so sorry. Please forgive me, Tara."

"Really? You really mean that, even if it makes you look like a total jerk in front of Rage?" I looked at Rage. "Sorry, Rage." I glanced back at Clay.

"I don't care how I look in front of these guys; you're the only one I don't want thinking that about me." Clay walked up to me, placing his hands on either side of my shoulders staring at me. "I don't know what I would have done if you had auditioned and gone away. I love you so much, and I promise I'll never assume anything else no matter how awful the situation looks."

"Oh, Clay."

"I love you, Tara."

He leaned forward, kissing me while we stood in front of the judges. They probably felt as if they were in a movie at this point, considering all the drama going on in the room. We pulled away from each other and turned our heads staring at the judges. The judges then stood up applauding for us as if we were performing in a play. We watched as they sat back down smirking.

"No, go on," Rage added.

Header

"Oh sorry about all this, you guys," Clay told the judges, who were smiling at us holding on to one another tightly.

"No problem, you've got to do what you've got to do, right?" Rage told Clay smirking.

"Yeah, of course."

The judges rose up from their seats and walked around towards us giving us a hug. "Any friend of Clay's is a friend of ours." They pulled away going back to their seats and sat down staring at us. "So why don't you sing your song anyway? That way, we can see what all the fuss is about."

"Alright, but Clay can sing with me."

The judges sat back down ready to listen to us perform curious as to what I sounded like. "So what will you two be performing for us today?"

"'The Sway,' by Clay Edison."

"Okay, whenever you're ready." Clay began the song as I did my thing, then I joined in a little while after as the judges watched amazed by how good we sounded together. We finished and stared at the judges waiting for their honest opinion of my voice.

"Wow, man, that was hot. You two took that song and made it your own. I'm a yes," Eddy finished. "Pamela?"

"You both are amazing together. I'm a yes, too."

"That was the best we've heard so far. Congratulations, you're going to Hollywood, just joking. Now get out of here, you two, we've got lots more people to hear."

Clay smirked at Rage then at me. "Come on, baby, let's go home."

"Hey, Rage, can I have one of those yellow slips for a souvenir?"

"Of course, you can have one on your way out, just in case you decide to come."

Clay turned to Rage shaking his head no as I stared at him smirking.

We then left the room as I held the yellow paper in my hand going out of the room waving it in the air towards Carrie. "I won! I got Clay Edison."

"Oh, Tara." Clay giggled at me. Clay smiled as he then glanced over at Carrie. "Hey, you're Kevin's girl."

I looked at Carrie wondering what he was talking about. "Kevin who?"

"My bodyguard, Kevin."

"Carrie, is that true?"

"Well, yeah, okay, you caught me. I planned this. I sent you here so Clay could find you, but it was all Kevin's big plan. I just went along with it; after all, how could I not? He is my dad."

Clay and I giggled just glad that we had each other back in our lives. We began to make out in front of everyone while they stared. Timmy Thermal caught up to us giggling as he watched us. We were too caught up in the moment to even notice anything that had been going on around us. Clay pulled away looking at me and whispering, "I want you so bad."

I giggled and pressed up against him. "I know, I can feel you."

"Let's get out of here, but walk in front of me, okay?"

I giggled as I smiled at Clay staring at me as though he wanted me right there, right then. We walked out of the building going outside. When we were outside still holding each other, I looked at the limo parked on the curb. I turned to face Clay smirking at how the limo had been parked. "You were in some hurry to get here, weren't you?"

"Well, I had to get you back. I told you I love you."

"And I love you, too, Clay."

He walked me to the door and opened it, and we entered. I moved over as he got into the limo closing the door after us. We were then driven away. I sat beside him looking at him realizing that he was really right beside me. "Oh, Tara, you're such a hard person to find some times, aren't you? Do you realize what it took just to make it here for you?"

"Well, you know how much I like to play hide and seek."

"No, but now I do. I had to find out the truth from Piercen, and then I took off out of the salon with my hair like this." Clay pointed to his hair then finished, "Then I went to your room, but you had been living in another one, so I went there. Finally, Tracy told me where you went, and I tried to leave, but all these girls in the foster home were surrounding me trying to kiss me and rip my clothes off my body. Now, if that's not love, I don't know what is."

Header

I began to laugh at the expressions Clay had been making while telling me the story of how he got there. I could tell that he was so glad it was all over and we didn't have to argue anymore. "Oh, Clay, you look so sweet when you're all riled up like that."

I pulled Clay by his shirt towards me then pressed my lips upon his, kissing him softly. He placed his hands on my hips gently while we kissed. I ran my fingers through his hair and began kissing and sucking on his neck. He laid me down on the seat of the limo, but he missed and we fell onto the floor of the limo giggling as the limo came to a stop. The limo door opened as Steve saw Clay on top of me and me beginning to wave up at him from underneath Clay.

"I'm so sorry, Mr. Edison. I'll come back later."

"Yeah, sure, why don't you drive us around the block a couple times, then we should be ready to get out."

Steve smiled. "Will do, Mr. Edison." Steve closed the door, got back into the driver's seat, and began to drive away. Clay looked down at me smiling. "Every time I'm with you, I swear, people just start acting weird around us. You even make me do things I know I wouldn't have done with anyone else."

I looked up at Clay as I fluttered my pretty blue eyes and smiled. Clay began kissing me and lifting up my red dress slowly as we made out with one another on the limo floor. It was the most wonderful time I had ever had in my life. It was true love, and I was ready to marry him right then as I spoke.

"Tara?"

"Yes, Clay?" I lay beside Clay on the limo floor below the seats after we had gotten dressed again.

"I want to marry you, right now. I never wanted a big wedding. I always pictured a small one with just our families there."

"Really? You want to marry me still?"

"Of course, I love you, Tara. I want to wake up next to you every morning and come home to you after a long, hard day at the studio."

"Oh, Clay, you want to marry me?"

"So will you be my wife and make my dream come true?"

"Of course."

Clay turned towards me kissing me again after I had answered yes to him marrying me. "Great, I'll set everything up tomorrow. I'll tell my family everything. I can't wait for you to meet my mom. She's going to love you."

"I hope so."

"No, she will. Don't worry."

"What day do you want to get married?"

"How about November 4th?"

"That sounds perfect, and it's even my favorite number."

Clay and I had sex again in the limo after being walked in on by Steve again, but Clay just told him to drive around the block a couple more times. Steve must have thought we were animals.

CHAPTER 13
Comfort

Clay and I had made up completely since the confusion we had in the past little while. We were so happy getting things back to normal, setting plans for our special day coming soon. Our wedding was so close. Our wedding I imagined to be the most memorable day of my lifetime. I would never have pictured my life turning out just the way I wanted it to a year ago. I always dreamed of walking down the aisle to Clay Edison, but never did I imagine it would come true. Only God could have given such a wonderful gift to me for everything that he had taken from me. He had made up for it with the best gift of all: Clay Edison, the man whom I was going to marry and share my life with eternally.

I loved where I was in life, and I was anxious to find out what else God had planned for me, considering all the wonderful gifts he had given to me so far. After all, what more could he give to me that would be greater than what I already had?

I lay next to Clay with my eyes almost closed but still open enough to see the morning sunlight shine through the creases of my eyes. I lay there thinking about everything that had gone on throughout the past year. Clay turned over towards me, and feeling him staring at me, I opened my eyes and stared at him smiling.

"Good morning, beautiful."

"Hey, baby."

"Do you want me to make you some breakfast?"

"That would be wonderful."

Clay rose up from our bed pulling on his basketball shorts that he always liked to wear instead of boxers or briefs. He looked so sexy with his shirt off. I watched him walk away leaving the bedroom as he turned into the kitchen to make us some breakfast. I pushed the bed covers off of me and sat up, getting up slowly. I put on my boxers and my undershirt that had been on the floor nearby from where I had taken them off the night before. After I got dressed, I stood in front of the bed thinking to myself about my love for Clay. It was so unexpected that Clay came back to me so fast. I couldn't believe that my mother had been right. She had told me, "Remember, Tara, when you fall in love and love gets taken from you, if you let love go and it returns to you, your love will last forever." I never really understood what she had meant when she said it, but now that I had experienced it, I completely saw what she had meant by letting love go and it returning again stronger than ever before.

I knew in my heart that Clay and I had been meant for one another from the first time I laid eyes on him. I felt like I was home when I looked into his eyes. When I was growing up, I always felt like there was a part of me that was missing, but as soon as I looked into Clay's eyes, I knew. I felt like the part of me that had felt so sad and empty had been filled with this happiness that sparked my life with fire from the only heat in sight, Clay Edison.

There is a person out there for everyone, and the one that makes your heart melt is the one that holds your fire in their hands, controlling your every devotion to them. They have the one thing you long for: your compassion and honesty that lets you be able to love another soul. They are then your life, your hopes, and your wishes, and they haunt you in the night while you're dreaming. There is no escape but to love them. You're yearning to hold them, touch them, and hear their heart beat within their chest. They are now what keeps you breathing, for they have given to you the one thing no one has ever given to you and that's love.

I then began to prance around the hotel room like I was in heaven. Clay peeked around the kitchen corner with a spatula in his hand staring at me. "What are you doing, Tara?"

"I'm dreaming."

"About what?"

Header

"About how great it will be when I get to be with you every day of the year."

Clay smiled then began to giggle still staring at me.

"What's so funny?"

I stopped prancing around the hotel room and walked up to him in the kitchen where he was. I looked down at the stove where there was a frying pan that Clay had been cooking in.

"Oh my God, I thought you said you were going to cook some breakfast, not torture the eggs until they give up the bacon."

Clay held back from laughing then put on a serious face. "I think they look yummy. Mmm, don't they smell delicious?"

"No, not really, they smell how they look."

"I can't cook, okay?"

"Well, I kind of figured that considering I always eat out with you instead of in."

"I'm sorry about your breakfast. I can always order some from downstairs if you want."

"No, that's alright, I'll still eat them there fine."

I picked up a part of the egg from the frying pan about to place it into my mouth as Clay swatted it out of my hand and it flew across the room. "Hey, what was that for?"

"You were really going to eat my eggs, weren't you?"

"Well, of course."

"That's so sexy."

"Sexy? How is that sexy?"

"Because it's you, everything you do and everything you say is to die for."

I walked up to Clay and stood in front of him as he reached his arms around me pressing me up against him. I listened closely hearing the soothing sound of him smelling my hair as he always did, breathing in every bit of scent that had been left on me from the day before. "Promise me you'll hold me like this forever. Please don't ever let me go again."

"Oh, Tara, I can promise you that I'll never let you slip away from me again. I need you. I love you so much, and without you, I'm nothing. All I know is love because all I see is you."

I tilted my head up pressing my lips gently on his beginning to kiss him as he held me so tightly in his arms. I whispered into his ear softly, "I love you."

Clay lifted me up into his arms carrying me to the bedroom as we made love again for the fourth time since we had gotten back together. It seemed as though all we had done that day was have sex over and over, but it was not like I was complaining or anything. It was so great. I used to be this one girl who was afraid to give her whole self to any man, but with Clay, it had been different, everything had changed. Looking into Clay's eyes staring at me as though I was the only one he could see, he made me feel so special, like I was home when I was with him.

A week had passed by since we had gotten back together, and the news was constantly talking about our lives on TV as if it was their business. Clay and I were sitting in our hotel room on the sofa snuggled up to one another eating popcorn. He kept distracting me by smiling at me and tossing pieces of popcorn at me giggling. I did the same back at him. We got so excited and caught up in the moment we forgot that the bowl of popcorn was on our laps. It went flying through the air spilling everywhere as the bowl came down hitting the floor in front of us. We were laughing so hard and started to pick up all the popcorn pieces that had fallen and place them back into the bowl as we heard our names from the TV. We turned towards it as we listened to what the news was going to say next about us.

"Clay Edison has been shacking up with a younger girl. She had been planning to be with Clay for about a year prier. Everyone is starting to wonder if she has used her parents' death as a way to get Clay's attention."

The TV shut off as I turned, seeing Clay holding the remote in his hand staring at me wondering how I was going to take what they had said about me. Tears began to build up in my eyes as I thought about what people had been thinking about me. I got up, put on my long jacket and my flip flop sandals, and was about to leave holding my hand over my mouth holding back from crying. Clay hurried over to me blocking the door so I couldn't get past him.

"Where are you going?"

I held my mouth struggling to answer him. "I'm going for a walk, that's all."

"I don't believe you, Tara. I think you're scared, and you're leaving like you always do. Don't listen to what they say, their bull-shitting, there isn't a part of you that would even think of doing what they said. Just ignore them, they don't know you like I know you."

"Ignore them? How do you suppose I do that? I can't just act as if I accept everything they're saying about us."

"This isn't about us. It's about you, and you think I'll believe them, don't you?"

I tried to move Clay away from the door, but he held on to me pulling me back. "No, please don't leave me again. I want to work this out, please, Tara."

"I can't, I can't take them always saying things like this about me. It breaks my heart to know there are people out there that think I'm someone who would use death as a reason for you to love me."

"I know it bothers you, Tara, but listen to me. If you leave, you'll be showing them that they were right."

"But I have to. I can't..." I stopped in the middle of my sentence, holding both my hands over my mouth crying, seeing Clay tearing up.

"You can't what, Tara?"

"I can't stay. I have to leave."

"No, Tara, I won't let you go, not this time, not like this, not until you tell me why."

"They're right, that's why. I liked you so much in the beginning. I talked about you constantly saying I wanted to marry you. When I lost everyone in my family, I wanted you even more. I prayed so hard for you to find me. I should have been praying for my family. I should have given them more love and consideration. I just let them die. It's my fault they're dead. If I never made such a fuss about meeting my daddy's girlfriend, they wouldn't have had to meet up with one another to discuss a matter about the way I had been behaving."

"Tara, shh. It's alright."

Clay pulled me close to him comforting me, making sure I felt safe in his arms. I did, and it was the first time I felt as if I could tell him anything and he would be fine with it. I never really knew why I had been crying, but I felt so upset inside. Every time I would hear about my family, I would see the finger being pointed directly at me as if I was to blame for their deaths. "I don't deserve you. You should be with someone that won't get in the way, that they won't judge you to be with."

"No, Tara, I don't ever want to hear you say things like that. I love you. I love you! You hear me? No one is better than you, no one." I stared into his eyes seeing he was really serious about everything he was telling me.

"You really do love me, don't you?"

"Of course I do. Why do you think I want to make you my wife?"

"You don't pity me, do you?"

Clay took a deep breath looking down at me. "I have never once felt sorry for you, ever. I know what it's like to lose someone you love. I've been there."

I looked up at him shocked that he had said that. I never even knew he had experienced such a tragedy. "What are you talking about?"

"I lost someone close to me. Everyone does once in their life."

"Who?"

"My sister."

"How come you never told me before, like in the limo when we first met?"

"Because it's not a subject I would like to discuss, especially in front of a beautiful woman such as yourself."

"But you could have told me. It probably would have made me feel a little bit better knowing someone who was going through what I was at the time."

"Tara, do we really have to bring up all this again? It's always the past with you, isn't it? You dwell in it too much. You hold on too long to the bad stuff without ever seeing the good things that you're left with."

"What do you expect me to do? Close it off like you, never opening up when you need to?"

Clay pulled away from me as his facial expression dropped drastically. He walked towards the sofa then turned around facing me once more. "Well, I didn't expect that from you. You're the last one I need making me feel small."

"I'm so sorry, Clay. I didn't mean it."

Header

I ran up to him wrapping my arms around him. "I swear I didn't mean to say that. I'm so sorry. I'm sorry. Please forgive me, don't leave me."

"What?" Clay pulled me away looking at me. "God, Tara, do you always have to act like I'm going to leave you all the time."

"I'm just…"

"Tara, I know, just…God, jeez." Clay took a deep breath and walked away from me then glanced back at me. "Look, Tara, if we're going to get married, you're going to have to stop thinking that I'm always going to leave you. Is it that you don't think I love you enough?"

I stood in front of him crossing my arms, staring at the floor. "Well?"

"Well, I just don't see how a man such as yourself could love me."

"Tara, do we have to go over this again? I'm really getting tired of this game you're playing."

"Game? What game? Is that what you think I'm doing? I love you, but I just don't know how you could want to love me."

"I don't want to love you, Tara, I just do, even with your attitude towards me sometimes."

"You know what, Clay, if you don't want to love me, then don't. I knew this was too good to be true. How can we get married if we keep arguing?" I walked towards the door unlocking and opening it. I walked out of the hotel room.

"Tara, I didn't mean it like it sounded." Clay followed me into the hallway of the hotel and grabbed my arm turning me towards him facing him. "Tara, just come back inside. I'm sorry. I won't bring this subject up again."

"No, I'm not coming back in. I need to get some air. I'm stressed out, and I'm so damn tired of bickering. I've got enough crap going through my head. I don't need any more."

"What are you saying, Tara?"

"I'm saying I need a break from you."

"Oh, I guess four months wasn't long enough for you, was it?"

"That's not fair, Clay."

"And you think what you're doing is fair?"

"You know what? Two can play this game."

I pulled the engagement ring off my finger and placed it in Clay's hand angry with him. I got inside the elevator going downstairs. I left the building and got into the limo parked outside as I told the limo driver, Steve, to drive me where I had planned to go. Clay never followed me. He just stood in the hallway staring at the engagement ring in his hand thinking it was over between us. He stormed back into his hotel room and yelled, slamming the door behind him.

A couple of hours went by since I had left Clay's hotel. I was on my way back to Clay with some news that I wasn't quite sure how Clay was going to react to. Steve, the limo driver, pulled up to the hotel letting me out and closing the door after I was out of the limo. I stood in front of the hotel staring up at the building beside Steve feeling him staring at me.

"So how do you think he'll take it?" Steve asked me wondering what I had thought.

"I don't know. I hope he won't be upset. After all, I can't help what has already happened, right?"

"Well, if he doesn't take it well, you've got my number."

"Thanks, Steve, for everything. You're such a good man, you know that?"

"No, Tara, it is you that will always make us men real men." Steve stared at me smiling and leaned towards me as we began to hug still standing in front of the hotel beside the limo.

"What the hell is going on, Tara?" I turned, as did Steve. We pulled away from each other. I turned and saw Clay storming towards us as if he had thought something was going on between Steve and me. Clay moved me aside and stood in front of me glaring at Steve angered by the sight of him holding me. "What the hell do you think you're doing holding my fiancé like that? She's with me."

I pulled on Clay's shirt trying to get his attention off of Steve for a minute so I could explain.

"Clay, stop it. Just stop it. He didn't try anything. We were just hugging, that's all."

Clay turned facing me. "You were just hugging? You say that as if it was nothing, Tara. It didn't look like just a hug, it looked intimate."

"I don't think so, Clay. You just made yourself see it that way."

"Oh. Then why were you holding him? Was he hurt in any way?"

"No. Clay, quit being so stubborn and listen to me."

"I'm listening, Tara, go on."

"Well, before you get all jealous again, we were hugging because he felt bad for me because I didn't know how you would take what I have to tell you."

"What haven't you told me, Tara? Are you hiding something from me?"

"No. Clay, you're not listening again."

"Okay, what is it, Tara?"

"It's me. I went to the doctor's today and…"

Clay wrapped his arms around me. I wondered why he did it in a way that was confusing to me. "Please tell me you're not sick. Please, God, oh don't get sick on me. Please, I'm sorry, just don't let God take you right now."

"Clay, it's alright. I'm definitely not sick."

Clay pulled away from me relieved that I hadn't been sick like he had feared the most. "If you're not sick, then what, Tara?"

I looked down at my tummy placing my hands on it then looked back up at Clay as he watched me. "I'm pregnant, Clay." I stood there staring at Clay worrying that he would be upset about it.

"You're having my baby?" I shook my head yes as he fell to his knees kissing my belly. "You're having my baby."

"I was so worried you would be mad at me."

"Is that why you were acting all, well, you know. Uh, it doesn't matter now. I love you so much."

He stood up hugging and kissing me, lifting me in the air excited about me having his baby. "Oh, Tara, now you've really made me the happiest man in the world." Clay then looked back at Steve smirking. "Sorry about that, man."

"Don't worry about it, Mr. Edison. I'll never hug her again, I promise. I think I'll go now."

"I think it would be best if you did. Tara and I have a lot of making up to do."

Clay picked me up into his arms placing me over his shoulders as he then carried me into the hotel building. "Oh, Clay!" Clay carried me as I was held over his shoulders without bending over him like I was supposed to be.

"Tara, relax your body. It feels like I'm carrying a board."

"But I don't bend."

CHAPTER 14

Rebirth

Weeks went by slowly after telling Clay I was having his baby. I was going to be due July 20th. He was so excited to become a father. I thought for sure he would be frightened by our unexpected pregnancy like most men were when it came to having children. I was sure scared to have one. It was a lot of work taking care of a baby. I prayed to God that I would be able to handle it when the time came for the baby to be brought into the world. The last thing I wanted was for a baby to come into the world and me not be able to handle it. I loved children just as much as Clay did. I just hoped that when it was our child that I was able to be a good mother.

Clay set up plans to move to Elko so we could be closer to his mother so she would be able to help me when I needed it when Clay was out. He was very happy that I had agreed to go back to his hometown. He had loved it there, whereas my home was no longer home to me anymore; it had been just a bad nightmare, except for all the wonderful memories that Clay and I had established. Clay and I were in the hotel room sitting on the sofa while I was listening to him talk on the phone with his mother. I noticed he called her "Mama" a lot, which was really sweet to hear. It kind of made me sad, though, considering I had lost mine.

Today was going to be a busy day. We had to cancel the wedding plans, and Clay had to call around about a flight to Elko. I had to go down to the foster home and sign out. I also wanted to stop by at my best friend Carrie's room so I could say goodbye before we left. I didn't want her to think I didn't care. I had to say goodbye. I was going to miss her so much. We spent so much time together after we met. I didn't want her to take me moving the wrong way or anything.

"Clay, I'm going to leave soon so I can do what I have to do before we move anywhere."

Clay held the phone on his shoulder covering it with his hand as he looked at me and whispered, "I know, just don't leave yet; I'll be off in a minute." I watched as he uncovered the phone and said goodbye to his mama on the phone. When he had hung up, he placed the receiver on the end table beside him and looked back at me. "Okay, sweetie, let's go set you free."

"Oh, Clay, you're so silly sometimes, you know that?"

"Of course, I know that, sweetie. Now let's head out, alright?"

I got up off the sofa and walked towards the door kneeling down and picking up my shoes. I sat down on the padded bench nearby to put on my shoes. Clay walked up to me kneeling down. "No, darling, don't do that. Here, I'll do that for you."

I smiled at him as he put on my shoes tying the laces. "Clay, it's alright. I think I can tie my shoes."

"I know that, but let me, I want to. I love taking care of you."

"Okay, baby, if you really want to."

Clay smiled while tying my shoelaces and rose up helping me up as if I couldn't get up by myself. He was acting so sweet since he found out I was pregnant. He always wanted to do things for me, even if he knew I could probably handle it on my own.

I stood by the door as he helped me with my jacket. After I was ready to leave, he got ready, and we left to go downstairs to get into the limo to be driven to the foster home. When we reached the limo, Steve opened the door for us. I got inside, as did Clay sliding in on the seat beside me. Steve closed the door, walked around the limo, and got into the driver's seat, driving towards where my foster home had been.

"Clay, I hope Carrie doesn't get mad at me about leaving her here. We became such close friends since Lindsey."

"Oh, I wouldn't worry about that too much, sweetie. I think she'll take it really well that you're leaving," Clay said smirking at me like he knew something I didn't. I didn't ask why he had been smirking, I wanted to find out for myself. "Tara, while you're saying good bye to Carrie, I'll take care of the paperwork with Tracy, alright?" I looked at Clay feeling like he was the man. It made me feel really good inside, considering the fact that I had always wanted a man with that type of quality.

"Okay."

We reached my house and were let out by Steve. I linked my arm around Clay's as he led me inside the house, glancing at me a couple of times smiling. We entered the house, and Clay kissed me and told me he would come to Carrie's room after he was finished talking to Tracy. I walked down the hallway to Carrie's room as Clay walked the opposite direction towards Tracy's office.

When he reached Tracy's office, the door had been closed, so he began to knock. There was no answer, so he knocked again, but there was still no answer. He turned around ready to leave, frustrated by the fact he had to wait until she was there before he and I could leave. When he turned around, Tracy was standing behind him wondering why he had been at the foster home again.

"Hi there. Clay Edison, isn't it?"

"Yes, it's me."

"So what brings you here again. Are you coming to yell in my hallway at Tara?"

Clay swallowed his frustration then answered, "No, I'm actually here to see you."

"Oh, I see, well, come into my office so we can talk in privacy."

Tracy walked past Clay opening her office door and inviting him in. "Have a seat, make yourself comfortable." Tracy walked around her desk sitting down in her black leather office chair, pointing to a candy dish. "Would you like some?"

"Oh no, that's alright, I'm good, but thanks anyway." Clay took a seat in the chair in front of Tracy's desk waiting patiently for her to say something, preparing to ask her his question.

"So what is it you want, Clay? Me?" Tracy smirked.

Clay giggled as he answered, "No, I'm here to discuss Tara and her living here."

"Oh, I see, you don't think she's in a good home?"

"No, that's not what I meant. I'm saying she's not happy here."

"Hmm, and what would you like me to do about that?"

"Well, I'm not asking you to do anything. I would like to take Tara into my care. After all, we're getting married, and we both feel it is a really good idea that we move back to my hometown in Elko."

Tracy leaned forward in her chair grinning. "Let me get this straight. You want me to hand over consent to you for Tara to live with you and get married. Uh, do you even realize she's just a child?"

"She's no child; she's nineteen years old and is old enough to make her own decisions now."

"No, I'm sorry, I won't allow you to have my permission to have care of her. She's so young. What are you two thinking about? You haven't even played the field, and how do you know this isn't just a crush?"

"I think we would know if it was just a crush."

"No way, there is no way I'm letting you come in here and take this young girl out of here when she has had enough crap happen to her. I don't care who you are. If you loved her, you would leave her be and let her grow up and make her own decisions instead of you telling her what she wants all the time."

Clay stood up from his chair hitting his fist on the desk looking at Tracy. "You can't just sit there and say no. We care about each other, and there is no way I'm just going to stand here and listen to what you think. Tara's coming with me whether you like it or not, and if you have any problems with it, talk to my lawyer." Clay pulled out a business card from the inside pocket of his long black trench coat, tossing it in front of her on the desk.

"If you take Tara out of this house and she's not back by midnight, I can promise you that you will be destroying Tara's life and destroying whatever chance she has for a future."

"Tracy, she's pregnant, and if you do anything to stress my fiancée out and she looses our baby, you'll be seeing me in court. You got that? She's coming with me whether you like the idea or not."

Tracy's facial expression dropped. "Tara's pregnant?"

"Yes."

"You got a nineteen-year-old girl pregnant? What's the matter with you? She's only a child. Now she has no chance for her in the future for sure. What were you thinking?"

Header

"Excuse me, are you lecturing me? I think it would be best if you would kindly keep your opinion to yourself. I did not get a nineteen-year-old girl pregnant. I got my fiancée pregnant, and we love each other, and there is nothing you or anyone can say to change that."

"You love each other? Oh my God, I'm so sorry, Clay. I didn't know it was that serious. Forgive me?"

Clay lowered his head then raised it staring at Tracy once more. "It's alright. I understand, you're just protecting her, but it's my job now to protect her. I'll do everything possible to make her happy. She's worth everything to me."

"It's alright, you don't have to explain. I'm sorry, Clay, and I'll have the papers mailed to your address in about a week."

"Thank you, Tracy, just call my manager, Kevin, and he'll give you the address for where to send them." Clay turned, about to leave.

"Clay, wait." He turned looking back at Tracy. "You take good care of her. She's had a lot happen to her, and if anything else happens, I don't think she could handle it."

"I'll do whatever I can to keep her safe, don't worry."

"I'm sure you will." Clay turned back around and walked out of the office closing the door behind him.

Meanwhile, I had been down the hall about to enter into Carrie's room preparing to tell her about what was going on. When I opened her bedroom door, I saw that she was on the bed placing her things into her suitcase.

"Where are you going, Carrie? You're not running away, are you?"

Carrie looked up at me seeing I had been standing in her doorway. "Oh, sorry, I didn't see you there."

"Carrie, why are you packing? Are you going somewhere?"

Carrie was silent just making eye contact with me. "No, of course not. I would never run away."

"Then why are you packing your things?"

"Oh, I'm moving to Elko with you two."

I began to smile excited, running over to her. "Oh my God, your moving for me? That's so sweet Carrie."

"No, Tara, my dad is your fiancé's bodyguard, so where he goes, I go."

154

"Oh, well, that's great; now you'll be there when I have my baby."

Carrie started to smile at me surprised. "What? Get out. You're pregnant with Clay Edison's baby? No way."

"Yes way, and we're moving and getting married; it's going to be so great."

"Oh my God."

"Yeah, oh my God."

"That's so great, Tara." Carrie was quiet as tears began to fall from her eyes. "I'm so happy for you." She leaned towards me giving me a hug.

"Why are you crying?"

"Oh, I'm just so happy for you two. My best friend's having a baby, not just any baby, Clay's baby. That's so wonderful."

"I know, I'm so excited, but then I'm scared, too."

"Oh, Tara, it's normal to be scared about having babies."

"Really?"

"Of course." Carrie pulled away wiping her eyes as we heard Clay standing in the doorway.

"Oh, it's a girly moment, isn't it? Just wait, let me join." Clay picked up a water glass that had been on the dresser dipping his fingers in it and wiping his hands on his eyes making it appear as though he had been crying. He ran to us kneeling down. "Oh, I'm just so happy. I love you all so much."

"Clay." I nudged him in the arm smirking at him being silly.

"I'm just kidding around. Come on, Tara, we have to get going."

"But what about Carrie?"

"Oh, don't worry, she'll meet us on the plane at the end of the week. Now which bags are yours." I pointed to the bags already packed beside my bed on the floor, nearest to the bathroom. "I'll get them for you. You just hug your girl, then we'll be on our way, alright, sweetie?"

I leaned forward hugging Carrie as Clay just watched smiling at us. "Oh watch out, don't squeeze her too hard; she's pregnant."

"I know that, you goober," Carrie added picking up a throw pillow nearby and tossing it at Clay as we all began to laugh. I stood up looking at Clay picking up my suitcases and walking towards me. He walked out of the room calling for me, "Come on, Tara, let's go. I have a lot more business to attend to"

"I'm coming, baby." I hugged Carrie and caught up to Clay so we could get back to the hotel so he could finish making the plans for everything before we had to leave. "Clay?"

"Yes, sweetheart?"

I giggled at the sound of him calling me sweet little nicknames as I asked, "Where will we live in Raleigh, Clay?"

"Oh don't you worry about that. I'll take care of all that before we leave."

We then reached the limo where Steve let me in the back while Clay placed the suitcases into the trunk. He got into the limo beside me. Steve closed the door and walked around the limo getting in, and he then drove away from my old home.

"Oh, Tara, you're going to love it in Raleigh. The people there are so nice."

"I hope so. I wouldn't want to live in a place where I didn't even feel comfortable going outside."

Clay placed his hand upon my thigh staring at me smiling. "You'll be fine. Don't worry about it. I'll make sure everyone treats you nice."

"Will you be working in Elko when we live there?"

"Uh, I was kind of going to talk to you about that when we got settled in Raleigh."

I looked down at my feet then back up at him curious as to what the answer to my question was. "Why wait? I want to find out now so I can prepare for whatever you decide."

"Uh, Tara, I was going to get you settled first and then, uh…"

"Clay, don't, just tell me what you have to. Let's not beat around the bush."

"Well, I have to go away for about three months to Toronto, but don't worry, I was going to tell my mama to check in on you every once in a while until I come home to you." I was speechless and was beginning to feel very nauseous at that moment.

"What's the matter, Tara? You look flushed."

"I feel sick. I need to get out of this vehicle."

"Okay, hold on." Clay pressed a button nearby and told Steve to pull over at a rest stop somewhere. When the vehicle came to a stop, Clay let me out walking me into a restaurant nearby and taking me inside to the bathrooms. I rushed into the bathroom hurrying into one of the stalls.

After I finished getting sick, I washed my face and hands and got out of the bathroom seeing Clay sitting at one of the tables signing autographs for a crowd that had formed. He saw me and hurried over to me concerned with how I was feeling. "Are you alright? Do you need anything? Do you want me to take you to a doctor?"

"No, I'm fine. It's just a little morning sickness; that's all."

"Oh, okay, well, let's get back into the limo so I can get you back to the hotel so you can rest before we have to leave."

"I don't need to rest, I'm fine."

"Tara, let me take care of you please. I just want to help."

"I know, but I don't need any right at this moment, so let's just leave."

I walked past him and went outside getting back into the limo, as did Clay shortly after. He seemed kind of bothered by something on the rest of the way home. I just couldn't figure out what was troubling him. I just hoped he wasn't upset with me that I didn't want to rest like he had asked me to do. After all, if anyone would know if I needed rest, it would be me, right? I was irritated for some reason. I felt like my emotions were a switchboard and people kept turning it up and down making me feel differently in a matter of minutes. The cause had most defiantly been pregnancy.

When we had arrived back at our hotel room, Clay placed my suitcases down beside the wall in the entrance. He watched me as I took off my jacket and hung it up. When I reached down about to untie my shoelaces, Clay ran over to me beginning to take off my shoes. "Here, I'll help you. You shouldn't be bending over too much."

"Clay, I'm pregnant. I'm not ill. I think I can handle taking off my own shoes."

Header

Clay took them off, placing them on the shoe rack nearby where we had been standing in the entrance. I stood in front of him with my arms crossed watching as he took off his jacket and shoes putting them away. "Clay, why don't you just cancel your plans in Toronto. I really don't feel comfortable with a stranger checking up on me while you're gone."

"Are you serious? You're asking me to cancel something that happens to be a part of the contract that I still have? The answer is no. I can't do it. I'm sorry, I wish I could stay, but I have to go. Plus, it's my mama, not a stranger, Tara."

"But I need you. Why can't I come with you?"

"You can't come on the road with me. You're in no shape to be going anywhere, and you might get hurt or something."

"But, Clay…"

"No, Tara, I'm going, and you'll be staying in our new place with my mother checking up on you for me."

"No, I'm not. I won't go then. I'm staying right where I am."

"Tara, don't be so stubborn."

"I'm stubborn? You're the one that's stubborn."

"I thought you would be happy about meeting the people I knew throughout my childhood, especially my mama."

"I am, but I want to be where you are. I don't know them. I want to go with you."

Clay walked up to me placing his hands on my sides looking down at me. "I know you want to come with me, darling, but you can't come, plus you'll have Carrie there to help you out, also."

I thought about it for awhile wondering if I should go, then my heart decided my answer. "Alright, I'll go, but I'm only doing it because I love you so much."

"Oh, Tara, you're so cute sometimes, you know that?"

"I am?"

"Yes." Clay lifted me up as I wrapped my legs around him. He carried me into the kitchen placing me on the counter. I sat on the counter with him standing in between my legs kissing me. "Mmm, you're such a great kisser."

"That's because it's you I'm kissing."

"Oh, Clay?"

"Yes, Tara?" Clay began kissing my neck as I tilted my head back.

I lowered my head back down as I whispered into his ear softly. "Make love to me." Clay then lifted me off of the counter carrying me into the hallway towards the bedroom. We were kissing as he carried me. He lowered me down in the hallway laying me down on the floor as the heat of our temperatures rising in excitement gave me chills. He made love to me right there on the cold hardwood floor beneath our bodies.

After we had sex, we lay on the hallway floor snuggled up towards one another as we began a conversation. "So what if the baby is a boy? What are we naming him?"

I lay beside him thinking of a boy's name that I had liked. "Uh, how about Clayton, like you?"

"No, I don't think he'll like it being named after his father."

"Why wouldn't he? Your name is so sweet."

Clay giggled and asked another question, "So what if it's a girl? What will we call her?"

I had a name picked out from when I had been younger. The name was special to me, so I shared it with Clay. "Well, I always dreamed of naming my first daughter after my mother; that way, I'll always have a part of her with me."

"What was her name?"

I looked at Clay wondering if he would laugh at the name I had liked. "Why are you laughing? Is it a bad name?"

"No, it's just unique; that's all. I just don't want you to laugh at it."

"I would never laugh at it unless, of course, it was Clay. I'm just kidding, I won't laugh. Now, what is this special name you like?"

"Adia."

"Adia?"

"Yes, Adia, it means 'gift from God.'"

"Really?"

"Yes, that's another reason why I like it, also."

"Well, I think the name Adia is a perfect name for our daughter if that's what God gives to us."

Header

I couldn't believe we were having a baby. It happened so fast. A year ago, I remember I had just lost everything, then we met, and now we were having a baby and later getting married. I was frightened of having a baby. You hear stories about labor and how painful it is. I felt in my heart everything would go fine at the delivery, but every mother-to-be always gets nervous about how it will all happen and if they will be able to handle the pain. All I could think about each day was if the baby would be healthy. I was so thrilled even though I was scared because I was the one that was going to be giving the greatest gift of all to a man that had so much already. I was worried about living in Clay's hometown alone without him there, but I knew I had to do this for him. There was only a week until we left, and it was going by so quickly. Clay still had to make more arrangements with his short tour to Toronto and a couple of other places in Canada, plus bring me to Elko before he left for Canada.

It was going to be a busy week for us, especially for him. He always wanted to be the one taking care of all the plans and details that needed to be done. He never once brought that kind of stress upon me. It felt good to be not only with a man that loved me the same as I loved him, but to be with a man that made me feel like I was so special to him that he would do anything and everything to keep me happy. What a strong man, always putting his woman first in everything. This was the most wonderful time of my life right about then. I'd never felt so alive in my life. I just prayed when we left, I would be okay when Clay was away for three months and I was stuck in a new place with his mama whom I'd never met in my life. I was scared. What if she didn't like me? Well, I guess I'd have to suck it up and prepare for the worst. Who knew? She could be everything Clay told me she was. Whatever she was like, I'd be finding out real soon. I just hoped I'd be able to handle it.

CHAPTER 15
Recalcitrant

We arrived in Elko about 4:00 p.m. on a Wednesday. It was sunny and warm there. I was feeling very nervous to be there, considering I had never lived anywhere but where I had grown up. Clay was in the happiest mood that day, excited about showing me off to everyone he knew there. When we reached a house that was a certain distance away from everything, Clay pointed to a blue house in the distance smiling.

"See that house right there, Tara?"

"Yeah, what about it?"

"That's our house. We live there."

"What? Are you kidding me? You're telling me that house over there is ours?"

"That's what I'm saying."

"Oh my God." I turned towards him hugging him and kissing his face everywhere. I looked out into the distance at the house. "It's so beautiful. I always wanted a blue house." I began to weep.

"Oh, Tara, don't cry. You're going to love it here."

"I'm not crying because I don't like it, I'm crying because it's just so beautiful."

"Oh, Tara, you're so cute sometimes. I'm glad you like it. I was hoping you would."

"Well, how could I not, Clay? It's, as some people would put it, simply smashing."

Header

Clay giggled laughing at what I had said. He was amused by how the tiniest things made me happy, whereas to others, they would take for granted those sorts of things. Plus, I was pregnant so I was a little emotional about everything that was happening around me.

When Clay got me all settled in our new home, he only had a couple more days until he would have to leave and fly to Canada where he would be living for three months. I wasn't at all thrilled about the whole idea, but I accepted the fact that he had to go. It was the job he chose for himself. I was prepared although I didn't really want to be. I needed him here with me. I just got him back into my life after four months when we had been fighting. I knew I was going to miss him, but I had to find away to look on the brighter side of the fence instead of always hiding in the shadow, waiting for the sun to shine over on my side of the fence.

When we first entered the house, I saw that it was fully decorated. Clay had set everything up before we arrived. It surprised me sometimes how fast he could get things done in life. He was such a hard worker. He made the house just as I had described to him in the past; I wanted a baby pink and baby blue theme throughout the house. I was so surprised that he would be able to feel comfortable about living in a world that was filled with so many feminine features. We spent the first night getting my suitcases unpacked and being alone celebrating in the best way we knew how: sex.

When morning came, we woke up feeling happy being in our first home together. Clay was planning on inviting some of his family and friends over to meet me later in the afternoon. Clay was going to leave later in the day tomorrow. He wanted to make sure I knew who everyone he knew was so I would feel more comfortable around them when he was gone. We had a shower, and I made Clay and me some breakfast since he never knew how to cook, or maybe he did, but he just made it seem that way so he didn't have to, I'm not to sure, but either way, I didn't care. I served the breakfast I had made placing the plates on the table as I took my seat beside Clay.

"You're a good cook. This looks delicious."

"Thank you, but I wouldn't say I'm much of a cook, because I'm not. I just know how to make basic meals, but I'll learn. That way, I can make you your favorite meal you love so much."

"Oh yeah, and what's that, Tara?"

"Steak, of course, with peach ice cream for dessert."

"You know me pretty well, don't you, Tara? I must say, it's so nice to have a woman to come home to who even wants to cook for me."

"I love taking care of you, Clay. You're so amazing, and I love you so much."

"And I love you, Tara." Clay leaned over his breakfast plate and kissed me while placing his hand upon the side of my face gently.

I loved him with all my heart and was looking forward to having his child and marrying him after the child was born. I couldn't wait to look that little angel baby in the eyes and see our love within the soul of our creation. I couldn't believe everything that had happened. It had come so fast, and I didn't know whether to celebrate it before it vanished or get comfortable because it was forever. I couldn't be sure about everything. It felt like I was dreaming, and I was about to wake up at any moment, but if this was a dream, I didn't want to wake up. I loved being with Clay. It was the most amazing thing that had ever happened to me, well, besides being born into a family that I would forever be proud of even though they were not where I could see them.

Clay and I finished our breakfast, then I got up from the table with him walking over to the sink, and we then placed our plates into the sink gently. "Baby, are you calling your mama soon?"

"Yeah, in a bit. Why?"

"Oh, no reason."

Clay walked up to me knowing I had been thinking about something. "What is it, Tara? I know something's bothering you, so what is it?"

"Well, it's just that she might not like me, and well, you know. I don't want to stay here if you're not here with me."

"But you agreed you would do this for me."

"I know, but I'm having second thoughts. I don't want to stay here without you. I'll miss you too much."

Clay took a deep breath of frustration as he looked away then back at me. "I don't want to upset you or anything, but, Tara, aren't you being a little unreasonable about this? I need to go on this tour. I have to; it's part of my contract."

"I understand that, Clay, but what I don't understand is why I can't come with you?"

"Tara, I'm not arguing about this. You already told me you would stay here and wait for me until I came back."

"But, Clay, we just got back together after four months of being apart. I don't want to wait another three months. One day seems like too long, so how do you suppose I take on three months? I want to go, Clay."

"No, you're staying here. I can't take you, I told you."

"Clay, listen to me for a second. I'm not staying here. I'm not asking to come, I'm telling you I'm coming."

"Not with me, you're not."

"Oh, it's like that, is it? You think you can tell me where I can go and when I'm allowed to and I have no say in anything. Clay, for once, just put yourself in my shoes. I need to be with you, and I'll miss you too much. Don't you understand what I'm feeling right now? Don't you even care?"

Clay walked away from me then walked back frustrated with me. "I bought this house for us. I got it decorated just how you wanted it to look, and I asked you to stay here with my mama because you are pregnant. You can't just stand there, Tara, and tell me that I don't understand you because I do. You're so stubborn, you know, that you don't listen when others are talking to you. You're not coming with me. You got that? There are so many reporters and so many cameras. They're going to be asking so many questions, and I don't want them upsetting you in any way. You're staying, and that's the end of it. You got that, Tara?"

"I'm nineteen years old, and I'll be the judge of whether or not I can handle it. I think I can, so I'm going to go even if I have to hitchhike there. You got that, Clay?"

"Tara." Clay's facial expression turned into anger, as he stormed out of the room away from me pissed off at how I had been acting towards him. I really wanted to be with him. I didn't understand why he wouldn't want me there with him instead of having to be around strangers I'd never even met before. I stood beside the dining room table wondering where Clay had stormed off to angry with me. I walked around the house searching for him. I checked every room in the house, but I couldn't find him. I got worried that he had left early so I couldn't leave with him. I turned around and saw a door that I hadn't checked yet, so I walked over towards it opening it slowly. There were stairs so I began to walk down them being careful not to fall. When I reached the bottom, I saw Clay sitting at an empty desk that had been downstairs. He was tapping a pencil on the desk thinking about whatever he had been mad about exactly.

"Clay, are you alright?"

He turned around staring at me with an upset look upon his face. "Tara, I want you to stay, but if you really want to come with me, I guess there is no way of stopping you."

"Oh, Clay, I really didn't mean to upset you or anything, it's just that, God, you are so stubborn."

He looked up at me with his eyebrow raised. "I'm stubborn, huh? If anyone is stubborn, it's you, Tara."

"Fine, then, we're both stubborn." I was silent for a minute, and then I continued, "But you're more stubborn."

Clay jumped off his chair and ran up to me pulling me down onto the floor playfully laughing. "Oh, Tara, do you have to be so..." Clay looked into my deep blue eyes silently as I lay beneath him on the floor. "...so beautiful?"

He pressed his soft lips upon mine kissing me as I lay on the floor beneath him feeling as his hands began lifting up my shirt. He always knew how to make an argument into a romantic evening within a matter of minutes. We never really had fights; they were more like little spats about silly things that could have been settled in a different manner, but this was the way we had chosen to settle our arguments. He was such a man, well, to me he was, but to others that had been blinded by his light within his soul, they begged to differ. I loved him so much. He was so full of life and always knew how to crack a joke at the right moment just as I had. We were very alike in many ways, and I believe that was the reason we had fallen in love so easily. Everyone usually searches for a soul who carries a little bit of him or herself within them. It's very understandable because how could you not love a person who reminds you of yourself, unless by chance, you don't love yourself? If I were going to be with anyone in the world it would be Clay. I was so excited now that I was going to be able to come with him to Canada. I had never been there, but I heard it was really beautiful there.

Header

"Tara, we have to hurry up and get dressed. My mama's going to be here soon, oh yeah, and also some of my friends." Clay rose up to his feet, helped me up, and walked with me upstairs making sure I didn't slip and fall while going up them. He was so loving to me, always making sure I was feeling well, except of course, when I irritated him and we called one another stubborn a million times.

When we got upstairs, we went into the kitchen, and he helped me prepare some snacks for our company that was coming any minute now. After we had finished preparing the snacks, we placed them on the table and heard a knock at the door. I jumped to the sound of the knock at the door, startled. I began to feel butterflies fluttering around in my tummy. I was so frightened of what his family might think of me. I ran past Clay into the bathroom trying to hide somewhere so no one could find me. Clay answered the door letting everyone in then returned to me, knocking on the bathroom door.

"Tara, let me in, sweetie; everyone's here."

"I don't want to come out; they won't like me."

"Tara, open the door." I cracked it open a little seeing Clay looking through the crack of the door at me. "Oh, baby, it's alright. It will be fine. I'm here. They're really nice people. Come out and meet them."

I opened the door and wrapped my arms around Clay hugging him scared of who was in the living room waiting to meet me. Clay pulled me away gently and walked me into the living room where everyone had been standing talking to one another. Clay pointed to everyone introducing him or her to me one at a time as they each shook my hand accepting me as his fiancée. "And this is my beautiful mama. Mama, this is my wonderful fiancée, Tara."

"It's nice to meet you, Tara."

I held out my hand to greet her with a handshake, but she moved my hand. "No, here, give me a hug; we're family now." She threw her arms around me giving me the biggest hug I had ever received from anyone. She pulled away right after and stood staring at me as if about to cry. Clay placed his hand on his mama's shoulder for comfort.

"It's okay, Mama, you don't have to cry."

"Oh, Clayton, you're so grown up now. My little boy has turned into a man, and just look at what happened when he did, he found a wife."

"Yes, Mama, I'm a man now. Don't you remember I've been a man for a while now? This isn't a new thing."

"Oh, Clay, your mother's just telling you she likes the kind of man you grew up to be." Clay smiled at me placing his arm around my waist as we all took our seats on the sofas near by. We sat there for hours just talking about how we had met and what we were planning next. Then the time came for Clay to tell his mother I was pregnant.

"Mama, I've been excited to tell you some wonderful news. Tara's going to be having my baby. Isn't that great?"

His mother sat back in her chair speechless not making any movement or sound for what felt like an hour to us. The tension was rising as everyone who had been in the room talking was now staring at Clay and me as if they had seen a ghost, but really it had only been their imaginations running wild.

"What? You're pregnant? But how?" She looked at Clay with a serious facial expression, as she demanded an answer. "I thought I brought you up better than to have unprotected sex. What were you thinking? How are you going to handle a baby with your careers just starting out?"

"Mama, stop it. Just stop it. I'm not a child so don't speak to me like I am."

"Is that why you're marrying this girl? Is it because you got her pregnant?"

"Of course not, you know it's not like that. I'm marrying her because I love her, not because she's pregnant. Hell, I just found out not too long ago, and we've been engaged for half a year now."

"Hmm, I see. Well, Clayton, I hope you know exactly what you're getting into here. Well, if you do marry this girl, you better get one of those prenuptial agreements before you do."

I looked at Clay feeling very uncomfortable. His face was really red from built-up anger at what his mother had said. "Mama, can't you just be considerate of people's feelings? I don't need any agreement. I trust her, and I love her, and neither you nor anyone else can change that. I can't believe you would even mention a horrible thing like that especially in front of Tara. Can't you see her sitting right here in front of you? I love this girl. You got that, Mama?"

"You don't know anything about this girl. Clayton, she could be just after your money. How do you know?"

"Again, Mama, she's right here. You know what? Why don't you just leave? I don't need you saying all these horrible things about my fiancée. Now, just leave."

"But I am your mama, Clayton."

"Not the way you're acting, you're not. Now leave us be, we need to get some sleep anyway."

"Fine, we'll leave, but just remember who raised you. Remember who kept you safe from all the people that have tried to take you away, remember that."

"Get out, and don't even try and make me feel bad about being with the woman I love."

After his family had finally left, Clay came up to me with tears built up in his eyes. I held him as he laid his head on my knees. He was sitting on his knees as I comforted him. I ran my fingers through his hair telling him it was alright, and I didn't take anything his mother said to heart. After all, she had just been worried about her son and wanted to make sure he was doing everything he wanted without just doing it because he felt obligated to. When it was time for Clay to leave the next day, I had decided to go with him. Actually, if I'm going to be completely honest with you, he told me he was not leaving me here alone with his mama. He was afraid she would hurt my feelings while he was away, and he didn't want anything or anyone to upset me while I was pregnant. He was such a sweetheart. I found the most incredible man in the world. Well, actually, if I do remember clearly, it was he who had found me. I was so excited to find out I was going with him, but when he told me, I played with him a little bit telling him I didn't want to leave. The conversation kind of went like this.

"Are you going to be leaving soon, Clay?"

"Yes, in a while. Why?"

"Oh, just so I can help you pack your things before you leave me for three months. I'm really going to miss you."

"What? Are you kidding me? You're not staying here now."

"But I thought you wanted me to stay here?"

"I did until I heard my mama spit out her words of judgment at us."

"But I want to stay now. I'm okay with it. I'll be fine."

"No, forget it. I'm not leaving you here. You're coming and that's the end of it, alright?"

"I'm not going."

"Yes, you are. I'm not asking you to come. I'm telling you. Now pack your things before I pack them for you."

"Clay."

"Tara."

"Oh my God."

"Oh my God."

"Alright, I'll come, but only because I love you."

"Thank you, now go pack before I pack for you." I giggled and packed my suitcases, as did he while we giggled still amused with our little argument that hadn't even reached boiling point. Luckily for us, we always stayed on simmer rather than boiling over. Who could blame us? We were the cutest couple when it came to arguments. Hell, we were the cutest couple no matter what we did.

We left the house that day, leaving in a limo that took us to the airport once again to be flown all the way to Canada. Before we entered the plane, I had whispered to Clay quietly, "Man, I feel like we went to your hometown for a night's stay in a hotel, and now we're leaving again."

"Yeah, it's kind of like what Rage said to us at the audition together when we were arguing. 'I feel like I'm on a soap opera.'" We giggled taking our seats beside one another on the plane getting prepared to take off and be flown to Canada for the last tour until after we had our baby and got married. We held one another's hand as the plane began to take off, as we left our troubles behind and flew towards our future that was not too far from where we were headed next. It was a world of many wonders in a place of many miracles that always seemed to happen to everyone who had lived in Canada, including us for the time being. It was wonderful, because I had the man of my dreams alongside of me.

CHAPTER 16
Reality Check

The months had gone by extremely quickly. We had so much fun together in Canada on his tour. I couldn't really go to his concert because we believed it wouldn't be good for the unborn child growing inside of me. I was four months pregnant, and if you would place your hand on my tummy, you could feel the baby moving around inside me. I wasn't showing too much, but my belly was starting to form slowly. Clay was getting so excited. I even remember waking up in the mornings sometimes seeing Clay talking to my belly. He was so excited to experience having a baby and seeing as it grew inside the woman that he was in love with.

After his tour, we went back to New York until we figured out what we were going to do because Clay wasn't ready to go back to Elko quite yet after remembering what his mama had said. He was a man of strong will and always stood up for what he believed in, especially when it came to the woman with whom he was in love.

A few weeks after we had arrived and settled into our hotel room in New York, Clay was taking me to the salon to get our hair done by Piercen for our dinner plans later on that evening. I was so excited to celebrate the wonderful success of his concerts that he had performed in Canada. We were in our hotel room getting ready to leave to head off to the salon. I reached for my jacket, but Clay, of course, like he always did, took it off the coat rack and held it out for me, and I slipped my arms into the sleeves putting it on. He then sat me down on the padded bench nearby as he lifted my foot, placing my shoes on gently smiling up at me. "You're so cute. You're always tying my shoes and making sure I don't do anything too over-exerting."

"Of course I am. I wouldn't want anything to happen to my beautiful wife and unborn child."

"But, Clay, we're not married yet."

"In my eyes, we are, and I believe in God's eyes, we are also."

I sat on the bench watching him staring up at me with the most love inside I have ever felt before. He carried so much love for me inside his soul, it made me lightheaded just staring into his soul. I almost felt as though I was about to float away, but then I came back to reality and began with whatever I had been doing. I stood up after he had finished putting on my shoes and getting himself ready to leave. We left the hotel room locking the door behind us. We went downstairs to get into the limo to be driven to the salon.

When we arrived downstairs, we walked out of the building as I walked alongside of Clay linking his arm as he led me towards the limo. We got inside after Steve had opened the door for us. He closed it and walked around to the driver's side where he got in. He drove us away towards the salon as we sat in the back of the limo staring at one another and talking.

"I can't wait to take you out for dinner. It's going to be so great to sit down with you and look into your eyes."

"I can't wait either. We haven't even been able to go out anywhere together too much since I had so much morning sickness and you were so busy with your concerts in Canada."

"I know. I'm sorry about that, sweetheart, but don't worry, it's not going to be like that anymore. We'll be able to be together all the time now."

"I know. Plus, it wasn't your fault that you had to work so much."

"God, you're so understanding, you know that?"

"Thank you, but it wasn't until you came into my life that I became everything I am right now."

"Oh, Tara, come here." Clay moved closer to me kissing me as we felt the limo come to a stop. Steve came around and opened the door for us, and we got out slowly, closing the door behind us. I looked up at the salon sign remembering back to all the fun we had in the salon with Piercen. "Come on, Tara."

I looked at Clay holding the salon door open for me. "Coming, Clay." I ran to him and went inside.

"Tara, you shouldn't run; you might fall. It makes me very nervous."

I placed my hand on the side of Clay's face looking at him smiling. "If it bothers you, then I'll try not to run."

"Thank you, Tara."

He closed the door and walked alongside of me to the counter where the register was. Piercen saw us and waved his hand in the air rushing over to us. "Oh hi, you come for hairdo? Good, I make you spikes, and you beautiful so Clay says 'Wow.'"

"That would be perfect, Piercen," Clay told him as Piercen stared at us with dreamy eyes.

"Come, I make your hair big and fluffy and yours stand up like peacock."

I giggled looking at Clay, but he was still staring at Piercen with a straight face. I don't think Clay really knew what to think of him and all the strange things he seemed to say. I believe Clay wanted to laugh deep down inside but thought laughing would offend Piercen. We followed Piercen as he led us to the two chairs waiting for us in front of the mirrors. We sat in the chairs beside one another ready to get our hair done by Piercen. Piercen worked on Clay's hair first because he said he wanted to spend more time on mine. He put some gel into his hands and ran his fingers through Clay's hair beginning to style it exactly how Clay liked to wear it.

"Your hair very soft, almost like baby's bottom, no?"

"I wouldn't know. Maybe Tara would know."

They both stared at me as I laughed my head off at Clay and how he was finally starting to warm up. Piercen carried on with styling Clay's hair as I stopped laughing, covering my mouth with my hands. Piercen finished up with Clay's hair, spiking his hair as Clay liked it. "There, just as you like it, tall and pointy like a peacock."

"Thank you, Piercen, it turned out great."

"Good, I'm glad you like it. I think you look very smooth as Tara always tells me."

"Piercen, you're not supposed to tell him that."

Clay smirked at me as I blushed about him knowing something that I had said about him when he wasn't around. "What else does she say?"

"Oh, she say lots, but you don't need to hear all the gushy stuff. Look, her face is turning red like a strawberry on a hot summer day, mmm. Oh no, now I'm making myself hungry."

Piercen then walked over to me standing behind me and started styling my hair as Clay watched still asking Piercen what else I said when I was alone. Piercen, thank God, never told him anything else respecting that I didn't want him to because I knew I would start blushing and would never be able to stop. "So what's new with you two love birds, you married yet?"

"No, not yet, we're getting married after our baby is born in July."

"Oh no." Piercen pointed at Clay. "I gave you present. Why didn't you use them? They were brand-new, no?"

"No, we did. It just happened, I guess."

Piercen smirked then looked at Clay seriously. "Nothing just happens." There was a sudden silence as he finished. "Oh, but that's okay. I give you more, for after baby, no?"

"No, you don't have to do that."

"Don't worry about it. It's no problem. I give you lots, then you can do bang bang all day long. I don't care."

"Piercen."

"Right, sorry, Mr. Edison, you the serious one, but that's okay, I make you smile again." He was silent thinking, then he looked at Clay smiling. "Tara said before that your butt is so nice and tight she always wants to reach out and touch it, and then she does. That girl is so funny, you good man." Piercen looked down at me smiling. "He good man, you know? He Clay Edison, no?"

Header

Clay and I started laughing at what Piercen was saying to us. He was so hilarious sometimes. Oh hell, what am I saying? He was always hilarious; that's what kept us coming back to get our hair styled. Piercen finished my hair looking at me in the mirror in front of us.

"There, now you look smashing, doll."

"Thank you, Piercen, my hair looks great."

I turned towards Clay as he was staring at me with an open-mouthed expression, his face was glowing. "Wow, you're…"

"Beautiful."

"No, the most wonderful, attractive woman I have ever seen in my life, wow."

"Oh, Clay, you get so silly when Piercen makes me beautiful."

"Oh no, it is all you. All I do is bring out your face. No one can make you beautiful. Beauty is something you just have."

"That's really sweet. Thank you, Piercen."

"Wow, wow."

"Clay, come on, we should get going now."

Clay shook his head trying to get back to reality again. "Wow."

"Clay, you're in the state of wow again; let's go."

"Oh, oh yeah, dinner."

"Yes, dinner. Mmm, I'm so hungry." Clay got off his chair, as did I. We then walked towards the door, saying goodbye to Piercen. Before we left, Piercen told us to wait by the door while he went into the back and came out with some more condom packages for us. He placed them into Clay's hands. "Here, these should do. Remember use them only once, or else they no work, okay?"

Clay's expression showed shock about what Piercen had given him. "Piercen, we don't need these, unless there's a way she can get pregnant while she's pregnant."

Piercen laughed. "Oh you silly man." He slapped him on the back lightly. "They're for you to use after baby pop out like popcorn."

"Oh, I see, well thanks, I guess."

Clay opened the door, letting me out then caught up to me on my way to the limo. We got in, and we were then driven to the restaurant we had reservations at. On the way, we stopped at our hotel room to get changed into our evening clothes for dinner. I wore a short black dress that came to my knees. You could notice the shape of my belly in the dress. Clay wore a suit. He looked really good in his suit with a baby-blue tie. I liked him in ordinary clothes. It made him look more real, rather than too, well, you know, dressed up. I'd love him to wear all blue jeans all the time. That man made blue jeans look royal. We got to the restaurant not too long after our reservations and were seated down in the back beside a piano that someone had been playing. The music was beautiful, but not as wonderful as Clay's was. But music can't always be all Clay all the time. I had to keep reminding myself that. Just because I was in love with Clay did not mean that everyone else was, too. Sometimes, I just couldn't help myself. He was just so sexy it made me believe that everyone must feel the same as I did. We had the most romantic time eating dinner together. I have to admit, it was the only time I had remembered ever eating so much food considering I was now eating for two. We went back to the hotel feeling refreshed and feeling as though our lives were flowing so perfectly, or so I thought.

There was a certain phone call that completely destroyed our excitement. Clay answered the phone still laughing from the joke I had told earlier before the phone rang. "Hello?"

"Yeah, it's me."

There was a sudden silence as I watched Clay listening to the person talk on the other line. "Are you sure? No. No, I can. Don't worry about it. Well, if I need to. I'll do it. I'll see you Saturday." Clay got off the phone placing it on the table nearby staring at the ground in thought.

"What's wrong, Clay? Who was that?"

Clay looked up at me with a frown upon his face. "I'm sorry, sweetie. I'm going to have to leave again."

"Why? Why would you have to leave? Your concerts are finished for a while, remember?"

"I know that, Tara, but…"

Clay was silent not finishing his sentence trying to figure out how to tell me what the person on the phone said. "But what, Clay?"

"That was Kevin, my manager. He said everyone is freaking out about us, and they want me to fix it. The fans are demanding explanations about us and why we're together. Apparently, Lindsey has been telling reporters that you are a girl who goes from star to star making her way around to get to the top. They want me to fly to Los Angeles and go on air and set everything straight or else it could affect my career."

"But, Clay, you said you would stay with me until after the baby was born. You promised."

"I didn't promise anything. I have to go. I'm sorry. I'm upset about this, too, you know."

"I know that, but what's more important?"

"Are you telling me to choose between you and my career I struggled so hard to earn?"

"I'm just saying you need to get your priorities straight, that's all."

"Excuse me, you did not just go there. I'm not going to stay here and risk my career for you. I can't. There's no way, Tara. I'll see the baby when it's born, I promise you that. Don't worry. I'll send you checks."

I was silent, beginning to cry. "I don't want your money. I don't need you. If you can't even figure out what's more important, I guess you weren't the man that I thought you were."

"Don't say that, Tara. It's only until the fans are happy again."

"Yeah, that could be awhile. You know how long it takes for people to get used to an ordinary girl engaged to a star? A long time. If you leave, don't expect me to be here waiting for you when you return."

"Tara, I'll find you a nice place to live before I leave. It will just take a phone call. Whatever you need, don't worry, it well be taken care of, alright? Trust me."

"Clay, God, don't you understand?"

"Understand what, Tara? That you won't stand beside me through thick and thin?"

"No, that I care more about us just being together even if we're living in a shack. I love you. Can't you see that? I thought you loved me, too."

"I do, Tara, but I have to make a living for my family."

I took a deep breath as I finished. "What's a family when you're not around?"

"Tara, please, don't be like that, please. Maybe you could come with me?"

"Get real. Clay. No airplane is going to let me fly when I'm five months pregnant."

"I'm sorry, Tara. What can I say?"

"Say you'll stay. Say you want to be with me more than anything in the world."

"I do want to be with you more than anything in the world, but I can't."

"Fine, that's just fine. Why don't you stay here while I leave you be? You fly to Los Angeles. You make your money while I go find a place to live, taking care of our child inside me all by myself."

I walked over to my suitcases opening them and throwing all my clothes into the suitcases trying to get out of there as fast as I could. I may have been overreacting, but I didn't care. I wanted Clay to realize what was more important than his career. Family was first, just like Dr. Phil always said, and I was going to have to say that I completely agreed with that saying. Clay walked up behind me placing his hand on my shoulder.

"Tara, wait, don't leave angry. Let me find you a place to live. Let me take care of you."

I pushed Clay's hand off of me as he tried to comfort me. "Don't touch me. I don't need your pity. If you wanted to take care of me, you would stay when I need you the most. You just care about hiding me from your other life you're living."

"Tara, I didn't mean to hurt you. You need to calm down. It's not good for our baby."

"Don't. Just don't tell me what I need. You know nothing. Get lost. Move out of my way." I closed my suitcases, crying and standing up. I carried them towards the door about to leave.

"Tara, please, just wait." Clay walked up to me placing his hands around me beginning to tear up. "Please, just let me do this for you. You can leave. I know you're upset, but please let me do this so I know you're okay."

I agreed telling him I would let him take care of me, but making sure he knew I wasn't about to just sit there and wait for him to return. He knew what he needed to figure out, but he was just so stubborn he couldn't see it. "Alright, you can do for me whatever you want, but don't think that you're forgiven for leaving."

Header

"I know, I know, that's okay. You have all the right to be upset with me right now." I stood there in front of Clay with his hands at the sides of my arms. He was staring at me. "I'll be back, don't worry. I wouldn't give you up for the world. You know that, don't you?"

"I don't know anymore. I'm confused. I just need a break from you, a break from all of this starlight around me."

"I understand, but don't leave, Tara. Stay, and I'll call around and set you up with a place to stay until I get back, alright?"

"I guess, but don't try and make everything alright, because it won't work. I don't want to celebrate my love for you and then tomorrow you leave, and I have to stay behind finding my own way around through everything."

"I know, I know, Tara, just come back inside, and we'll just talk, that's all. I promise."

"Okay."

I went back inside sitting down on the sofa as Clay closed the door locking it and turning towards me. He walked over to the chair in front of me. He was sitting down leaning forward staring at me as if trying to tell me he was sorry without having to say it to me. I felt as if I had been dreaming. There had been so many twists and turns since I had met Clay. I wasn't sure if it was all real, but it was, and here was another bump in the road for me to stumble on. I was hurt for the hundredth time. I was starting to wonder why we were even together if we kept on arguing. I then realized it was because no matter how many holes we fell into together, God was probably showing us love would always bring us closer together. I believed even though it hurt us so much to be apart, it was indeed making our love stronger than it had ever been, and for that, I was truly thankful. Although in a strange way, you wouldn't think I would be. I was the type of person who would always see the light through whatever darkness, no matter how hard I had to struggle to see the good out of the ugly. I didn't understand anyone who would see a problem as a block that would never move.

I would move that block, I would lift that stone, and I would forever climb that mountain, no matter the outcome. That was who I was and that would forever be who I would always be in life, the entrepreneur, the rising stone of the universe. Or maybe I wasn't, maybe I had been the one who was always on the sidelines making my way by following others around to get to where I was going. I highly doubted I would follow. I had too strong of a will to just stand there on the sidelines without taking whatever was thrown at me, with not only a fight, but with a comfort in it. I would read between the lines of whatever circumstances I had been forced to stand with.

I came back to reality from my thoughts and was sitting on the sofa, staring at Clay on the chair in front of me leaning forward staring at me. "Tara, I'm really sorry, I have to go. I didn't want this, and you know that, right?"

"Clay, let's just drop it. I don't want to cry anymore. I'm really tired of it."

"I know. I'm sorry. Is there anything you want me to do for you?"

"No, just a place to live would be fine, considering I am having your child."

Clay got off his chair, walked towards me, and fell to his knees in front of me as he wrapped his arms around me. "Oh, Tara, I love you so much. Please don't be angry with me. I don't think I could leave if I knew you were angry."

"I think you could, and I think you will. Clay, your career's too important to you. I thought you wanted to work with children more, change their lives in a way that is unbelievable. I found out you're just like everyone else, just pretending to be someone special. I thought you were different. Now, I have to have my first baby without my family and without you. I need you. I want you here. I just don't understand why your fans can't wait until after I have our baby."

"I know you can't understand it, but I know what I need to do. I have to leave tomorrow no matter what. It's my job."

"Yes, that's right, it's your job. It's not your wife, it's not your child, and it's not something that you can't stand to lose. I am, your baby is. Have you already forgotten about what you care more about, or are you failing to see it?"

"Hey, that's not fair."

He rose up onto his feet, as did I. We were staring at one another standing in front of each other. "You don't have the right to just stand there and tell me what I'm not. I'm not like that. I know you're more important."

"But what, Clay? When you come back from fantasy world, maybe you'll see that you leaving wasn't such a great idea."

"Tara, you're really getting on my nerves, you know that? You're so..."

"So what? Stubborn?"

"No, you're so unreasonable. You stand there telling me all the things that I'm doing wrong when you should be looking at your life in a microscope, pointing out everything that you've done wrong."

"That's not fair, Clay."

"Life isn't fair, Tara, but we have to live with it anyway. I love you, but right now, I'm wondering why."

"You did not just say that."

There was then a knock at the door and it creaked open. It was a maid coming in to clean the room. "Excuse me, sorry to interrupt, but I heard yelling. Is everything alright?"

"Everything's fine."

"Yes, Mr. Edison, I'll come back later."

The door closed as Clay looked back at me. "Tara, look, I know you're pregnant, but you can't use that to keep me with you."

"Are you telling me that you think that's what I'm doing?"

"No, I didn't say that."

"Then what, Clay? What are you saying?"

"It's nothing."

"No, tell me, I'd like to know what it is that's bothering you about me."

"Jeez, just, God, Tara, I don't know what to do anymore. We keep arguing. All we do is fight. I'm leaving tomorrow, and if we could settle this before I leave, that would be great, but at the rate you're going that won't happen."

"Oh, don't worry, it's settled."

I sat back down on the sofa looking away from Clay upset and angry with him. I could feel our argument coming to a close, but I wasn't sure as to when it was going to be over. I felt Clay sit down beside me on the sofa rubbing my side as I leaned over onto the sofa away from him and started to cry.

"Oh, Tara, God, I'm so sorry. I want so much for you to support me about leaving. I'll be back, and I love you."

"I know you will; that's what I'm afraid of."

"Why on earth are you afraid of that?"

I turned staring at Clay while tearing up. "Because I'm afraid if you come back, they'll end up changing you to believe I'm exactly like Lindsey tried so hard to make me out to be."

"Don't you understand that I'm just going to straighten everything out between my fans and me?"

"I'm also scared that when you come back, we'll have the happiest time of our lives, and then you'll have to leave again for some reason. I hate being afraid all the time. I shouldn't have to worry all the time about if we'll be together for a birthday or an anniversary. I love you, and I want to celebrate our love every day, not once every year."

Clay took a deep breath not knowing what to say. He was stressed out, I could tell. I wanted so much to turn around and hold him, but I didn't know how to. I didn't know whether he would even want me to after our argument. He got up off the sofa walking away. I looked up seeing him about to leave the room. I rose up off the sofa, ran over to him, and turned him towards me.

"Don't leave me, please. Oh, Clay, I don't want you to leave, not like this, not right now."

Clay wrapped his arms around me comforting me as I cried against his chest. "I'm not going anywhere right now, sweetie."

"Just don't say anything, Clay. Just take me in your arms and hold me for the time we have right now."

Clay smelt my hair breathing me into his soul as he held me tightly comforting me. He dragged his fingertips down my back then ran them back up still holding me closely. He lifted my chin up with his fingers beginning to kiss my lips without saying anything to me. Clay picked me up into his arms and carried me to the bathroom laying me down on the floor. He lay on top of me looking into my eyes.

"Clay, why are we in the bathroom?"

"I just realized that this is the only room we haven't marked with our love." We giggled for a minute, then he made love to me on the cold bathroom floor. After we had sex, he lay on top of me looking into my eyes as if he could almost see heaven within my eyes. "Oh, Tara, you always make me never want to leave, every time I look into your eyes."

Header

"I love you, Clay, but you will leave, and neither me nor my eyes are going to stop you."

"Tara."

"I know. I'm sorry, too, and I love you, Clay."

"I love you, too, Tara, and I'm so sorry about earlier."

I placed my hand over his mouth gently staring at him not wanting him to bring the whole subject up again. "Shh, no more talking. Just be with me." We lay beside one another for hours, just holding each other and sharing the greatest gift of all: time.

CHAPTER 17

The Birth of Our Creation

Clay left that day and went to Los Angeles and left me in New York alone and scared as to what I was supposed to do next. My heart was breaking, and I wanted him to stay with me and tell his fans that they could wait, but his baby couldn't. I loved him so much, but maybe I was expecting too much from the man I loved.

I didn't understand why he couldn't just choose to stay, but I guess if I placed myself into his shoes I would see he'd been having a hard time getting used to what his fans thought about him instead of just letting them think whatever they wanted to because it was not true. He felt he had to go, so he left leaving me alone in a condo up on the fourteenth floor, fully furnished. Whenever I needed food, a lady would come drop some more off making sure I was fed. Clay thought of everything that I would need or might want. He even gave me spending money so I could go shopping for the baby or myself whenever I wanted to. Yeah, it was unreal, but it wasn't as great as you're probably thinking it was. Yeah, I got a place to live, and yeah, I got everything I needed, but the thing was I didn't want all that. All I wanted was Clay and no amount of money in the world was going to hide that feeling. I needed Clay. I wanted him here with me sharing the birth of our child that would be coming soon.

Months had passed by of my not being with Clay, and I had even stopped accepting his phone calls. It hurt too much to hear his voice and not be able to touch or see him like I wanted to. It was getting closer to my due date, and I probably had about a week or two to go. Clay must have been getting very aggravated with me about not accepting his phone calls, it seemed. I figured that out when someone knocked on my door. I hurried to the door with my big belly full of baby and opened the door to a man in a black suit staring at me. "Miss Heart?"

"I'm Miss Heart. Why?"

"Sorry to disturb you, but Mr. Edison is on my cell phone and would like you to talk to him." He pulled out his cell phone, holding it out towards me looking very frustrated. "Here, talk, he's been on my ass about this for a week now. If you don't answer the phone…" He was silent leaning towards me then finished, "I might as well be fired, so please do us both a favor and answer the phone."

I took a deep breath staring up at the man. "Uh no, I don't think I can. He's there, I'm here. It's too hard to hear his voice, just tell him I'm busy or I wasn't here when you knocked."

"Don't you think it would be a little odd if he can hear you? The phone is right here, remember? I think he can hear that you're here. Now you might as well talk to him."

"Fine."

I took the phone from his hands and threw it down the hallway. "Tell Mr. Edison he can talk to me when…" I suddenly felt a gush of liquid drizzle down my legs, dripping onto the floor from my dress. The man in the black suit in front of me glanced down after seeing my reaction. "Oh my God, did your water just break?"

"What's that?"

"Oh my God, hold on." The man ran down the hallway picking up the phone as I stood by my door looking down at the tiny puddle of liquid below me. "Mr. Edison, we have a problem; she's in labor, and her water just broke."

"What? Oh my God, she's having the baby?"

"Well, not right now she isn't, but soon."

"Put Tara on, right now."

He ran up to me handing me the phone. "It's Mr. Edison. Talk to him now."

I placed the phone to my ear. "Clay, something's happening; where are you?"

"Tara, why didn't you answer my phone calls. I'm so frustrated with you. Never do that to me again."

"Clay, it hurts. Look what you've done to me! Now I'm leaking."

"It's not my fault."

"Yes, it is, now I have to give birth to a twenty-pound baby."

"It's not that big."

"No? Well, it could be."

"Are you still standing there?"

"Yeah, why?"

"Tara, what are you doing? Get to a hospital. What's wrong with you?"

"No, I'm not leaving until you come get me."

"But, Tara, I'm in Los Angeles. By the time I get there, you'll have had the baby. Now get to the hospital before I go ballistic."

"No, not without you."

"Tara, you're making me angry."

"I don't care."

"If you don't leave, you'll end up having the baby right where you're standing."

"That's just fine. I'm sure this nice man here will help me deliver my baby."

I stared up at the man in front of me seeing him beginning to back away from me frightened he might have to deliver my baby. "Tara, jeez. God, put Bob on."

I handed the phone to the man that had brought me the phone as he stared at me frightened. "Bob?"

"Yes, Mr. Edison?"

"Take her to a hospital, even if you have to carry her."

"But, Mr. Edison, she's giving me the evil eye; it's kind of scaring me."

"Bob, do what I said or you're fired. This is the mother of my child, and if anything happens to her, I'm holding you responsible. Now, do it."

"Sorry, Mr. Edison, I'll do what I can."

"Great, now put Tara back on."

"Clay, what did you tell him?"

The man then picked me up carrying me as I kicked my legs. "Put me down. Put me down, you jerk."

"Tara, calm down. There is an ambulance waiting downstairs for you."

185

"Clay, just shut up. Ow, ow, it hurts. I hate you, ow. Make it stop, Clay, make the pain stop. Look what you've done to me, ow."

"I didn't do it."

"Yes, you did. Put me down." I was silent for a minute and then felt like I had to push. We had only made it into the elevator. "Oh no."

"What? What is it, Tara? What's wrong?"

"I feel like I have to push."

"Oh crap, hold on, I'll get 9-1-1 on the line for you. Now give the phone to Bob."

"Okay."

I handed Bob the cell phone as he placed me onto the elevator floor. I lay on my back in the position about to push. All I could see was Bob on the phone with a paramedic that Clay had transferred the phone to. Bob was on the cell and was told to get me into the hallway out of the elevator and get a couple things from my place. He left me on the hallway floor coming back with towels and some other things I didn't pay much attention to considering I had enough things on my mind about what had been going on. Bob held the phone on his shoulder as the paramedic on the phone told him what to do. Bob stared at me with a serious expression on his face, while holding out his hands.

"I need you to push now, Miss Heart, slowly."

I bore down, pushing with my chin to my chest as the man whom I had just met got a free show of my, well, do I even have to explain. It must have been uncomfortable for him, or maybe it was just I who was uncomfortable. Well, whichever way it was, I had bigger things to think about rather than a stranger staring at me. I pushed again, then I heard Bob tell the paramedic on the phone that the baby's head was out. "One more push, Tara." I pushed again as I felt the baby slide out slowly. Bob wrapped the baby in a towel cleaning out the baby's nose and mouth, then I heard it cry. It was the most beautiful sound I had ever heard, well, besides Clay's voice. The baby was so gross covered in blood, but it was so cute. Bob placed the baby into my arms as the elevator door opened, and three paramedics came running over to me kneeling down beside me. They took the baby out of my arms cutting the umbilical cord and cleaning the baby off more. They then gave the baby back to me and lifted me onto a bed that they then used to wheel me into the elevator and bring me downstairs.

When we were downstairs, I looked around seeing everyone who had been in the lobby staring at me. The paramedics then wheeled me through the doors of the building and into the back of the ambulance as I cradled my baby close to me. The baby was so beautiful, and I couldn't have pictured it to be more beautiful if I had painted the picture myself. I was lying in the bed in the ambulance holding the baby in my arms when one of the paramedics handed me their cell phone. "Hello?"

"Tara."

"Clay, what's wrong? You sound like you're crying." I heard sniffling coming from Clay on the other side of the phone.

"I am. How's the baby?"

"The baby's fine."

"Are you alright, too? I was so worried. I'm such a jerk. I just realized how selfish I've been. I'm so sorry."

"It's alright, Clay, don't worry about it."

"So what did we have?"

"It's a boy, Clayton Vincent Edison."

"It's a boy? You named him after me?"

"Of course, who else would I name him after? Bob?"

Clay giggled. "No."

"When are you coming, baby?"

"As we speak, sweetie. I'll be there tomorrow some time; don't worry."

"Oh, Clay, I miss you so much. I can't wait to see you hold your son. He's so beautiful."

"Oh my God."

"What is it?"

"I just realized that I'm a father. I'm a daddy. Oh my God, it gives me the chills every time I say that."

"Oh, Clay, you're so silly sometimes; now hurry up."

"I am, sweetie; I'm on my way."

I arrived at the hospital not too long after my conversation with Clay on the phone. I was so relieved that he was excited about being a daddy now. I knew he would do a great job. I had no doubts about that one. I was getting excited to see him again. He was coming back finally, and I was so happy.

When I woke up, I saw Clay sitting in a chair in front of my bed holding his son in his arms smiling and singing in a quiet voice to him. He looked up at me seeing I was awake as he then rose up off the chair walking over to me. "He's so beautiful, sweetheart. He's perfect, just like you." I smiled watching as Clay kissed the top of Clayton's head. "I can't wait until you two can get out of the hospital and go home with me."

I looked up at Clay as I questioned him in a quiet voice. "Where's home, Clay?" I lay in bed waiting for his answer, afraid it might be one that I wouldn't like.

"Los Angeles."

"What do you mean Los Angeles? I don't live there. You're not taking Clayton away from me, are you Clay?"

"Tara, for heaven's sake, no. Why would you even think that? I'm bringing you and the baby with me; we're moving to Los Angeles if that's alright with you."

"Of course it is, as long as I'm with you, I don't care where we live."

"You're such a wonderful woman, you know that?"

I smiled seeing how happy I had made Clay and feeling how happy he had made me. We both gave each other what we had wanted that day. I wanted to share a life with Clay, and he wanted to have a family to come home to. I loved my family so much; all I could feel was love inside me, and all I could see was Clay holding our child in his arms as if he could see the future of his family in his eyes. He pulled the chair over to me and placed the baby into my arms as he sat down beside me. "I'm going to be a better father to our child than my father ever was. I promise you two that." He leaned forward kissing me.

"I know you will, Clay."

That moment I was going to remember for the rest of my life. I loved hearing Clay talk to me with so much love for me in his voice. I needed him as much as he needed me. We were clearly meant for one another, and every time I looked into his eyes, I began to see our wedding day coming soon. I couldn't wait to hear the words of the priest announced in front of everyone: "I now pronounce you husband and wife." I already felt as though Clay and I were married, but I knew when those rings got placed on our fingers, we would forever be connected through body and soul in God's eyes. Clay was everything in the world

I could ever ask for and more. He held my heart, my soul, and even saw the parts of me I never wanted anyone to ever see in me. I had to admit, I did get angry and so did he. We were so similar, and we were so close. We could tell each other anything we wanted and the other one wouldn't even judge us. Yeah, so what we argued? At least the little things made us stronger. We loved each other, and we wanted so much to be with each other forever, and I believed that was why we never gave up when things got tough. Who could blame us? We were in love.

The next day, the baby and I were released from the hospital. We got picked up in Clay's limo which drove us to the airport right away almost as if it had already been planned. "Clay, what about my things at the condo?"

"Oh, don't worry about them. They're already being shipped over to our new house."

"You planned this, didn't you?"

"Well, of course. I didn't want to have to stay in New York for another day. I wanted to fly my family home now."

"You're so romantic, Clay."

"Well, you know, for you, anything is possible."

I giggled feeling butterflies fluttering inside my tummy as we reached the airport and got out. We walked past all the people who were beginning to stare. There were no cameras or reporters waiting for us to arrive. The only ones who were there were the people at the airport looking at us as we walked through the closed-off area in the airport that led to our plane. "Where are all the reporters that always meet us here?"

"Oh, they think I'm bringing you to the condo."

"You told them a lie?"

"No, just a little fib. I didn't want them to bother you on our way home with our child."

"Well, thank you, Clay. It's nice hearing nothing but you when we go somewhere."

"Yes, and it's going to be really nice seeing no one but you and our son when I come home from a long day's work."

"You're so sweet, Clay, especially when you're not being stubborn."

"Hey."

We reached the airplane and got on, taking our seats. We waited for the plane to take off. We were finally feeling as though we were going to be together without anything getting in our way. Clay sat beside me staring at me with a smile. "Clay, when we're living in Los Angeles, you're not going to have to leave every month, are you?"

"That's the thing, Tara, since all my work is basically going to be centered mostly in Los Angeles, I won't have to leave so much."

"But what if you do?"

"Well, then if I do, I'll take my family, too. It's no big deal. From now on, where I go, my family goes, too."

"Oh, Clay, you don't know how happy that makes me feel."

"Yes, I do, because I can feel it every time you look into my eyes."

The baby then started to cry so I lifted my shirt up letting the baby latch onto my breast. Clay glanced over at me startled by the sight of my nursing the baby. "Tara, what are you doing? There are other men on this plane. They can see your breasts."

"I'm feeding our son; he's hungry."

"Well, cover yourself up. Here." Clay took off his jacket placing it over my chest and the baby lightly so no one could see anything. "There, jeez, you scared me there. I don't want other men staring at my wife's breasts, no one but myself, and of course Clayton."

"Oh, Clay, you're so funny sometimes."

"I am not. I'm being serious."

"Sure you are, uh huh. You just keep thinking that, alright?"

"I'm not joking. I don't want other men seeing your, well, you know."

"Breasts?"

"Tara."

"What? It's just my breasts. It's a beautiful thing."

"I know that, but other men might be getting the wrong impression."

I giggled laughing at how my breastfeeding Clayton in public made his voice all high and squeaky. He was so adorable when he was being manly and protective of his woman. "Now, every time you need to bring out your breast, just cover the jacket over you so no one can see, okay?"

"Yeah, yeah, I will. You're lucky you're so cute, Clay."

Clay smiled. "Yeah, well, I guess I'm thankful you find me so cute. Whatever keeps you from doing that again, I'm for it."

I just stared at him laughing as I breastfed Clayton. While I was feeding Clayton, I noticed Clay glancing down at me smirking. "I wonder what your milk tastes like."

"I don't know. Why? You want some?"

"Tara, shh." He was silent then whispered, "Well, maybe later."

I giggled again at the fact that Clay wanted to try some of my breast milk. Then again, what man in his right mind would refuse a woman's breast? Well, not Clay, I guess. We were quiet the rest of the way, and I was beginning to get so excited to see where we would be living in Los Angeles. I was sure wherever it was it was just perfect. After all, Clay picked it out.

When we had arrived in Los Angeles, we got off the plane, and we looked around seeing crowds of people who had been waiting for us to arrive. "I guess they found us."

"I'll say."

"Stay with me. Don't worry, my bodyguards won't let anyone touch you."

"Okay."

We walked together with the baby in a car seat that Clay had been carrying, while everyone around us was screaming for us. "Look over here! Look over here." That's all I could even understand them saying.

"It's alright, Tara; we're almost to the limo." I followed Clay as he and his bodyguards led the way towards the limo waiting for us ahead, or at least I thought it was a limo at the moment. When we got closer, I noticed just a black car parked nearby, so I turned to Clay worried.

"Clay, the limo, it's gone. How will we leave? There are so many people."

"I don't know. Where would it be?" Clay looked at me oddly as I started to worry. "Oh, Tara, I'm just kidding; the car is mine. I bought it so I could drive you around instead of some limo all the time."

"Really? You're going to drive me?"

"What's wrong with that? You look worried about that. Why?"

"It's nothing, Clay, honest."

"Tara."

"Alright, it's just, well, are you even a good driver?"

"Tara, that's a pretty rude thing to say to someone you love."

"I'm just worried about our safety, that's all. I've never seen you drive."

"Yes, Tara, I do know how to drive. Now let's get in the car before you say something else hurtful, and you make me angry."

"No."

"No? What do you mean 'no'?"

"I'm not getting in the car if there's smoke coming out of your ears, not with our son I'm not."

"Come on, Tara, look around you, there are cameras everywhere. Don't make a drama scene for them to twist around. Now smile and get in the car until we get home, alright?"

I looked around at all the cameras then got inside the passenger's side as Clay placed the car seat in the back making sure it was secure. Clay then got in the driver's seat closing the door as he began to drive away. When we were far enough away, Clay pulled over parking at the side of a street staring at me.

"Why are we stopping?"

"Tara, I just want to get something straight before I take you home, and we make that commitment."

"What is it?"

"It's us. Are we going to keep arguing about stupid things all the time or are you going to try and be a little easier on me now?"

"What? I've been hard on you?"

"Yes, don't you notice it, Tara? Ever since the airport incident with Steven, you've been acting, well, I don't know."

"What?"

"Different, edgy, if that may explain it. Is there something that you need to tell me?"

"Yeah, well, I guess I would be edgy considering I was pregnant with your child and you left me."

"It's not that, Tara."

"Then what, Clay?"

"It's alright, Tara, if you did date Steven. I won't care. I know you were more serious about me."

I sat there shocked that he was bringing this up all over again. "You think I dated him?"

"No, I'm just saying if by chance you had, that it's alright."

"Huh, okay, let me get this straight, you're accusing me of being with Steven; plus, you're saying it's okay if I did. What is the matter with you, Clay? Yeah, you're right about one thing, I am still upset about the airport incident, but I have all the right to be. I never cheated on you. I loved you then, and I love you now, so don't you dare accuse me of anything different."

"I'm sorry, it's just that I get worried sometimes that you may have, but it's only because you always make me feel like I'm doing something wrong. I just want to know right now if you're going to work on this so we can make this marriage work."

"I don't know what to say except I'm sorry for being such a B."

"Tara, don't talk like that about yourself. All I wanted was for you to realize that you were treating me like this so you could work through whatever it is that's making you act as you have."

"I'm not a child, Clay."

"Well, sometimes you act like one."

"If you want an old lady, then go to an old folks' home and be with one."

Clay started laughing at me, and he couldn't stop. He laughed so hard I began to laugh without even knowing why we were laughing. I stopped laughing staring at Clay still giggling at me. "What? What's so funny, Clay?"

"You. 'Go to an old folks' home and be with one.' It made me remember all the granny underwear I received over the years. Oh God, Tara, you're so funny. What would I ever do without you in my life?"

"I don't know. Be with a granny?" I started to laugh with Clay. I figured I'd rather be laughing than arguing with him. Well, that was the end of that argument, and all we did was laugh the whole drive home.

When Clay pulled up to the house, I looked out the window at the most amazing home I had ever seen. I opened the door, got out, and walked away from the car a little looking up at the house. I looked back at Clay standing by the driver's side door out of the car watching me. "Is this..."

"Yes, that's our house, Tara."

Header

"Oh my God, where did you find it?"

"I didn't. It found me. I was driving one day, and I got lost, and I ended up here and saw a 'For Sale' sign and bought it."

"Is that the truth?"

"Of course." Clay closed the car door and went around getting the baby out of the car. We then walked towards our front door. The house was two stories and was a five-bedroom home with three bathrooms. It was the most beautiful house I had ever seen in my life. I couldn't believe we were going to be living together in a house in Los Angeles. It was amazing. It felt so unbelievable to me, but it wasn't. It was all happening, and to my surprise, it was all happening to me. Clay was making me the happiest woman in the world. I never felt so alive. When I was with him, he gave me energy in the day, and I fed off his light. I was the brightest star in the sky every time Clay was in my life.

We approached the door. Clay inserted the key and opened the front door. I stood with Clay as I watched him carry the baby in the car seat inside the entrance and place the baby on the floor staring back at me. "Aren't you coming, Tara?"

I looked around at the inside of the house, walking inside slowly. "Yeah, of course." I walked in as the door to our new home with new adventures closed behind me closing off the outside world and sealing off the inside with my family in it. I felt different the moment that door closed. I felt a security, and I felt so safe. I knew from then on that this was where I belonged, in this house, with this man, and with our children. I was indeed captivated by Clay's heart. He held all my dreams, all my hopes, and all the prayers that I had ever dreamt about. It wasn't until that door closed that I knew that I was definitely where I was meant to be in life, in Los Angeles sharing my soul with the love of my life, Clay Edison!

CHAPTER 18

Remaking Our Love

Two years passed by so smoothly, we never argued after we moved into our new house in Los Angeles with our son Clayton Vincent Edison. I was so excited about living there. We were so happy being together as a family. Clay and I had a lot of fun times within the two years from Clayton's birth. I remember Clay had changed Clayton's diaper, and he peed right in his face. Then he put his diaper on backwards, like anyone probably would if they had urine in their eyes. He was so funny when it came to taking care of Clayton. It was so cute. We would all play in a tiny swimming pool in the backyard together splashing water at each other. He was such a great father to Clayton, just as he said he would be. He was a better father than he or I had ever imagined he would be. He loved teaching him to do so many things, like to ride a tricycle. Clayton was so afraid of it at first that Clay had to ride it even though he was way bigger than it. I used to get a kick out of it, because when he did, he kept banging his knees every time he tried to pedal, but after Clay had gotten off, Clayton got right on it and started riding it. They were so cute together. We had food fights, and when we did the dishes together, we put the bubbles in our hands and blew them at one another. Those days were so wonderful and will forever stay with me.

I was twenty-one and Clay was twenty-six at the time. We were now planning for our wedding, which would take place on Christmas Eve, since Christmas was our favorite time of the year. Clay and I had decided that our wedding would be in Elko so all his family and friends would be able to share with him the happiest day of his life: our wedding.

He was so excited about being married to me finally. We read a lot of tabloids talking about us having a child together and us still not being married yet, like it was some kind of sin or something. I didn't get it how someone could think a child coming into the world would be some kind of sin. God wouldn't have brought children into the world if it were a sin. Childbirth was the most interesting, exciting, joyful experience of a person's life. Well, for some people it was, but for others, it was the worst thing in the world that they could ever be cursed with.

I came back to reality where Clay was on his way home from work while I was at home taking care of our son and looking through bridal magazines planning in my head what kind of dress I imagined myself wearing on our wedding day. I had just laid the baby down for the night when Clay came home from work. I greeted him as I normally did, giving him a kiss on the lips that lasted about five minutes. We were so in love. We loved to kiss. Then again, who could blame us? We were a flame burning like a bonfire through a forest.

"Hey, baby, so how was work at the studio?"

"It was great, and how was work at home?"

"Wonderful, especially now that you're home."

Clay took off his jacket and hung it up on the coatrack while taking his shoes off. "So did you end up writing any songs today?"

"No, not yet. I can't think of any. I wish I had someone to write with; it would probably help me think a lot better."

"Well, hey, I can help you. I've been writing songs since I was sixteen years old."

"You have? How come you never told me this before?"

"You never asked."

"Oh, Tara."

"Come into the office. I'll show you what I've written recently. It's called 'No, Baby, It's You.'"

"Well, that's cute; let's hear it."

When we reached the office, he sat down on the loveseat in the office as I went into the file cabinet and pulled the song out of my folder. I held it in my hands while walking over to Clay. I sat down beside him on the sofa. "I'll sing it, and then you can kind of get a feel of it and join in, alright?"

"Great, go ahead, sweetie." I sang the song to Clay, and he seemed to enjoy it then joined in after he knew the chorus well enough. After the song ended, he stared at me with the biggest smile upon his face. "You really wrote that, baby?"

"Well, yeah. Why? Did you like it?"

"It was great. Can I use it?"

"Well, of course, you can have all my songs."

"You know what? You could be my songwriter, and we can work together as a team."

"Well, I have thought about being a writer since I was younger. As long as the songs are sung by you, I'm happy."

"But of course."

The next week, I was cleaning our house watching Clayton, and I turned on the radio for some music. I couldn't believe my ears. I heard the song I had written for Clay playing on the radio. It felt so strange but exciting to hear a song that I had written being played on the radio. I picked Clayton up and started dancing to the song laughing as Clay walked into the room running over to me hugging us.

"Do you hear that, baby? It's your song, and they recorded it."

"No, Clay, it's our song. You sing it so beautifully. I love it."

"I'm glad. Whatever makes you happy I would gladly hand it over to you. I love you so much."

"Oh, Clay, that's so wonderful. I love you, too."

"Why don't we go out for a nice romantic dinner to celebrate our success together?"

"I would love to, but what about Clayton?"

"We'll just get a nanny to watch him, don't worry."

"Alright, dinner sounds just perfect then."

"Great, I'll go set everything up. You stay here and relax while I make everything perfect."

Clay kissed me and his son then left the room to set up our date. I carried Clayton into his bedroom and put him into bed to sleep then walked out of the bedroom closing the door behind me. A nanny showed up not too long after I had laid him down so Clay and I got dressed up and left the house walking towards his car in the driveway. I placed my hand on the car handle about to open it when I heard Clay.

"Tara, what are you doing?"

Header

"I thought we were going out for dinner; that's why we got a nanny and dressed up, isn't it?"

"Well, yeah, but we're not leaving in a car; we're leaving in that." Clay pointed to a limo pulling up to the house as I then looked back at Clay after seeing the limo.

"You rented a limo?"

"It's for old times, remember?"

"Of course, how could I not, Clay? We had so many fights in there it's not even funny."

"I know, but we've had many good times, too. Haven't we, Tara?"

I thought for a minute remembering all the times we made love in the limo before. "I have to admit it, we have, and those were great times."

"Come on, sweetie, let me take you out for dinner." Clay held out his arm, and I walked up to him linking his arm, then he led me to the limo letting me in. I slid across the back seat as Clay climbed in closing the door and climbing on top of me.

"Clay, what are you doing?" I giggled.

"I'm loving you. Is that a crime?"

"Yes, it's a very big crime, you naughty, naughty man."

"Oh, Tara."

"Mmm." I giggled as Clay began to kiss my neck as I made sweet little noises. "Mmm, oh that's nice, uuu."

We made love on the back seat of the limo, and it was the greatest night we ever had in two years. Being away from the baby was nice for a change. We got dressed again and made sure our hair was fine by looking in the mirror as we felt the limo come to a stop. "We're here, baby, let's go."

Clay placed his hand out for me as I placed my hand over his. We sat there in front of one another just staring into one another's eyes dreaming. The limo door opened as we slid across the seat towards the door, getting out as the door closed behind us. I looked up at the restaurant smiling over at Clay. "It's beautiful, Clay, thank you for tonight."

"Anytime, sweetie." Clay led me into the restaurant as we were then seated beside a window. We ordered our dinner, and while we waited, we sat there talking to one another about life and love as we always did.

"Tara, I was thinking all day about our wedding and how great it's going to be to be married to the woman I love finally. I was hoping to talk to you about something, but I'm not sure if you would want to do it."

"Well, what is it, Clay?"

"Well, I was thinking, what if we move the wedding up more, say about…I don't know…September maybe?"

"September, isn't that a little too soon? We won't have enough time to plan then." "Sure we will. We have a month and a half or so, depending on what day in September we choose the wedding day to be."

"I don't know, Clay. September is so soon."

"Tara, you love me, don't you?"

"Of course I do."

"Well then, what does it matter what month we have it as long as we have it, right?"

"Wrong."

"But, Tara, I want this more than anything I've ever wanted in my life."

"Clay, I don't want to move the day."

"Tara, this isn't the time to get cold feet when we're so close to having each other forever."

"Clay, do we have to talk about this in a public place? We're about to have dinner. Really, this isn't the right time for this kind of subject."

"What do you mean, Tara? It's the perfect place. Now, say yes and be my wife in September."

"I will be, in December on Christmas Eve like we planned before, remember?"

"Please, Tara, don't make me get on my knees, because I will, I swear it."

"Go ahead."

"Alright, you asked for it."

Clay got off his chair and kneeled down in front of me as I leaned towards him and whispered, "I was joking; now stand up, people are watching."

"No, I don't care. Let them watch. Let them listen. I want everyone to know that I want to marry you."

"Clay, shh, be quiet."

"Say you'll be mine, Tara."

I rose up off the chair to my feet and stormed past him in a hurry, running out of the restaurant about to cry. When I got outside, I ran to the limo and stood in front of the limo door with my hand on the handle and my head faced downward.

"Tara, what was that all about? What's the matter?" Clay walked up behind me placing his hand on my back as I turned around with tears falling from my eyes.

"Why did you have to embarrass me in there? People were staring at us. Everyone probably thinks I'm so ridiculous not to say yes to you."

"No, Tara, you're not. You're the most sensational woman I've ever known; that's why I long so much to have you, for your name to be mine, Mrs. Tara Edison."

I giggled a little. "Yeah, well, that does sound really nice."

"See, now, what's the problem then? Are you having cold feet?"

"No, I'm just now realizing the closer it gets to our wedding, the closer it gets for me to walk down the aisle to you."

"Well, what's wrong with that?"

"I'll be walking down the aisle to the man I'm so in love with, and when I look to my right, there will be no one standing beside me. No one's giving me away to you. I miss my father. I miss them all so much, Clay."

"I know, shh, come here, sweetie."

He held me close to him as he whispered, "I miss my sister, too, just as much as you miss your family. I miss my father. All we can do is just hold on to their memories with us, and they'll forever be with us. I'm sure when you're walking down that aisle to me, your father will be standing right beside you. Hell, why don't we walk down the aisle together? It would feel almost as if we were walking away from our past and bringing with us the memories that will forever make our future."

"That's really sweet, Clay. Thank you for that. You see, this is why I love you so much."

"And this is why I love you." Clay placed his hands on the back of my head and moved them through my hair gently. He pressed his lips upon mine kissing me. We turned towards the restaurant hearing, "Aww," from a couple of people that had been staring at us from across the way watching us kissing and leaning against the limo door. "You want to get out of here?"

"I think we should, before a crowd forms." We got into the limo and closed the door being driven away to wherever we chose to go next.

We decided we should go somewhere quiet, so we drove to a secluded park and got out of the limo. We looked up to the sky above us seeing the stars fill the sky all around us. It was so beautiful. Clay walked over onto the grass placing his jacket on the ground. "Come on, sweetie, lay down with me."

I walked over to where Clay was sitting down on his jacket. We lay down on our backs and snuggled up to one another just staring up at all the beautiful stars out that night. It was very romantic.

"How many stars do you think are even up there?"

"I don't know."

"Yeah, I guess it's probably better that way. Life's more of a mystery that way," I finished then glanced over at Clay seeing him stare up at the stars.

"So what about September, Tara? Are we on?"

I thought for a minute. There was silence filling the air as I answered in a quiet voice, "September what?"

"Uh, how, about September...I don't know...14th?"

"The 14th, hmm, well, okay, that sounds great as long as there's a four in it somewhere, I'm happy."

"I knew you liked fours. I wasn't sure, but I kind of figured it."

"How?"

"Well, you wanted the condo on the fourteenth floor rather than the sixteenth. You want four children, and you lost four people."

"Four? No, only three."

"No, not if you include Lindsey, too."

"Lindsey didn't die; she just turned into Jennifer."

Header

Clay was all of a sudden silent, clearing his throat acting as if he wanted to change the subject. I sat up looking down at Clay curiously. "Clay, are you hiding something from me?"

Clay sat up staring at me. "I don't know what you're talking about."

"Yes, you do. What about Lindsey? Why would you say I lost her?"

"I meant as a friend; that's all."

"Are you sure that's what you meant?"

"Of course, what else would I mean? Now come here, my beautiful." Clay wrapped his arms around me as he kissed me lowering me back down onto the ground still kissing me. We made out on the grass as a flashlight shining in our faces interrupted us. We looked up seeing two police officers staring down at us smirking.

"Okay, you two lovebirds, let's get a move on." They noticed Clay was right in front of them then finished, "Sorry about that, Mr. Edison. I didn't know it was you."

"That's alright; we were just leaving."

"It didn't look that way to us," one of the policemen said as the other cleared his throat.

"We're just checking out the area. You two shouldn't really be alone in the park. It's kind of dangerous. We'd appreciate it if you two would kindly go home where it's safe."

"That's fine; we will."

"We're sorry about this, Mr. Edison."

"No, don't apologize; you're just doing your job."

We got up off the ground as Clay bent down picking up his jacket. We then went back into the limo closing the door after us. "Well, let's say we call it a night, Tara."

"That sounds like a great idea to me."

We arrived back at home in the driveway, getting out of the limo as it drove away. We started making out walking towards the front door, unlocking it as we entered still kissing, closing the door behind us with a lock.

"Oh sorry."

We turned having been disturbed by the nanny standing in front of us staring. "Clayton's asleep and everything's clean, Mr. Edison."

"Well, thank you, you can go home now." The nanny picked up her things going into the other room to call a cab to pick her up.

"You want to go upstairs."

"Oh, so what are you planning for us to do up there?"

"Oh, Clay, you know what I'm thinking, baby."

"No, I don't, please explain yourself."

"I'm not going to explain myself; you can just come upstairs and find out for yourself."

"Oh, so you're going to be like that, huh? Well, I guess I'm going to have to take charge then."

Clay picked me up, and I wrapped my legs around him, as he carried me into the kitchen placing my ass onto the island in the middle of the kitchen while kissing me. "Oh, I see." Clay unbuttoned the buttons of my dress in the front and slowly pulled the shoulder straps off of my shoulders. He started kissing my neck and chest while holding his hands against my back pulling me closer to him. "Mmm, that's nice."

"Just wait, Tara, this is only the beginning." Clay ripped off his dress shirt as if he was a male stripper of some sort trying to entertain me.

"That was your new shirt, wasn't it?"

"I don't care; now kiss me."

"Uuu, I love it when you're so demanding."

"I know."

We were about to, well, you know, when the nanny came into the kitchen to say goodbye. She saw me up on the island with my hair all messed up while Clay was in between my legs with his pants down and his shirt off as we stared at her. The nanny covered her eyes turning away. "I'm so sorry, Mr. Edison. I was just going to tell you I'm leaving now. Sorry about that. It won't happen again."

"Bye."

The nanny left as we continued what we had been doing. That was the most exciting time that I had ever remembered before, and I didn't know if we could ever top that, but I was sure we'd come close.

CHAPTER 19

Dreams Happen

A month later, we had two more weeks until we were going to be pronounced husband and wife, finally after so many years of waiting. We had been together so many years, we already felt like we were married, but the feeling of it going to be final in everyone's eyes was so exciting and joyful. I was on the phone with Carrie after not talking to her for awhile. Clayton was playing in the back yard, and Clay was out signing autographs again for his fans. Carrie and I were getting into talking about the subject of friends that we had had in the past. I was just beginning to tell her about Lindsey while keeping an eye out for Clayton in the backyard, making sure he was safe.

"Yeah, Lindsey was such a wonderful friend, or so I thought. I didn't think she was ever like Jennifer, but boy was I wrong, huh?"

"Yeah, but you can't predict things like that; they just kind of happen. Someone could show you they're a nice person when really underneath, they're just not."

"I know, tell me about it, I'm so mad at her for trying to mess up the one good thing I had."

"Yeah, well, at least you don't have to worry about that anymore."

"I know. If I ever run into her again, I'll have to hold myself back from slapping her."

"Well, that won't happen; you won't be seeing her around anymore, don't worry."

I was silent, then I began to question what she had meant by that. "What do you mean I won't be seeing her around anymore? You say it as though well, you know?"

"Oh my God, you don't know?"

"Know what?"

"Didn't Clay tell you?"

"Tell me what?"

"I think you should sit down, sweetie."

"Why would I need to sit down, Carrie? What the hell is going on?"

"Tara, Lindsey died two years ago. Didn't you know? She was struck by a car."

"What? Oh my God, you're kidding, right? My Lindsey? Lindsey, my best friend?"

"Yes, I'm sorry, Tara. I thought you knew about it. Clay should have told you."

"Oh my God, I've got to go. Carrie, I'll talk to you later."

"No wait, Tara."

I hung up the phone holding it in my hands and looking down at my feet. I was upset by the fact that my friend had died. I know what you're probably thinking, why would I even care that she died when she treated me like crap? The thing was when we were friends, we had been best friends for twelve years before that, and we were practically sisters. Why wouldn't he tell me my own friend had died? I was so mad at him at the moment. I picked up the phone calling for a nanny so I could get out of the house and go somewhere just to get away for awhile.

When the nanny arrived, I left the house feeling very upset and angry. Just as I opened the front door about to leave, I saw Clay pull up in the driveway and get out of his car. I closed the front door, locking it, and ran up to Clay hitting him lightly with both my hands. "Why? Why didn't you tell me? Why, Clay?"

"Tara, stop it, just stop it. What's the matter? What happened?" Clay held me by the sides of my arms trying to prevent me from hitting him anymore. "Why didn't you tell me Lindsey died? Why did you keep it a big secret? I trusted you."

Clay stood there in front of me. Glancing up, he realized what he had done. "How did you find out about that?"

"It doesn't matter how I found out, Clay. The fact is, I know now, so quit avoiding the question and tell me."

"I'm sorry, Tara. I didn't want you to get hurt anymore. You had so much happen already, and you were pregnant. I just couldn't tell you. I'm sorry."

"You should have told me. You lied to me. I never thought you were capable of that."

"I only did it because I was protecting you."

"I don't need protection, Clay. I don't need your pity either. You should have told me. I'm supposed to be your fiancée, remember? We were going to get married."

"I know. I'm really sorry, but like I said, you were pregnant. I didn't want to upset you."

"I wasn't pregnant for two years, Clay. You just wanted to get away with me not knowing. You were never going to tell me, were you?"

Clay took a deep breath. "I wanted to, but I didn't want to be the one that hurt you."

"Well, you hurt me anyway. I can't believe you lied to me."

"When did I lie to you, Tara? Please explain to me. How I could lie to you if you didn't even find out until now?"

"In the park, Clay, you lied, and then you made love to me. How could you? How dare you cover it up like that?"

"I'm so sorry, Tara. I didn't mean to. I'm sorry. What do you want me to do?"

"Nothing, just never mind. I've got to get out of here. I'll see you whenever."

I turned as Clay grabbed my arm turning me towards him and kissed me. I pushed him off of me glaring at him. "Don't, just don't. You can't just kiss me and make me forget about it. It doesn't work like that."

"Tara, don't. Just stay here."

"No, I'm leaving, and you can have your stupid ring back."

I pulled the ring off my finger picking up Clay's left hand and placing the ring in it. I began walking away when Clay said something to me that I would never forget.

"Fine, leave; it's what you're good at."

I turned around towards him. "Excuse me?"

"You heard me, Tara. You're always running away from me, hiding from your problems so you don't have to face them. When, Tara, when are you going to stand up to them. When are you going to see the only thing you're running away from is yourself. The person you end up hurting is me. I've stood here by your side through so much crap, Tara, and I'm getting sick of you always thinking about yourself. For once, I'd like to see you put someone else first instead of yourself."

"Is that what you think I'm doing? What about you, Clay? You don't run away from your problems, you dwell in them."

"I may with some problems, but at least I stand up to them instead of hide in a hole until they're gone like you do."

"If you don't like who I am, then why are you even with me? Why do you even care that I'm leaving?"

Clay walked up to me placing his hands at my side looking into my eyes as I felt chills down my spine. He picked my left hand up placing the ring back onto my finger gently as I just stared at him. "Because I love you, because I want to be with you no matter what kind of problems you have. We both have different ways of coping with our past, but it's the way we choose to deal with it that will make our future. I love you, Tara, and if you don't love me, walk away, get out of my life, and let me move on. But if you do love me, like I feel you do, stay here and forgive me. See the good side of why I hid the death of Lindsey from you and stay with me. Marry me on the 14th. I want you to be my wife. I will never love anyone the way I love you. Now make your decision."

I stood in front of him with his hands still holding my left hand with the ring he had placed back on. I wrapped my arms around him crying, "I'm sorry, Clay. I didn't mean to be so hard on you about everything. I just…"

"I know, Tara, you don't have to explain. Let's just go inside, and I'll make you something to eat, alright?"

I sniffled looking up at him with my head still upon his chest. "But you don't know how to cook."

"I know, but there's some peach ice ream in the freezer, and all I have to do is take it out and serve it with some spoons."

I giggled, laughing at Clay trying to make me smile again.

"I knew that would make you smile. Now let's go inside, sweetie."

Header

I looked up at Clay, smiling with tears still falling from my eyes. "Clay?"

"What is it, sweetie?"

"I'm so sorry for hitting you earlier."

"It's alright, Tara. You don't have to apologize, I understand." He led me towards the front door with me still clinging to his side. "Tara?"

"Yes, Clay, what is it?"

"Do you want to have a hot bath with me and relax?"

"But I thought we were having ice cream?"

"Oh we still can. We can eat it while in the hot tub, then we won't feel cold."

I giggled at him, smiling real big.

"Now that's the smile I like to see from you."

He was so sweet how he always knew exactly what to say to me to make me feel better about my problems. I was so wrong to have treated Clay the way that I had in the past. I never wanted him to feel like he had to always worry about me leaving him. I had to stop overreacting about everything. I didn't know why I always had, and I wasn't sure if the quality had come from my mother or my father, but then I wondered if it even came from any of them. Maybe it came from their death and that's the way it had affected me. I always tried to keep the ones I really loved at a certain distance from me so if anything happened to them and I lost them, it wouldn't hurt as much. That way of thinking never worked with Clay. It was different even at a distance. I still cared so much. It hurt me so much to be away from him. I loved him more than anything in the world. There was no one else I could ever want to be with more than him. I was just too stupid to realize it before. I was too selfish, but not anymore, not after that day, I wasn't. I was myself again finally, and it felt really nice to have my heart filled with more love than heartache.

Clay and I gathered our things together and left to go to Elko for our wedding that was coming up. When we arrived in Elko, we stayed in a hotel that we would be staying in until after our wedding. Our wedding was getting closer and closer. We were feeling so excited. Everything had been set up for us to be married on the 14th of September, in the field outside of a church. We always dreamed of having an outdoor wedding, so we were going to make it happen in reality. The day came so fast, almost as if God had turned the clock so that we could be pronounced husband and wife.

The wedding day was so hectic in the morning. Our wedding was going to be starting at 4:00 p.m. that day, so we had to be separated so we could do our own thing. I went to Clay's mama's house where all the bridesmaids were getting ready and a hairdresser was making my hair beautiful, placing the veil and a tiara in my hair. After my hair was perfect, I put on my makeup feeling as though I looked so beautiful, and I hadn't even put on my wedding dress yet. It was about 3:30 p.m. when I had to put on my dress, and all the girls helped me lift it over my head. It was a dress like a princess's. It had spaghetti straps and a tight-fitting top, and at the waist, it flared out like a ball gown; it was fabulous. When I had finally gotten it on, I walked over to the mirror that had been set up especially for that day. I admired myself, staring at myself from head to toe. I was beautiful, and I couldn't believe my own eyes at how wonderful I looked in a wedding dress. Clay's mama came up behind me, placing her hands on my shoulders and looking at me in the mirror smiling.

"You look so beautiful today. Clay made a good choice wanting to marry you. I want you to know from the moment I met you, I already knew in my heart why he chose you. You're going to make all his prayers come true when you say I do." I knew right then that his mama didn't only accept our wedding, but she actually liked me and was proud of her son for choosing me.

When the time got closer for us to leave, we all left Clay's mama's house. We left in the limo parked outside waiting for us, which would drive us to the church where the ceremony was going to be held. When we arrived and I stepped out of the limo, I looked around seeing flowers everywhere. The wedding was beautiful. There was a red runner down the aisle, and everyone was already there waiting for us to begin. I saw Clay standing at the beginning of the red runner waiting to walk me down the aisle. As I walked up closer to him, he turned and looked at me. I was never going to forget the way he had looked at me; it was an expression of, "Wow." I loved it when he stared at me like that. I had butterflies in my tummy and goose bumps forming on my arms. I was

Header

so nervous, but as soon as I reached Clay and I linked his arm, I felt safe and comfortable all over again. I felt the greatest feeling of all, love. It was a moment I was going to remember forever.

We walked down the aisle together as the music played for everyone to hear until we reached the front where that priest was standing waiting for us. As the priest read from his book, we looked into each other's eyes seeing our future and all the times we'd experienced together flash before our eyes. I loved him so much at that moment. I never even paid any attention to anything the priest had been saying. I had been too caught up in his love for me. I was too focused on listening to his soul whisper little nothings to me as if we were speaking through our eyes. Then I heard the priest tell Clay to place the ring on my finger and for me to do the same. I lifted my left hand as Clay slid the wedding band on my finger smiling. I held his left hand and slid the wedding band on his as we then held one another's hands smiling at each other as we shook with happiness.

"By the power invested in me, I now pronounce you husband and wife. You may kiss your beautiful bride." We then leaned forward as we gave our first kiss as husband and wife and turned towards the guests seeing everyone smiling and crying tears of happiness.

Even Piercen was crying; in fact, he had been the loudest one there. He was clapping and cheering while bawling his eyes out. "Oh, I'm just so happy for Clay and Tara. They will make such cute little babies. Just think of all the spikes I could make for them all. I make hair stand up like peacock."

We took our focus off Piercen and went back to each other, staring into one another's eyes. Clay held out his arm as I linked it getting prepared to take our walk back down the aisle as husband and wife. I smiled at him as he did me with tears falling from his eyes making me start to tear up. I walked down the aisle linked in Clay's arm with the feeling of completion of my only dream I had ever had. I listened to the sound of the hummingbirds in the trees nearby. My heart pounded from within my chest as my tummy fluttered at every inch closer we came to the end of the aisle towards our future. We were married that day, and if I listened closely enough, I could almost hear the sound of angels singing from a distance. I felt like the luckiest woman in the world. There was nothing I could want more than having the gift of love that I had just received minutes ago. I trembled every minute that passed by knowing I would be spending eternity with the man I loved and with the child which God had given to us. But too bad it never really happened.

I was indeed a true believer that dreams do come true, and it only takes a little bit of hope to make them happen, but you have to believe in yourself. Whenever you feel like your life isn't going the way you had hoped, always remember these words: "Never give up on your prayers, never throw away your wishes, and never close off your thoughts because dreams do happen. They can happen to me, and I believe they can happen to you, if you only have faith in who you are as a person."

"*SPECIAL!*"

About the Author

Amandah Berkowski was born and raised in Port Coquitlam B.C Canada and grew up in a large family of three brothers and two sisters. She has a certificate in Early Childhood Education and has been writing since the age of sixteen. Her interests include singing, dancing and writing and is known for her sensuality and respect for others. Spirituality and family play a large part in her life giving her inspiration to write.

Printed in the United States
60429LVS00003B/64-72